Emrysia

Awakening

C.A. Morgan

Railroad Street Press
St. Johnsbury, Vermont

Printed in the United States of America

Artwork and cover design by C.A. Morgan

LIBRARY OF CONGRESS
CATALOGING-IN-PUBLICATION DATA

Morgan, C.A.
Emrysia/Morgan, C.A.

ISBN 9781936711314

Railroad Street Press
394 Railroad St., Ste 2
St. Johnsbury, VT 05819

Dedication

For Roger, Jordan, Christian, Katrina, Jaime & Lydia,
You *"illuminate"* my life.

Volume One of the Three Sisters Trilogy

C.A. Morgan

The Luminaries

Aryelle – (Beautiful Sky Servant) Daughter of Elazaryn

Elazaryn – (Servant Sky Father) El'Kandhar of the Empaya, Brightest Candle of All

Karril – (Laughing Light) Son of Kayanna, and Aryelle's cousin

Leandhra – (Much Beautiful Music) Elazaryn's deceased first wife, mother of Aryelle

Kayanna – (Beautiful Light) Aryelle's aunt and member of the Kandharril

Ladhonna – (Song of Sorrow) Elazaryn's second wife, Aryelle's stepmother/aunt

Rachaan – (Sun Eater) Current advisor to Elazaryn

Gaelen – Commoner representative to Elazaryn's council

Jonazat – A Naturra

The Mer

Lureli – Princess of Mer
Jorda, Crispin, Katri & Jaim – Lureli's bearers

The Aurrac

Eleanor – Huntress & female warrior
Borrac – Head Chieftain of all the clan-herds
Nodd (Rogar) – Ostracized fauen; stepfather to Eleanor
Althea – Former favorite of Borrac and Nodd's common-law mate, mother of Eleanor
Lavina – Althea's twin
Accora – Aurracan High Priest
Torc - Patrol guard from the Upper Village

The Language (Empayan)

Words that end in "rre" or "nne" are feminine in form, "rra" or "nna" gender inclusive. Double vowel 'aa' is pronounced as in "cane". Syllables ending in *'a'* or *'e'* may have a long or short vowel sound. A vowel followed by another vowel is long, the succeeding vowel is always short. The exception is when separated by an apostrophe (a'a), the vowels *may* combine to create one long "I" sound, as in "pine". The Common word for *Empayan*, spelled *Empa'ayan* in the luminaries'ancient tongue, is pronounced accordingly.

An apostrophe in the middle of a word denotes that two words have been combined to create shared meaning, for example *Lumina'da* is Father of Light (more accurately - Light Father). *Lumina'dharra* is a combination of the names for the sun and moon. Emphasis is heaviest on the syllable immediately following the apostrophe. One exception to the previous rule is in children's names, which in royal houses are created by combining (in abbreviated form) parents' names; Ex. – Aryelle = *Le*andhra & *E*l*azar*y*n; Karril = *Ka*yanna (pronounced Kay-ah-nah) & E*ril*dhil.

The letter combination "dh" always receives a strong emphasis; the "h" is not silent. The letter combination "ch" has a hard "k" sound at the middle or end of a syllable and a "sh" sound at the beginning. "J' can sound like a *Y* or *J*.

A glossary and partial listing of Empa'ayan terms are listed at the back of this book.

Contents

Emrysia
(Awakening)
By C.A. Morgan

Prologue

Rainbow light filtered down through the crystal dome of the Prism Rotunda, bathing each member of the gathered Kandharril in a separate hue. For long moments, perhaps hours the elite healers stood unmoving, trancelike, wingtip-to-wingtip. On a marble dais at their center lay a still form all but obscured from view.

Suddenly, the bow of light recollected into one brilliant white glow, radiating up and outward from the center of their Healing Circle. Waves of energy pulsed around and through them in an audible, otherworldly thrumming. Just as suddenly, like the upstroke of a valleo drum hammer, a final heartbeat reverberated throughout the chamber.

Silence.

And then… a breath. And another, and another. Now shallow, but rhythmic they came, as from one deep in slumber. Gradually the light faded as one by one the members of the Circle staggered from their places. No words were spoken – none were needed.

The assumption was complete.

The young luminarie would live.

On the observation balcony above, Aryelle turned away disappointed.

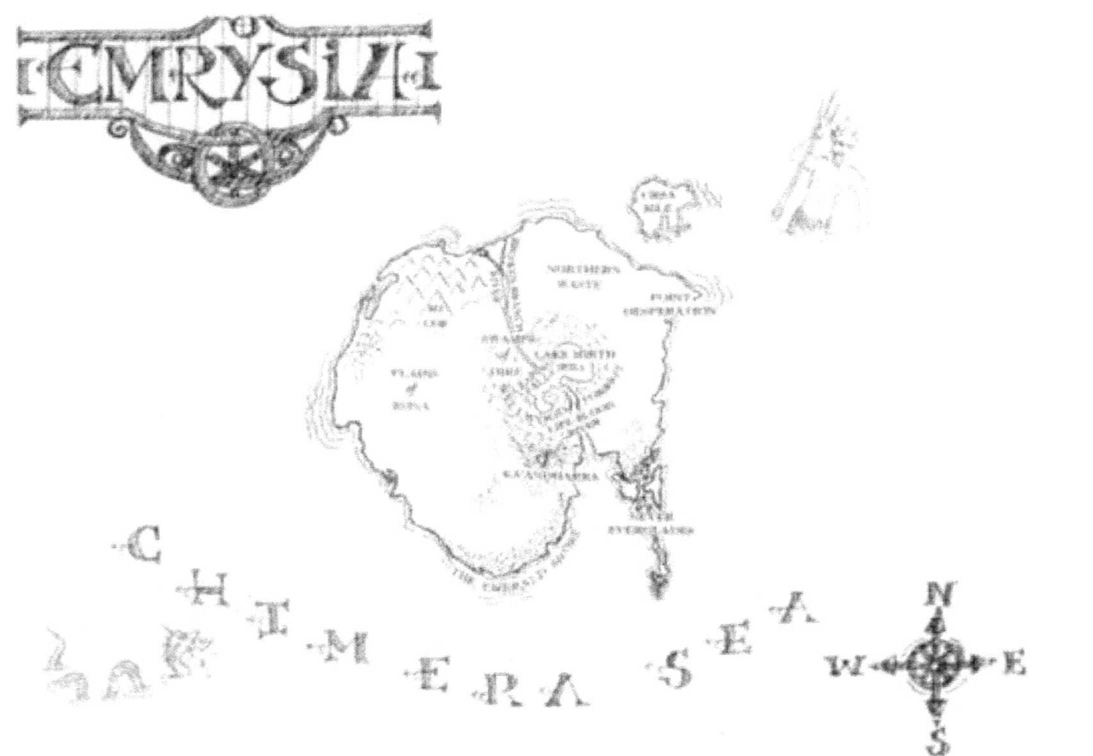

CHRYSIA
CHIMERA SEA
N
W
E
S

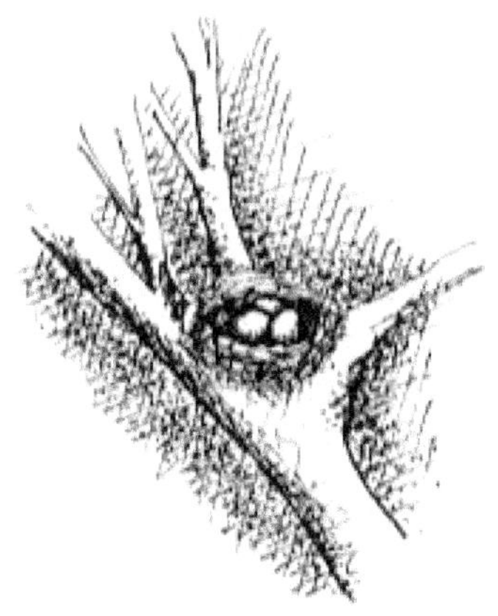

Chapter 1 – The Messenger

The tree-born city of Ka'Andharra nestled snugly into the interwoven branches of an ancient grove of valleo. Only here near the heart of Emrysia did the meandering limbs cover so vast an area. Smooth silver bark and platter-like, heart shaped leaves of yellowish green camouflaged the luminaries' dwellings year round. Along the branches of the mother tree, the El'Kandhar's residence sprawled in every direction. From central throne room to the gardens along the forest floor, its corridors twined over the oldest and sturdiest branches to sprout rooms as naturally as fruit. The rest of the city blossomed in clusters around it, prominent homes soaring skyward, commoner dwellings grafted onto the branches' undersides, carved and chiseled, of crystal and of wood.

Elazaryn sat poised like a statue on the exalted Seat of Ka'Andharra, his vacant stare fixed just left of the defiant youngster before him.

"He will not survive till dawn…."

"But Father, his injuries do not seem mortal," Aryelle countered.

"His spirit is wounded beyond reach. We cannot help him."

"You mean you will not help him!"

"I seek not your council, Aryelle," he warned.

"And I seek not your permission! I will heal him myself!" Aryelle cried out, squirming uncomfortably as the echo of her outburst crashed like waves off the columns and walls of the vast, empty reception hall and died away.

Slowly, Elazaryn raised his chin from where it rested between slender, bejeweled fingers. "Your love is great, *m'yana*, but your judgment is clouded. It is not yet your time of Passing, yet you hasten to enter the Gate without considering which way it will open."

"But Father," she pled changing tactics, "please, only let me-"

"I forbid it! Speak of it no more!"

Sparks flashed in Aryelle's emerald eyes. Her wings - translucent, yet leathery flushed with anger, quivering as she struggled to hold it in check. Hastily, she lowered her gaze. It would not help matters to give in to her frustration. That much she knew.

"Long burn your flame, El'Kandhar," she managed though barely, the age-old response passing reluctantly through clenched teeth. Seething, she spun on her heel and fled the throne room, purposefully neglecting to bow to the blind ruler.

But other eyes witnessed her irreverence.

"She disgraces your name, El'Kandhar." Elazaryn's chief advisor strode forward from the shadows.

"She is still young, Rachaan. A season or two yet may pass ere she be held accountable." Elazaryn's face, unlined despite his age, furrowed with consternation. The thin circlet of gold resting upon his brow did little to conceal it. Would a season or two change much in the way Aryelle viewed life, he wondered? Would time alone tame her? With a sigh, he pushed aside his concern. More immediate matters demanded his attention. For instance, the stranger who had arrived last night with a mysterious scroll that he would deliver only into the El'Kandhar's hands. The stranger who now lay dying in the east branch's Prism Rotunda. The Kandharril had made the messenger comfortable, but nothing more. Elazaryn would not risk an assumption. The decision had been a painful one, but his alone to make no matter what his headstrong daughter thought. And considering the scroll's contents, he must now make one even more difficult.

Mistaking his sigh for a sign of weakening resolve, Rachaan pressed the issue. "Perhaps her time of discernment has come, El'Kandhar."

Elazaryn swatted aside the suggestion like an annoying insect. Turning away, he beckoned a page, one of many ever at the ready beside the throne. A fair-haired youth scrambled up the polished steps of the dais and nodded respectfully. Though his El'Kandhar's eyes unsettled him, he loved the old luminarie with all his heart.

"Uncle, a joy to serve you."

Elazaryn's face relaxed into a smile. "Karril! I did not notice your watch had come. Has the morning passed so quickly?"

"I have just come from Lessons, as you surely know. What ever escapes you, Uncle?" Karril kissed the proffered hand, which was smooth and ageless as his soveriegn's face.

Elazaryn stroked the boy's cheek affectionately… and then gave it a sharp pat. "Keep your tongue in your cheek, Karril, and you will always speak out of the side of your mouth. Your words may be honey to others, but I find such sweets too rich in my dotage."

"And that, Uncle, is why I would never lie to you. I would hate to have you spew me from your presence!" he replied, rubbing his jaw. An impish sparkle danced in his eyes.

"As would I, my lad, as would I." The corners of Elazaryn's smile quirked merrily.

"Eh-hem, my Lord, if there is nothing further?"

"Rachaan? I thought you had left," said Elazaryn. "No, no… you may go. I have business to discuss with this young scoundrel." Dismissing the councilor, Elazaryn drew his nephew into the empty seat at his right, Domina - The Heirs' Throne. Karril shifted uncomfortably on the narrow, un-cushioned ledge. Neither one noticed Rachaan's scowl as he slipped from the room.

"I know you do not fancy your lessons Karril, otherwise why would you rush from them to wait upon an old beetle like me, required or not? The Illuminator informs me that you perform exceptionally well, though of course, you are easily distracted. But no time for lectures now" said Elazaryn in a conspiratorial whisper, "Now you must do something for me. You must find your cousin Aryelle and do your best to distract her. She bears a yoke unnecessary for one so young."

"She is no longer a child, Lord. She is older than I am by three revolutions. How may I ease her burden?"

"Not ease, Karril. Someday you will have burdens of your own. I would not ask you to bear any before your time. But you are young and, as I am well aware, able to find mischief enough to occupy much of this household. Take her to the Galleries, visit the hot springs or the aviary. Aryelle should take pleasure in her youth, as you do, while responsibility still weighs on other shoulders." Elazaryn clasped the boy's hands in his own, his sightless eyes regarding him. "You may be the son of my cousin Erildhil, but would that you were my own. Your carefree spirit refreshes me as no draught of blaiz ever has. Find Aryelle. Be the children you will be for such a short time yet. You can do me no greater favor."

Karril drew his hands slowly free, rose and folded his arms across his chest, bowing deeply as was customary. Then he leapt down the steps and skipped the length of the hall toward the great chamber doors. "Long burn your flame, El'Kandhar," he called belatedly, passing like a spring breeze through the doorway of the hallowed hall.

Karril finally found Aryelle storming down a wide, polished corridor along the western-most branch of the royal complex. Her slippered feet were swathed in finest silk, though an iron-shod Aurrac would have stomped less noisily.

"What do you want?" she asked, casting him a scathing glance.

"Nothing from you," he taunted, falling into step beside her.

"I have no time for games, Karril." Aryelle stopped mid-stride making it clear she considered his presence an annoyance.

"I am too old for games anyhow," he answered glibly.

"Then what do you want?"

"I am supposed to distract you."

"I do not want to be distracted," she hissed.

Determined to carry out his mission, Karril choked back a retort. "I am sorry, Aryelle. The El'Kandhar thought-"

"My father thinks I am a child! I am sixteen revolutions – ready to accept the duties of my calling, and yet he shelters me as if I was still a clinging infant!"

"He loves you *too* well, cousin."

His sudden sympathy caught Aryelle off guard, deflating her tantrum like a windless sail. She collapsed with a sigh onto an ornately carved bench, one of many that lined the corridor. Late-afternoon sunlight filtered through the amber leaves outside the arched windows to flood the hall with liquid gold.

Raised together like nestlings in the shelter of these halls, the cousins used to be close, though Karril could barely remember the last time they had played. He yearned for the easy camaraderie they once shared. Watching Aryelle now he realized she had almost become a stranger to him. Long, silken lashes shaded her cheekbones as she sat, head bowed, graceful hands limp with defeat in her soft-robed lap. A silken strand escaped the confines of her jeweled hairnet and brushed her cheek. Absently, she tucked it behind her ear and twirled it for distraction. Then, as if needing more comfort than a single strand could offer, she reached further up to loosen her hairnet. Spun from the gossamer threads of wood spiders' silk and decorated with bits of amethyst set in hammered silver, its web-like strength soon gave way, and a luxurious sheet of glossy, chestnut hair fell around her shoulders. She shook it out raising her face to gaze through the window, but caught Karril's eye instead.

-I know- his unspoken message resounded through her brain *-I know-*

Karril sat down beside her. His hands reached out for hers.

-Aryelle…- he thought.

-You do not understand, Karril- she thought back, looking away.

-I do understand. You want to heal the messenger who arrived last night. The El'Kandhar forbids it.-

-He forbids it because he fears what it will do to me.-

-Because he loves you.-

-But I am ready! I am strong enough!-

-The entire Circle has tried-

"No! They have not! The Kandharril love too little and fear too much!" her words erupted down the peaceful corridor and the moment was shattered. She sprang to her feet and began to pace. "Their fear weakens them, and their weakness makes them even more afraid. How can they hope to illumine the lives of others when they themselves live in shadow?"

"But he is not one of us! Why should they expend their light?"

"Because he has come to us!"

"But we do not know-"

"We do not need to know any more than that, Kay! The Elders would have saved their questions – no! They would have needed no Circle! The messenger would have been at table by now, enjoying repast, the horror of whatever attacked him blazed from his memory..." Her eyes shone with a distant vision.

Karril followed her gaze but saw only the passing shadow of a large bird. He shuddered and shook his wings open with a snap, startling Aryelle out of her reverie. She turned toward him, a look of profound peace flowering across her face… a look that worried him.

"The Elders have passed on their gift to me, Karril. I must honor them by using it well, not hiding it under a basket," Aryelle stated calmly.

"What of honoring your El'Kandhar, your father?"

"And who are you to remind me of that? You disregard our family name by behaving like a kitchen serf - sneaking off to cause mischief when you should be minding your duties."

"I am not heir to the Seat of Ka'Andharra; you are!" snapped Karril.

"Not by choice and you know it," she replied. "I can no more change my feathers than a sparrow, but that does not mean I do not dream of becoming an eagle."

"More like the eagle wishing to become a sparrow."

"But this eagle is not allowed to soar! Oh, Kay, I am so sick of being treated like a child! Soon I will have to marry, yet Father does not even trust me to use my flame."

He knew how she felt. Karril had the gift too, as did all luminaries to one degree or another, of assuming another's pain before dispelling it into the ether. He longed to test his own healing flame, but as a still growing child was allowed to use neither flame nor flight. Aryelle had completed her studies, had excelled even. She was no longer a child. But still… "Luminaries of old may have burned brighter, but their life spans were far shorter as well. If you spend your light too soon it will fade and flicker out!"

"The Elders cared little for themselves. And that is why the Circle is ineffective - the Kandharril care nothing for this stranger!"

"And you alone do," he said blandly.

"Yes, I do! I care about all Emrysians. And I will assume his pain, with my father's blessing or without it!"

-Zu qualith kra'dempa! - Karril thought in their ancient native tongue, but to himself alone. *-Dhe zu n'et dhruy nochta…..-* You are too proud cousin! I just hope it leads not to your destruction.

The door to the Rotunda whispered open, its carved facade pushed effortlessly aside by a delicate hand. A slim, cloaked figure slipped into the light-filled chamber. Glancing toward the vaulted Prism dome, she strode purposefully toward the center of the room where a still form lay unattended on a marble dais.

"What secrets do you hold?" she wondered aloud.

-None that will ever be told- A second hooded figure had sidled in behind her.

If startled by the intrusion, she showed no sign. "Perhaps Rachaan. But perhaps not. The Circle has little to gain by his recovery, and Elazaryn already retrieved the scroll he carried. I know it spoke of a Summit, but…what else might *he* tell us?"

"I do not know, my love. Nor do I care. He is nothing to us."

"But this Summit -"

"We will send no-one! What need have we of alliances? The rest of Emrysia is beneath our concern. Are we not the Enlightened? Let those who have chosen darkness stay there, I say. If I held the Seat of Ka'Andharra-"

"As you should, Rachaan," she interrupted, "and perhaps this messenger is the key. Elazaryn does not want him healed. Think! It has been far too many revolutions to count since anyone other than the Naturra have entered our skies. Elazaryn is afraid, as I have never seen him before. This…situation may help us restore the throne to its rightful owner – you!" She wove her pale fingers through his dark and lustrous hair.

Rachaan grew thoughtful for a moment. Then grasping the woman by her shoulders, his fingers digging into her flesh, he turned her abruptly to face him searching her face for signs of treachery.

"It will be dangerous; Elazaryn has forbidden it," he said finally.

"Just as our love is forbidden. But it too shall come to light when all is set aright," she answered, taking his hand and stroking it like a favored pet.

"Then let it be so!"

Together they turned to face the strange, wingless foreigner. He lay supine, a position no luminarie could hope to maintain since voluminous wings, even folded, allowed for slumbering only on one's belly or side. His short, curly hair was an unusual shade, and his pale skin was mottled with slightly darker spots, especially on his arms and across the bridge of his nose. To the Kandharra, whose long, straight tresses ranged in color from dark chestnut to silvery-blond and whose pale visages were flawless, the stranger seemed peculiarly malformed.

Rachaan scowled down at the outlandish face. The thought of expending his energy to heal this wretch repulsed him. Yet… the woman was curiously drawn to know more about him, and her instincts were worthy of attention. Certainly it made the threat greater. But they would deal with that when the time came. For now this *andhruypa*, this *alien,* might be useful, especially if the current El'Kandhar truly did fear him.

"He is a coward if he fears this deformed little slug," he spoke his thought aloud.

The foreigner moaned and his eyes rolled back into his head. Rachaan and the woman both gasped. His eyes!

Before either had time to recover their shock, the heavy wooden door crept open once more. Rachaan yanked his hand free of the woman's and drew his hood forward to cloak his face in shadow. Head bowed, he shuffled quickly from the room through an auxiliary doorway. The woman, doing likewise, followed close behind.

The curling tip of a juvenile wing appeared around the outer door's edge. A tousled blond forehead with mischievous eyes peeked into the chamber. It disappeared for an instant, and then Karril's whole face popped from behind the door like a turtle snapping at a dragonfly.

"All clear," he whispered. "Two healers just left. Maybe they were able to help him after all…?"

"They will only have made him comfortable," Aryelle said brushing past him and approaching the dais. "Father's orders were that none should sacrifice their own well being.

They say he has suffered greatly and that to assume him would involve great risk."

"But I thought that the Circle-"

"What, this morning? That was only an ordinary assumption, a commoner injured by a falling branch. They left *him* here to die of starvation and thirst, if his mind does not eat him up first!"

"How could they!" cried Karril.

"You see? They have forgotten the old ways, cousin. No-one will challenge the El'Kandhar, and this time he is wrong!" Aryelle reached out to stroke the stranger's fevered brow showing no sign of fear or repulsion. He shivered once, but was otherwise still. "But we have not forgotten, have we?" she asked Karril, her eyes never leaving the stranger's face. "It is written into our very bones. Our gift is not for ourselves, but for any in need. Help me, cousin! Stand watch at the door."

"But I could -"

"No, Kay, you are at greater risk. You have not even been tested yet. I can do this alone, but I dare not be interrupted."

"But -"

"Please Karril! Trust me."

"Be careful," he said hesitating near the doorway. "Aryelle, could you not just heal his body and let-"

"No," she answered, cutting him off. "Spirit, mind and body; all are one just as water, land, and sky make up one Emrysia - Lesson One from the Book of Illumination. Once I begin the assumption, I must continue until it is complete."

"And if the healers return?"

"You saw for yourself that they just checked him. Just watch the outer door in case one of Father's advisors comes for a report."

Reluctantly Karril took up his post outside the door while Aryelle turned her full attention back to the messenger. He was smaller in stature than one of their race, though equally thin and wiry. A translucent tunic similar to her own replaced the bloodied rags he had arrived in last night. His wounds had been cleaned and the worst of them bandaged. She noted his peculiarities, enthralled by them. Imagine – no wings!

As she continued to study her subject, a sense of how he moved, thought and felt infused her being. He was common for one of his kind, and young, but accustomed to hard labor evident from the calluses on his hands. His feet spoke of long journeys unshod. He must have been determined to deliver his message at all costs. Why else would he have pushed himself beyond all endurance, faced unimaginable horrors, coming to them from who knew where? Either his love was great or his fear, she thought… or both. Looking closer she noticed three long scratches on his chest beneath his tunic. The wounds were superficial, but she sensed they inflicted a pain far greater than physically possible. Something - but what?- had entered his spirit and begun to devour him, leaving this broken shell of a being. He flinched when her hand brushed across his chest, his face contorting in pain. Cooing softly, Aryelle rested her hand lightly over the stripes and closed her eyes. Standing perfectly still she matched her breathing to his. Slowly her bowed head rose, a warm glow emanating from her upturned face. Light from the prism dome funneled over it, dazzling, blindingly white, yet – so beautiful! Wildly colorful! She could feel each swirling hue differently against the bare skin of her face and arms; the cool of violets and blues, vibrant, refreshing greens, gradually warmer yellow, orange and red, and feel the pulsing energy as they blended into one pure, white light. She had no need to squint against the brilliance, was not burned though its heat was intense as a smelter's fire. She gazed through the light and saw that his eyes were beginning to flutter open. Tears of ecstasy streamed down her cheeks. I have done it, she exalted. I have succeeded where the Circle could not! The gift is mine!

Aryelle willed him to awaken, to revel with her in this moment of triumph. Lifting her hand from his now-unmarked chest, she brushed an errant curl from the stranger's forehead. At her touch his eyes flew open, locking on hers with a fear-filled gaze. Only his terror registered at first. Then suddenly her panic mirrored his as the whirling colors surrounding them darkened ominously. She faltered back a step as brilliant day plunged into deepest night.

One revolution for the seed to grow
(Birth)
Two revolutions till light he will know
(Eyes covered for first year)
Three revolutions without voice he sings
(Begins to speak audibly at 2 years)
Four revolutions – then grow his wings
(Wings become functional at 3 years)
Five revolutions, and Six more in turn
Ere his lessons he must learn.
(Formal education begins at age 10)
Seven revolutions more make a man
(Age of accountability begins at 17)
(Eight till woman's ending Chan*)
*(*Female fertility ends at age 18)*
Nine revolutions must pass from thence
Until a man has common sense
(Age 26 considered middle aged-age of enlightenment)
Ten more he will spend ere fades his sight
And enters in eternal night
(At 36 luminaries begin to dim)
Eleven then pass with the blink of an eye
(Considered elderly by age 46)
Twelve more revolutions – he will surely die.
(Luminaries rarely live to see 60)

Chapter 2 – Drawn to the Light

"Thru here, my liege!" called a frantic voice. An instant later the heavy door crashed open, flung aside by Elazaryn himself, followed closely by a wide-eyed acolyte. The El'Kandhar felt his way to the center of the chamber where Karril sat cradling his cousin's head in his lap. The messenger lay forgotten.

"Aryelle!" Her name escaped his lips like a prayer as Elazaryn fell to his knees.

Karril relinquished his cousin to her father, and standing, shifted uncomfortably beside them. Gathering her into his arms, Elazaryn crushed Aryelle to his breast.

"I…I…sh-she called out…there was a flash…" stammered Karril.

Anger blazed in the El'Kandhar's opaque eyes. "Why did you not stop her?!"

"I…I am sorry! I did not think… she said she could-"

"Fool! She is just a child!"

Comforting arms folded around Karril's sagging shoulders from behind. "As is this brave young man, brother," soothed a voice more familiar to Elazaryn than his own. Though Karril's head reached the top of her shoulder, he turned and clung to his mother with relief.

Elazaryn raised his face, his anger melting away.

"Kayanna…"

The exquisite female luminarie stayed with arms wrapped protectively around Karril.

"What happened, Karril?" asked Elazaryn more gently, his unspoken apology filling the distance between them.

Karril took a deep breath. "I found Aryelle like you asked me to, but she was not to be distracted, so… I decided to stay with her. I thought she would see for herself that there was nothing she could do. But when we got here and she said that they- the Kandharril - were going to leave him here to die, it just… well, it felt wrong! I wanted to help, but she would not let me. She made me keep watch outside the door, but I peeked in. I saw light all around them growing brighter and brighter, and the colors! All the colors of light were swirling around them." He paused, reliving what he had seen, his face clouding over. "And then it changed, not beautiful anymore, but ugly and dark. I saw that Aryelle was afraid too, and then there was a flash! It was so bright I had to close my eyes! The image of her standing there was branded into them. When I could finally see again, she was lying on the floor - I thought she was dead! But she is not… not… she *is* still alive?"

"She lives," confirmed Elazaryn caressing Aryelle's cheek, "but I must act quickly. I will do everything in my power-"

"-with the help of the Circle, brother."

"No! She is mine! I will heal her!" insisted Elazaryn.

"We all will."

Elazaryn and his sister-in-law locked eyes, blind though he was. Unspoken volumes passed between them until reluctantly Elazaryn nodded his consent.

Kayanna motioned to the acolytes waiting to help the El'Kandhar to his feet. He rose with difficulty, not allowing them to take his daughter from his arms. Other acolytes came and swiftly removed the messenger, who appeared to be sleeping peacefully. Elazaryn himself placed Aryelle tenderly upon the vacated marble, keeping a protective hand at her side.

In moments, nearly a dozen robed and cowled Kandharril filed silently into the chamber, forming a ring around the table. A female acolyte came forward and Kayanna gave Karril over to her care, and then joined the Circle. Reluctantly, Elazaryn let his hand fall to his side and turned to join it as well. As one the gathered healers lowered their hoods. Their incandescent wings unfurled, and time stood still.

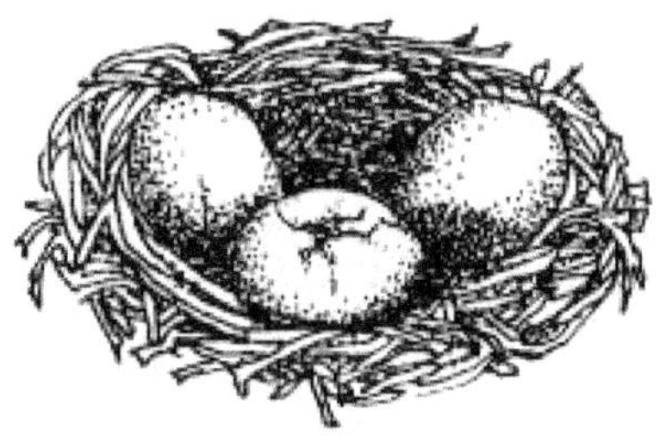

Chapter 3 – Awakening

...the moon, Silva Kandharre, low in her descent... an aching desire deep within... racing through the night over winding stairways and swinging walkways to the path on the forest floor... just beyond the river's edge, a lone luminous figure against the shadows of the forest, a beautiful maiden awaiting a broken-hearted young man...

Elazaryn dozed fitfully in a chair at Aryelle's bedside. Suddenly he raised his head, listening. Aryelle had finally stirred, beginning to awaken. Her hand, the one he wasn't holding, reached up to brush the front of her robe. Elazaryn held the other to his cheek. Then kissing its palm, he cradled it tenderly between both of his own.

"Come back to me, *m'yana,*" he pled.

Her eyes flew open. "The messenger!" she cried in a raspy voice.

Elazaryn patted her hand reassuringly. "Shhhhhh child, rest easy. He was sent back to his people. You have slept for days."

"But is he all right?" she croaked urgently.

He wagged his head. "It was too great a price to pay, Aryelle. You could have both been killed."

"He is dead?" Her look pled disbelief.

"No, he still lives. You succeeded in healing him. But the light was more than his eyes could withstand," his chiding tone softened, "though he seemed to remember nothing of his former injuries."

Aryelle hung her head. Her success had cost the man his vision. Then suddenly she remembered. "His eyes!" she said, bolting upright. "Father, they were green like mine!"

Aryelle had always felt like an outsider, different from every other luminarie in Ka'Andharra with their irises of blue, gray or violet. Only the Naturra, distant relatives to the Kandharra who lived in the far wilds of Wellwood Forest, ever rarely exhibited this strange trait of green eyes… or so she had heard in tales. Aridhina, the Holy One, who had come to them from the Naturra and was her ancestor, was reported to have had eyes of emerald.

"Surely you do not think you are *andhruypa*! Aryelle, he had no wings!"

"I know I am not born of another world. But his eyes-"

"He had flaming blaiz hair… and spots!"

"But-"

Elazaryn sighed and cupped his daughter's lovely face in his hands. She searched his clouded eyes, knowing he saw with a vision no other living luminarie shared.

"You are *m'yana, mi'qua,*" he said tenderly. "No one found you in the wilderness like the great Aridhina. You were your mother's dying gift to me. A more precious gift has never been given. Now," he said, easing her toward her pillow, "you should rest."

She acquiesced, closing her eyes and folding her hands under her chin. Her father tucked a light blanket around her, kissed her forehead and settled back into his chair. As he wrung a hand across his weary face, he heard her familiar request.

"Tell me the story again, *Dadher....*"

"Your mother was a strong woman, beautiful and strong willed like you, and I knew from the moment I saw her that my soul loved hers. She was a mere fledgling. I had just entered the age of accountability, and was about to embark on my first diplomatic mission. But Azadhar, your grandfather, insisted that I first declare a wife. His councilors approached Kadharron and Leanna regarding a match between their first-born daughter and the El'Kandhar's only son and heir. An agreement was struck, and a marriage feast arranged to cement the union. Ladhonna quavered beside me, draped in colorful silks and ribbons, a fragile centerpiece appropriate for that garden party. Her eyes, just visible above her tinted veil, were wide with panic. Leandhra, Ladhonna's younger sister, sat across from us fidgeting in her everyday robe. It was simply cut from an inferior quality silk, and kept slipping off her shoulders. Then to my surprise, her father bade the girl sing.

Leandhra had a voice like bird song. She sang with the ease of a troubadour, and when she had finished she sat down and glared at me. Her fidgeting grew worse. I thought she was angry at having to entertain the royal guests. But in reality, she had picked up a briar while playing in the forest with her other sister, Kayanna. The pair of them had been sent to collect jewel flowers for Ladhonna's hair, a ruse to keep them out of the way of the preparations for the evening's festivities, no doubt. They made the most of their romp in the woods and returned late, with no time left to change robes.

I caught Leandhra's eye and winked, and she poked her tiny, pink tongue out at me. I tried not to laugh and, unfortunately, began to choke on a bit of un-swallowed food. Leandhra leapt to her feet – to save me, I suppose. Instead, she accidentally overturned a full decanter of blaiz, and sent a serving spoon from a nearby dish flying through the air. It whacked Ladhonna right on her jewel flower-adorned forehead. A brilliant stain spread across the tablecloth while Ladhonna sat there stunned, chilled sauce dripping down her face – what a picture! I burst out laughing and coughing, but mostly laughing. Meanwhile, Ladhonna turned to her other side and up came what little she had consumed. She was mortified! She gathered her silks and bolted from the banquet pavilion, Kayanna and Leandhra at her heels. Our poor bewildered parents sat there in shock while I tried to regain control."

Elazaryn always enjoyed retelling this portion of the tale. The images were so clear, the colors indelibly imprinted in his memory. Aryelle had to prompt him to continue.

"So you did not marry Ladhonna then."

"The marriage feast was more formality than celebration. Ladhonna had been chosen for me-"

"But you did not love her?"

"I did not even know her. She sat so still under all those veils that she could have been made of marble. But, I knew your mother. I could tell by the way she fidgeted that she was not one for putting on airs. As eldest daughter of all the noble houses, Ladhonna was the logical choice. But love, when it comes, has little to do with logic."

"Mother stole your heart."

"I insisted Azadhar withdraw our offer and extend it to Leandhra. But Leandhra's compassion for her sister was great. She would not even consider me until Ladhonna insisted she would no more marry me than a treefrog."

"And so you married mother instead?"

"Yes, Leandhra finally agreed, though of course, I had to wait the customary five revolutions to make her my own. I took Ladhonna as second only later, at Leandhra's insistence. You see, she hoped to heal her sister's broken spirit. Perhaps it has helped," he reflected, "and Ladhonna has been invaluable to me. But my heart still belongs to your mother. She shared my desire to reunite the Kandharra and Naturra, to become once again a unified Empaya. She even accompanied me on my visits to the Naturra when she could. But that was before Emrysia fell under the *Kra'nochta Empaana*, the Reign of Shadow."

Aryelle knew better than to ask about that topic. "Tell me about me," she asked instead.

"I returned from my final mission to find that Azadhar had passed through the Gate and that I was the new El'Kandhar. Leandhra was my only comfort, though she herself was still grieving the loss of our second child. When we realized she was with child for the third time, we took every precaution to ensure that you, at last, would survive. She had thought her *chanzu* was ending, but instead it was *you* beginning..."

All of the faces save one gathered around the banquet table were the same as on the day of the initial marriage feast. At the parents' end, Elina and Leanna were animatedly discussing the chances of this union producing grandchildren, while Kadharron sat back contentedly sipping blaiz. No one was seated in Azadhar's place, left vacant out of respect. Erildhil sat to the right of Kayanna, his bride. This time no veils hid Ladhonna's fragile beauty. She glowed with expectation, while across from her Leandhra – the first Lady Ka'Andharra, sat staring vacantly at the feast before her. Elazaryn caught her eye and attempted to smile, seeking to reassure her. But seeing his sorrow mirrored in her eyes, his smile died. And then, in an ironic twist of fate, Leandhra leaned over and threw up beside her chair…

"Keep going, *Dadher*," urged Aryelle.

Elazaryn collected himself. "Allora herself assumed your mother's care, and for many candles all went well. Then, about one candle before you were due to be born, Leandhra disappeared." Elazaryn's clouded eyes grew misty. "She was seen in the gardens at midday, but had not returned by nightfall…and we feared the worst. The palace emptied, everyone searched. When she was finally found wandering through the forest the following evening, she was out of her mind… bleeding, blistered by the sun. In her arms, she held a bundle. She would let no one take it from her, or even touch her until she was brought to me. She placed you into my arms. 'My gift to you, my love' she whispered. 'Her name is Aryelle'… and then she was gone. I tried to bring her back, but she was beyond reach. She had lost so much of her lifeblood."

Elazaryn's face crumpled, the pain of his true love's passing fresh in his memory.

Aryelle squeezed her father's hand.

"The last thing these mortal eyes of mine ever saw," he choked out finally, "was your beautiful little face. You too were near death, premature and tiny as you were. Your mother had somehow bound your wings and made a makeshift jaboqua for you. She had swaddled you in her cloak, but in her weakened condition, was able to do no more than that."

"But you healed me."

"Yes, I healed you."

"And it cost you your vision?"

"Yes."

"I am so sorry, Dadher," she whispered.

"I am only sorry that you never knew your mother… that I could not save her for us both."

He had told the story many times. When she was little, she had begged to hear it again and again, to feel for a while as though she actually belonged. This time was different. Her father's answers were the same - the script rarely varied - but nagged by the memory of emerald eyes, eyes that could also no longer see, her father's words echoed hollowly in her ears.

Aryelle closed her eyes and pretended until she drifted back into a fitful sleep...

…she was three revolutions old, barely two outside her mother's womb. Unlike most children she spoke clearly at an early age, her

innocent, yet astute observations enchanting most of the royal household. But not her stepmother. For some reason Aryelle could not understand, her stepmother did not like her. While the ladies in waiting, the servants, and even her father's courtiers and visiting dignitaries found her delightful and indulged her horribly, her stepmother blanched visibly whenever she entered the room. Aryelle had tried everything she could think of to endear herself, but was rewarded with only the woman's cold shoulder.

That spring she was allowed by her nursemaid to wander the walled gardens alone, a privilege granted because, being able to speak so clearly, she obviously understood what she was told. And what she was told was that under no circumstances was she to pick, step on or roll in any of the many flowering herbs and shrubs that comprised her stepmother's garden.

Normally this would have been no problem. But today was different. Today was Ladhonna's twenty-first name day. Arielle knew her stepmother had been more unhappy than usual lately. Perceptive as she was, there was no way she could've understood the reason, but had vowed she would make things better. She would pick a beautiful bouquet and present it to Ladhonna… who would then take her into her arms and show her all the affection that she surely must feel.

Aryelle tiptoed around the garden filled with fragrant cooking and healing herbs. Most luminaries gathered such things from forest and glen, but Ladhonna liked to keep her favorites close at hand. She was an excellent cook, unusual considering how little thought most of their kind put into what they ate. Her salves and tinctures were used by many to treat everything from insomnia and insect bites to varicosities and vertigo. Aryelle herself slept peacefully each night with her head resting on a pillow filled with hops, costmary and sweet woodruff from this very garden.

Woodruff has pretty little blue-white flowers, Aryelle remembered. She had seen some just the other day growing in the shade at the garden's farthest corner. She scampered off to find some. Partway there she was distracted by the wonderful scent of sweetbriar – but, better not to pick Ladhonna's roses she decided, glad for an excuse. The small, pink blooms grew on stems covered with even smaller, but sharp thorns. Beside the sweetbriar was a plant with clusters of yellow-green flowers and bluish leaves. She broke off a few stems with little difficulty, rubbing the oily residue on the front of her tunic. The palms of her hands tingled slightly, but she ignored the sensation as she spied an overflowing bed of tall, spiky flowers whose blossoms grew in white, pink and red whorls. After bending several stems without succeeding in breaking a single one, Aryelle firmly grasped a plant near the root and pulled with all her might. It came out of the ground suddenly, sending her sprawling into a patch of hyssop. Still clutching her prize, she added it to her growing bouquet roots and all. Then she crawled to her feet, leaving the violet hyssop flowers trampled, but intact. The smell reminded her too much of the medicine that was forced upon her whenever she had a cough.

Looking around, she saw that most of the plants in this part of the garden towered over her, some even growing higher than her wingtips. I had better go get the woodruff - she thought - it is more my size. She hurried down the path only to pull up short when ladies' voices drifted from ahead. One of them belonged to her stepmother. Quickly, she searched for a last moment addition to her skimpy bouquet, wishing she had added at least one stem of hyssop. Before she could grab so much as a plantain, she was spotted by one of the ladies.

"And here is our little Aryelle, with a pretty bouquet for you by the look of it, my Lady."

Ayrelle quickly thrust the flowers behind her back, deciding belatedly that perhaps it had not been such a good idea after all.

Ladhonna stepped past her companions, a tight smile on her lips. Behind her, the others giggled and cooed about what a sweet little flower they had found in the garden. Aryelle knew they meant her, but the look in Ladhonna's eyes said that she found her anything but sweet.

"What have you done child?" she demanded.

Reluctantly, Aryelle brought forth the drooping blooms. "For you," she said timidly.

Making no move to take them, Ladhonna stood mutely staring at the gift. Then her hand shot out, striking and strewing the flowers onto the path. She brushed roughly past Aryelle, crushing a whorl of white beneath her slipper.

Aryelle stood statue still, eyes brimming with tears that she refused to let fall. One of the maids gathered her gently into her arms as another stooped to retrieve the bruised blooms.

"Mother's milk," she whispered, reaching for one of the yellow topped stems, "and rue."

"How did you know, little one?" asked the third as they watched Ladhonna retreat down the path. "How ever did you know?"…..

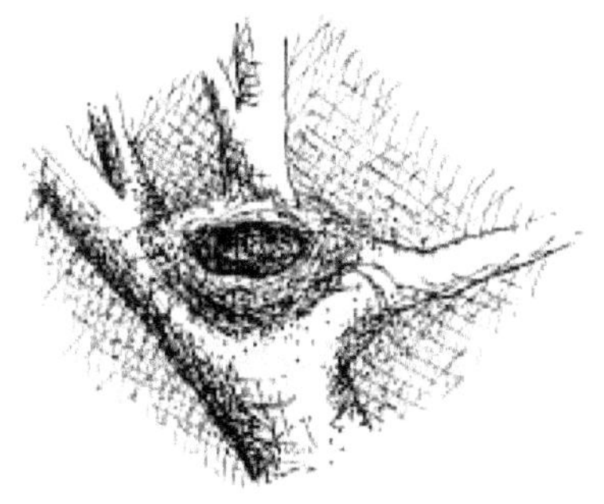

Chapter 4 - The Darkened Path

Dawn's rosy fingers tiptoed across the ceiling of the bedchamber as Karril bounded in. The room was unusually tidy but for an arm hanging limply over the edge of the oversized hammock that was Aryelle's bed. Karril pounced, triggering a tsunami of blanket and mesh. Aryelle clutched her pillow in alarm. Her eyes were rimmed with shadows. The embers of restless dreams still smoldering, she growled at the unwelcome intruder.

"Whoa! A fierce cheetah has eaten my cousin, and now it is after me!" Karril laughed.

"Go away!"

"I am glad to see you are back to yourself, Ari."

"Yes, thanks to you, I know! Now go away!"

Aryelle was always cross in the morning. Karril grinned, reassured that her ordeal had not changed her. He tugged playfully at her pillow as she burrowed deeper under the blankets.

"Wake up! I have news!"

Aryelle peered out from under the covers.

"Look where the last news you brought landed me!"

"This is different!" Karril said defensively. He yanked the pillow out and dropped it on her head. "You are to be sent away!"

"What?" she cried, bolting upright.

"Elazaryn's councilors are with him right now – they have been at it all night. Mother and Gaelen are against it, of course. They say you are too weak yet. But Ladhonna and Rachaan agree with the El'Kandhar-"

"Father *wants* to send me away?"

The next moment an insistent rap tattooed the door, and a nameless female page stepped shyly into the room. "The El'Kandhar summons you to his council chamber, my Lady."

"A moment!" Aryelle called as the page began backing out. "Ouf! Off my wing, Karril!" She shoved him onto the floor.

"Tell my father we will be right there."

"Yes, my Lady."

"And tell him…tell him you find me looking particularly well today." The page nodded. "No need for him to worry," Aryelle explained. "Hurry, Karril! Help me find my robes!"

Aryelle straightened her robe, positioning the cowl partway over her shoulder-length hair as was proper. She tapped lightly on the door, and hearing the summons entered. Karril was close at her heels.

The council chamber of the El'Kandhar was little more than a warm, richly paneled study. No imposing conference table overwhelmed its intimate space. In contrast to the vast emptiness of the main audience hall where the Seat of Ka'Andharra resided, this room overflowed with comfortable chairs and low tables, the walls adorned with richly textured weavings of woodland scenes mimicking the lush beauty outside large oval windows. Beams fashioned from living limbs of the majestic valleo spread haphazardly across the ceiling.

"I do not recall inviting you to this council, young master Karril. But I suppose since it affects you as well…" said Elazaryn, beckoning both young people further into the room. He and his weary councilors were taking full advantage of the fern backed chairs with their longer seats and narrow, curved backrests which allowed them to recline, wings parted comfortably, supported by the frond-like structure.

Aryelle approached her father and kissed him on the cheek.

"Good morning Aryelle. It is good to have you up and around again."

"Good morning, Father," she piped a little too cheerfully. "I trust you slept well?"

"I am sure our young informant here has told you just how I passed the night." Karril looked about innocently, though Aryelle had the grace to blush. *T'sura,* the 'other-sight' Elazaryn alone among living luminaries was gifted with, served him well.

"Listening at doors, however, is beneath even you, young man," he chastened, "which is why I have decided that you will accompany your cousin on her journey."

"Am I really being sent away, Father? But where? When? Why?" asked Aryelle in rapid succession.

"Patience, Aryelle. All will come to light."

Elazaryn gestured to servants hovering beside the door. Quickly they fetched chairs for the young newcomers. Aryelle took hers, but did not recline. Karril sat anxiously forward, swinging his dangling feet.

It was Rachaan who finally spoke. "The El'Kandhar has finally heeded my council and decided your time of discernment has come," he said self-importantly. "The arrival of the…eh-hem…*messenger* was timely indeed, for you are also being charged with a mission."

"But, I do not understand. What of the labyrinth?"

She referred to the labyrinth designed by her stepmother to simulate the spiritual journey that must be undertaken by all young luminaries discerning their vocations.

"It seems that the labyrinth is insufficient in the case of royalty," said Ladhonna petulantly.

"So, Sister, now you agree with me?"

"That is not what I meant and you know it, Kayanna. It is just that no one actually leaves Ka'Andharra anymore."

"My point exactly."

"But Aryelle is special?"

"Yes, she is. And she also nearly died!"

"This is not the time," Elazaryn reminded them. The sisters left off bickering and fell silent.

"As I was saying, the *andhruypa,*" Rachaan spat the word as if it tasted disagreeable, "brought news of a Summit to be held in one candle's time on Mount Cor in the village of the Aurrac. You are to go," he drawled, toying with her, "only as far as the nearest Naturra settlement with tidings that the Kandharra will not be attending." A thin smile curled his lips, twisting his handsome features. "And you must hurry;

your convalescence has wasted nearly a quarter-candle already."

Aryelle's questions poured forth in a torrent. She ignored Rachaan, turning instead to her father. "But should we not go to this Summit? Should we not seek peace with the Aurrac now that it is offered? And why would an andhruypa carry an Aurrac message?"

Rachaan's thin veneer cracked, emitting hostile sparks. "What do you know of the Aurrac, you impudent, foolish girl? It is forbidden speak of the other races!"

Elazaryn raised a hand for silence. When he spoke, his tone brooked no argument. "The affairs of the outside world are no longer our concern; that knowledge cost me dearly. I am content that our relationship with the Naturra, though tenuous, is at least somewhat restored. There is still much work to be done there. You, Aryelle, will go on your questanna, stay with the Naturra for a quarter-candle as my ambassador, and then return to Ka'Andharra. The Naturra will pass along our apologies to the Aurrac, and by that time you will have learned who you are."

Aryelle sat dazed. Her father had opened the cage with one hand and plucked her wings with the other.

Karril leapt down from his chair, barely able to contain himself. He knelt before his liege. "I will protect her, Uncle," he swore solemnly, "though I lose my life in the making."

"I know you will, Karril," said Elazaryn wryly. "You have proven your love and loyalty. However, I send you along not as champion, but as her chastisement." He turned toward Aryelle. "You believe you are a child no longer. To demonstrate it, you must put your needs and desires aside.

You must learn wisdom as well as compassion. *Ra dhin n'et dher zu*; the sun circles not only you. The path you walk may indeed grow dark, but your cousin's well being lies in your hands alone, Aryelle. Search yourself. And return Karril safely to us in one candle's time."

"It is foolhardy! They are children - they know nothing of what lies outside New Forest!" Kayanna had held her tongue long enough. Now that Aryelle and Karril had gone to prepare for their journey, she would speak her mind freely.

"Of course they know nothing! The Seal of Silence was the only way to ensure the children's safety, keep them ignorant of the world beyond Ka'Andharra, so that they would fear it. The Council of Elders foresaw this, which is why they commissioned the labyrinth in the first place," Ladhonna reminded her.

"Well, Aryelle already seems to know more than is good for her," grumbled Rachaan. "Besides, I thought you agreed that it was best for her to go."

"Enough!" said Elazaryn. "It has already been decided."

"How will they even find them?" asked Gaelen. The others seemed to have forgotten he was there. He alone among Elazaryn's councilors had actually visited a Naturra settlement.

"They will be given a guide, of course, and servants and a tutor for Karril. Oh, and certainly a healer will have to travel with them," sneered Ladhonna.

"Quite a retinue for a journey of self discovery, you must say," said Rachaan dripping sarcasm.

"Would you care to join it then?" asked Elazaryn.

"I will remain as always in the skies of Ka'Andharra. Those who would sully themselves may walk the pathways of darkness, but the royal houses of Kandharra have no place among them."

"Some royal houses of Kandharra are blinded by their own brilliance," said Kayanna, and looking past him to Elazaryn, "and some brighten even the darkest gloom." She went to kneel before the El'Kandhar. "I wish to accompany them, my lord, as healer and protector."

"I cannot allow it, Kayanna. Aryelle alone must assume responsibility for Karril."

"He is my son… and she is my niece. Aryelle need never know it is me traveling with them," she said, drawing her cowl over her silvery smooth hair. "What heed will they pay a silent contemplative?"

"I should be the one to go," said Gaelen, slapping his knee as he jumped to his feet.

"Oh, sit down!" commanded Rachaan.

Like an obedient puppet, Gaelen returned to his seat.

"Let Kayanna go," Rachaan counseled Elazaryn. "She is the most accomplished healer among the Kandharril, barring yourself, of course. And should the need arise, revealing her presence would surely be an additional thorn in the side to hasten your daughter's maturing. What fledgling wants an over protective mother goose to keep them from flying too far afield?"

Elazaryn weighed his chief advisor's words.

"So be it," he announced at last.

Chapter 5 – Wellwood Forest

Leaden skies wrung a steady drizzle over the cloaked figures navigating through the dense underbrush of New Forest. Around them, rain-darkened limbs donned swirling, autumnal dresses of red, gold, deep green and umber. The saturated forest floor swam under its thick, mossy blanket. Low-lying foliage soaked their robes as they brushed aside brambles and stepped lightly over fallen boughs. Undertones of decay, of fungus and rich humus mingled with the sharp snap of fern and occasional whiff of fir concocting a pungent potluck for the senses.

The travelers, having set out well before dawn strode silently, not single file but four abreast, each several wingspans from the next. Their wings, however, appeared as packs, furled tightly and bound with spider-silk netting to avoid the painful nuisance of a snag. Such was customary on questanna, as was the forging of one's own path.

At least, thought Aryelle, she didn't have to wait for the next in line before letting wet branches snap back into place behind her. The understory was much too close for flight, nor would she have wasted precious energy on such extravagance even without Karril along. Only in dire need would she dare use her wings without weighty consideration. Did the Naturra feel the same way living in this wilderness, she wondered? She imagined their carefree silhouettes flitting among the trees.

But… the Naturra would not be carefree, would they? Here in New Forest, the vast woodland encircling Ka'Andharra, they harvested timber for building, furniture making, and trade. For the most part the Kandharra disdained commerce, considering it beneath their attention, and had left such mundane tasks to the Naturra in the generations since the schism that divided the Empaya into factions. Erudite and philosophical, the Kandharra inhabited the tree-borne city. Ordinary Naturra preferred the surrounding forest, leaving the capitol for the elite. Though they were, after all, the same people, many revolutions ago when pestilence and famine ran rampant through their ranks, the Naturra became aggressive, raiding the city for provisions, abducting women, children, and anyone whose work or studies took them outside its boundaries. Retaliation was unheard of; luminaries were by nature pacifists. But anger and resentment eventually choked off all contact between the factions. Hard times followed. The city inhabitants were forced to neglect their studies, undertaking by necessity the manual labors once performed by the forest dwellers. Meanwhile, the Naturra withdrew to the further reaches of Wellwood Forest where life grew increasingly difficult. Recently they had begun resettling New Forest, and an uneasy peace now existed.

Today was the fifth day of their journey. Soon they should reach the Naturra settlement closest to Ka'Andharra. Aryelle should have been jubilant despite the gloomy weather. After all, she was finally getting her wish. Her father had sent her on an important mission, given her adult responsibilities. Granted, he had also sent along a Naturra guide and a healer - and *of course,* Karril - but venturing beyond Ka'Andharra and its park-like woodland was itself extraordinary. Though Naturra occasioned the city, she had never spoken to one before or even seen one up close, let alone visited one of their settlements. Why then was her heart so heavy? Finally, it dawned on her. These her brethren were as much strangers to her as the andhruypa had been. Her father had once been determined to change that, but so little progress had been made before he gave up. Perhaps she could rekindle that flame.

Earlier Aryelle had sensed snatches of thought between Karril and the guide. So far, however, resentment kept her from joining in their conversations. Now she detected nothing, nor could she sense the healer. A thought-shield guarded the Kandharril's mind as effectively as the deep hood that concealed the elite healer's face.

Aryelle glanced to her right, expecting a glimpse of her companions, startled to see nothing but gray. She found herself dwarfed by an enormous beech, it's trunk a full wingspan across. Never had she seen a tree so immense! The valleo that supported Ka'Andharra were giants, yes, but in a sprawling mass of gnarled branches that gave the city a feeling of being wrapped in a massive embrace. This colossus soared upward, straight and true, branching out only after several flytes of enormous, smooth trunk. Aryelle spied other towering beeches and maples breaking through the leafy canopy, and a number of lofty conifers as well. The dense underbrush had given way, and before her rose a wall of textured sepia, grays and evergreen.

A hand touched her shoulder before the guide's thoughts reached her mind, causing her to startle.

-We are entering Wellwood, the most ancient forest in all of Emrysia. From here springs forth all life, all happiness.-

"It is breathtaking!" replied Aryelle, peering from the trees to his weathered face. His skin was rough as tree bark from a lifetime in the elements.

-Hush! Speak only with your thoughts until the sun is full ripened. We must not interrupt the morning adoration.-

As the clouds parted to allow the first rays of sunlight to penetrate the dripping foliage, a chickadee's trill, like a concertmaster's baton, called for attention. A robin answered, and a thrush, and soon the hushed stillness that had ushered in the day gave way to a cheerful symphony. Karril came to stand beside Aryelle, sharing her awe. The cousins linked hands and together entered Wellwood Forest.

****

"Was it not brilliant? Ridding ourselves of three obstacles in one effortless swoop! Four really, if you count the andhruypa, but of course, he really does not count, does he? It is not as if he were Empaya, or even Emrysian for that matter. And what ghastly eyes! I thought Aryelle's were bad enough, but with that blaiz hair and pale spotted skin, they jumped out so menacingly, even in his delirium. Do you not agree Ladhonna? Ladhonna! Have you drifted off, my darling?"

"Of course not," she snapped from the simple, woven cushions of her divan. "I have been blocking out your prattle, trying to think!"

"Touchy, are we? Do you have headache again? Here, let me take it-"

"Leave me be!" She shied from his touch. "I am not in pain. But neither am I so foolishly certain that we are rid of them."

Rachaan's fist clenched like a vise around her fragile wrist.

"I am no fool, my dear. You would be wise to remember that. You may have your potions and poisons, but I hold something just as powerful – the purse strings. Who do you think selected and *paid* the guide for their little excursion? Hmm? Ah, I see you are beginning to understand." He loosened his grip and sauntered across the room, leaving Ladhonna to rub her bruised forearm. "Just about now, they should be feeling the effects of their journey into Wellwood, which alas, it seems I neglected to mention. And their guide, I am afraid, is turning out to be an unreliable drone, incapable of keeping his way. Your sister, as you know, has promised not to interfere. By the time she realizes what is happening, she will have succumbed as well. Now," he said arrogantly, "who is the fool?"

"What makes you think Aryelle will not find her own way?"

"A surprising young woman is she not?" he drawled. "But *if* she survives Wellwood, the surprise will be hers when she reaches to the Naturra settlement. Not even Elazaryn could protect her from what she will find there."

****

Aryelle reeled gazing up through the spiraling branches at the dizzying height of the forest, newly aware of her own insignificance. The trees stood like massive columns in a vast sanctuary as a lofty chorus of birdsong issued from the canopy overhead.

Neglecting the custom of no trail travel, Aryelle and Karril continued in awed silence, pausing occasionally to wrap their arms around a massive trunk. Oak, pine, beech, and others they did not recognize eventually gave way to even more mammoth redwood and sequoia. Time slowed and their legs grew leaden, the soporific effect of decaying needles. The further they plodded the slower their pace, as if they were growing roots or wading through deepening water.

Once last summer, on a dare from Karril, Aryelle had plunged into the icy depths of an abandoned quarry pool. The pressure had threatened to crush her chest as she struggled to return to the surface. The same pressure threatened her now.

Karril fastened on Aryelle with widening eyes.

"I…cannot breathe…," he gasped, his voice pale and frightened. He doubled over with a sudden cramp.

"Just try to….relax. Breathe… slowly…" A giant fist squeezed her own chest. She turned in slow motion, scanning the forest. "Where…is…guide?"

Karril shook his head weakly. "Drowning…"

"Cannot…drown…here…"

Aryelle caught her sagging cousin just as her own knees buckled beneath her, and they collapsed together against the toes of an enormous sequoia. She swung her head drunkenly, searching for signs of the healer. There - a movement, perhaps the flutter of a white Kandharril robe, she could not be certain. Her thoughts grew thick and sluggish, panic slurred to drowsy calm. For some reason Kayanna's distraught face floated eerily before her eyelids. Then darkness took her.

The enormous forest impressed Kayanna too. She had journeyed south to the Emerald Shore for her own questanna, her sole venture beyond the familiar woodlands of Ka'Andharra. Tales of the giant forest thrived in her youth, but she had never paid close attention to them. Her love was for the sea. Now however, she found herself lagging further and further behind. She observed the youngsters from a distance, privy to their conversations while effectively shielding her own thoughts. But soon the sheer size of the rugged giants distracted her. Had they not been likewise distracted they would have found her thought-barrier slipping. Like them, she extended her arms around the rough and spongy, reddish-brown bark, measuring her own insignificance. By the time Kayanna felt the same crushing weight as Aryelle and Karril she had completely lost sight of them. She called out beyond caring about discovery, but her cry was swallowed in the cacophony of birdsong. She stumbled forward, bracing herself against the wall of a mighty sequoia as she struggled against the sleepy stupor that threatened to engulf her. Her last conscious thought was that she had failed the children.

Chapter 6 – Out of the Depths

"Stop! Stop here! Ooof!"

The occupant of the ornate, triangular litter nearly fell off her plush perch as her bearers rounded a giant sequoia just as she was beginning to rise. Righting herself, she flicked a tasseled rope at her lead bearer, knocking his feathery headdress askew. He adjusted it back into place, not missing a stride.

"You great oafs! You can't hear me, can you? Oooh! - why aren't there reins on this thing!" The woman sniffed in irritation producing a slim, reedy looking whistle and blowing it with all her might. Immediately, all three bearers and a fourth servant carrying an enormous feathery fan came to an abrupt halt. The woman lurched forward, hurling unheard epitaphs upon their heads. One of the rear bearers activated a switch on the contraption's side, and a set of crisscrossed legs dropped from its underbelly and locked into place. Lowering each to one knee, the bearers relinquished the litter to its supports and awaited the pleasure of their mistress.

She rose shakily. Finding her balance, she stepped daintily to the edge of the platform and stamped her foot in impatience. Instantly all four servants bound forward to form a living staircase. The first, on hands and knees, arched his broad back reducing the distance his mistress must step from the platform. She wriggled her toes against his bare skin and stepped lightly onto the back of the second. The third bearer hunched a step lower, and the fourth lay prostrate on the ground, his fan propped against the rear of the litter. As the train of her shimmering, sea green gown tickled his skin, his expansive dorsal muscles rippled. Turning, she prodded him in the ribs with her foot and cast an appreciative glance, then jerked her head in the direction of the fan.

The woman, a voluptuous russet-haired beauty, motioned to her attendants to accompany her. They fell into formation, the lead man attending point position once more, while identical rear bearers bookended the woman. The fan bearer took up his prop and shaded her from behind. Rounding the roots of yet another massive sequoia, they stopped just short of trampling a crumpled, white figure. The woman peered around the lead bearer, and then hastily pushed past him. Crouching, she tore back the figure's hood.

"Tsk-tsk…what a pity. She must be one of the city dwellers," she murmured to deaf ears. "Probably didn't know the giant forest's secret."

Noting her straight, silvery blond hair and unadorned robe she commented wryly. "What a plain creature!" But admiring looks from her servants confirmed that they did not share her opinion.

Feeling peevish, she picked up the luminarie's limp wrist… and felt a pulse.

"She's still alive – quickly! Fetch my vials!

No one moved. Scrabbling for a pinecone she pitched it, hitting the closest man squarely in the chest. She pantomimed effectively someone drinking a potion for a miraculous recovery. Quickly the servant ran back to the litter, returning with a small, sealskin case. The woman tore into it. The case was lined with pouches and pockets, each holding a miniature conical vial. She carefully selected one and removed its stone stopper, pouring a few precious drops into Kayanna's parted lips. Almost at once she sat up taking big gulping breaths.

"You must not have drowned long ago," said the russet haired beauty in Commonspeak.

"Drowned? Drowning! The children! Please, we must find them!" Kayanna cried.

"How many others?" the woman asked.

"Three. My son-"

But the woman was already motioning wildly to the men who spread out swiftly in each direction. Soon, one returned with Karril and Aryelle slung over either brawny shoulder. He knelt and eased them onto the ground near Kayanna. Both had a slight bluish tinge to their skin.

Once again the woman un-stoppered the vial, allowing a few drops to fall into their mouths. Nothing happened.

"Were they drowned longer than you?" she asked.

"It could not have been much longer," answered Kayanna anxiously.

The woman turned Karril's face skyward and blew into his parted lips. His chest swelled, and when she lifted her head, he began to cough and sputter, though not fully awaken. Quickly she moved around to Aryelle and filled her lungs with air, but nothing happened. A large hand pushed the woman aside and swung, striking Aryelle on the center of her chest. Her eyes flew open and she gasped. Then they closed once more.

"No!" screamed Kayanna, clinging to her unconscious son.

"She's breathing," the woman reassured her. "See, her color returns. Nicely done, Jorda! I may even forgive you for handling me so roughly!" she patted the man's strong arm as Kayanna gathered both youngsters into her arms. "You must rest now. Returning from the deep is no easy matter. The girl must be weaker, but with rest she'll be fine."

"Our guide…?" began Kayanna.

"Couldn't have gone far… unless he knew the forest and its ways?"

"He was Naturra."

"Then he has abandoned you, lady. Didn't he warn you of Wellwood's depths?"

Kayanna shook her head. "I should have known, but the Kandharra have forgotten much. I still do not understand what happened. How could we drown in a forest?"

"Few outsiders know its secrets, besides my people that is. We shared this knowledge with the Naturra ages ago," the woman explained knowingly. "Wellwood's name has two meanings. A well may have untold depth, and so does the forest encircling Lake Mirth, the birthplace of Emrysia. These are the oldest trees in the land. Like all things elderly they sleep a great deal. But they also dream. When their dreams are deepest they remember their beginnings as tiny seeds, buried deep beneath the soil, waiting for the great spring to overflow her shores and bring them to life. As they wait, their dead boughs fill the air with the fragrance of sleep - sleep so deep that only those accustomed to great depths can withstand it. Entering the forest, the unsuspecting drown in the fragrance and become part of their dreams." She shrugged. "Eventually they become part of the soil."

Kayanna eyed her skeptically. "Why did our guide not warn us?"

The woman answered with a question of her own. "What do you know of your guide?"

"Naught save that Rachaan said he was the best, and came from the Naturra settlement to which we travel."

"Perhaps this Rachaan didn't have your best interest at heart."

Kayanna considered her suggestion. "You are from here?"

The woman laughed a throaty, gurgling sound. "No, but I have known depths such as these. Now, see here! My men return with empty shoulders, a poor thing for a slave, wouldn't you agree?" She smiled at Kayanna's confusion. "We shall speak more later."

She turned to her servants and gestured a command. At once, they hurried to the litter and began to unload it. A lavish silken tent was unrolled and erected, fluttering banners at its pinnacles. A smaller, yet no less elaborate tent was pitched nearby, and a screened pavilion as well. Kayanna watched in fascination. In just moments they were nearly done.

"Have you never seen men work before?" remarked the woman.

"I have not," she replied, "at least, not like those…like them. 'Slaves' are servants then?"

"No, they're my brothers! Of course, they're servants. And you? Have you no servants other than children?" She frowned. "Or are you someone else's servant?"

Kayanna returned her dubious look. Surely, this strange woman could not mistake her for a member of the working class.

"I am Kayanna of the Kandharra, High Order of Kandharril. This is my son Karril."

"K- k- k! That's a lot of kays. And the girl?" she asked, mildly amused.

Kayanna regarded the wingless stranger. She had saved their lives, but that did not make her rudeness any more acceptable. Though her colorful, wavy hair was striking, the rest of her appearance was garish. A crown of many-colored coral coiled across her brow. Shells and pearls hung in thick ropes at her neck. Rings and bangles adorned each slender wrist and finger. Her skin appeared flawless, but when she turned her head, a silvery shimmer flashed across it. Kayanna wondered if her recent brush with death had left lingering effects on her vision. The woman's gown was strapless, clinging to her like a second, glittery skin, and it matched the color of her eyes exactly. Something about her was disturbingly familiar.

"Her name is Aryelle. She is my niece, and heir to the Seat of Ka'Andharra. She is…" Kayanna paused, wondering just how much to reveal, "…on questanna, a journey of the soul. She knows a healer travels with her, but she does not realize it is I. Nor does my son," she added, cradling Karril's unruly blond head. "I have reason to conceal this from them."

"Ooh, a secret identity! How delicious!" The woman leaned in conspiratorially. "Fear not; *I* won't reveal your secret."

"And your servants?" Except for elaborate headdresses and brief loincloths they were practically unclothed. Kayanna blushed.

"Them? Why, they can't hear or speak! At least… well, never mind. But, perhaps you'd like them to set up an additional shelter?"

"I do not need-"

"Nonsense! Crispin! Katri!" She clapped her hands, despite the fact she had just proclaimed them deaf. "Oh, there I go again!"

From the bosom of her gown she produced a slender whistle and blew. Kayanna heard no sound issue from it, but all four men immediately snapped to attention. Using gestures, the woman instructed them to raise another tent.

"I will stay with the children while they recover," Kayanna said, watching the men work with amazing speed. "What are their names?" she asked belatedly.

"Jorda, Crispin, Katri & Jaim, though I often forget which is which. Bulging, blond, beautiful - and dumb as rocks! Except for maybe Jorda, but then he's the eldest. Isn't the eldest always the brightest?"

Kayanna did not know how to respond. Instead, she inquired her name as well.

"Lureli-, er-…um…just Lureli. And now, I suggest we all get our beauty rest."

Chapter 7 – The Stranger's Tent

Kayanna awoke totally refreshed. She had not meant to sleep at all, but it felt wonderful to unbind her wings after so many days of confinement, and the sleeping mat had proven irresistible. Lureli told her that these pads were called sponges. The name meant nothing to her. She only knew they were incredibly comfortable, conforming to her body no matter how she shifted. Dreamily she considered her luxurious surroundings. Gauzy silks and shimmering satins draped in an excess the likes of which she had never seen. This surfeit use of fabrics and pillows she considered poor taste, though she had to admit, it suited her hostess. Kayanna reprimanded herself. How childish to be critical of Lureli's taste in decorating when they owed her their lives! The curtains billowed as the breeze played across them, ripples of light across the waves. It reminded her of the sea. Actually, now that she thought about it, the hangings added a softness that the sparseness of her suite in the royal compound could benefit from. She herself wore only the white linen robe of the Kandharril, but many Kandharra preferred the sheer weight of silk. When they returned she would speak to a clothier about procuring some for her apartments.

Stretched out on their own sponges, Aryelle and Karril rested peacefully. Kayanna probed their minds for any lingering signs of injury. Confidant that they were out of danger, she rolled up her sponge and carried it with her. She was glad Lureli had suggested the third tent. To continue to keep her identity hidden, at least for the time being, she must keep her distance.

Trying to ignore their appreciative glances, Kayanna stepped past the scantily clad servants standing guard outside the tent's entrance. Lureli must have appointed them to wait upon her. One of the matched pair snatched the sleeping mat and, with a grin as broad as his brawny shoulders, rushed off to put it in the third tent. Kayanna felt her insides squirm when the second man fell into step behind her. She turned and made a shooing motion. He fell back a pace. Each time she shooed, he gave her more space yet cheerfully tagged along. Finally she gave up and hurried toward Lureli's tent where yet another servant stood guard. He parted the tent's flowing entrance curtain and allowed her to pass. Thankfully, the men remained outside.

The interior was cave-like after the dazzling sunlight, and it took several moments for her eyes to adjust. When they did she saw that Lureli lay not only on a sponge mat, but also in the center of a very large puddle. She pretended not to have noticed and began surreptitiously backing out of the tent only to bump into the last of the servants. Across his shoulders he bore a yoke from which hung two large vessels. Kayanna stepped out of his way and watched as he emptied first one, then the other into the puddle.

"What? What!" Lureli cried bolting upright as water splashed over her.

Before she could stop herself, Kayanna burst out laughing. Her hostess was hardly recognizable. Lureli's face was coated with a thick, green paste. Two smooth, flat stones covered her eye sockets, and her hair was coiled in prickly rows along her head. Gone was the garish jewelry, but the coral headpiece had slipped down like a chinstrap, looking for all Emrysia like a multi-colored beard.

Lureli plucked the stones from over her eyes and screamed. Kayanna responded with a squeal of nervous laughter.

"Out! OUT!" Lureli screeched, clutching her silky robe around her.

Kayanna did not need to be told twice. Retreating, she left the bewildered servant to bear the wrath of his mistress. The others were nowhere to be seen. She fled the encampment past the giant sequoia – the very tree that ought to have been her last living vision. She needed privacy to think, perhaps by the river where the servant had drawn water. Wandering in the most likely direction, she made sure to keep the tent banners in sight.

Karril awoke to find himself in a strange tent, on a strange bed, with an even stranger lady bending over him. Her hair, though not true blaiz, resembled that of the andhruypa messenger in coloring. Her dangling jewelry practically brushed his face. He gulped when he spied the huge blond men flanking her on either side.

"I'm glad to see you're awake," she said, with a queer upside-down smile. "I was hoping to find your m-, um... healer here with you. Don't suppose that's um... ah, well, seeing as you're up... I expect you're a bit confused."

Confused did not even come close! He understood what she was saying all right, though she contracted words in a manner that was unfamiliar. Since contact with other Emrysians was rare, Kandharrans studied languages mostly for intellectual stimulus, yet spoke Commonspeak more often than their own ancient tongue. But...who was she and what was he doing here? The last thing Karril remembered was drowning in the middle of an immense forest and Aryelle with him. He looked around in alarm. Where was she now?

"The young woman is right over there," offered the stranger, "still sleeping soundly. I suspect she will for some time yet."

"She is my cousin," he said hesitantly. "She is taking care of me. Do not hurt her!"

"Who's caring for whom?" asked Lureli, amused. "I won't hurt either of you, you know. I'm a friend. These," she gestured, "are my servants. You are in my tent. *I* am the one who saved you," she announced.

"But our healer-"

"I saved your healer as well, though I've received little gratitude there."

"Then where is he?"

"He? Hhenh! *He* is probably out roaming the forest again, though you needn't worry. The potion I gave you all will protect her- I mean him, for the rest of his days. You too."

Karril was more confused than ever, and more than a little bit worried. It must have shown on his face, for the woman's expression softened and she gazed almost tenderly at him.

"Your guide has disappeared, by the way, but don't worry," she said. "You're safe here, and when your cousin wakes up we shall sup together. Rest now and I shall find that *healer* for you."

Karril breathed a sigh of relief as she and her escorts left the tent. Then he rushed to his cousin's side.

"Aryelle! Aryelle! Wake up!" he whispered urgently, shaking her. "Come on, we have to get out of here!"

She sat up groggily. "Where are we?"

"An andhruypa tent- a *lady* andhruypa!- with wild blaiz hair and huge men, and none of them have wings!" Karril tripped over the words as he ran out of breath.

"Slow down so I can understand you," said Aryelle, rubbing sleep from her eyes. "Begin again, only slower this time."

"There is a lady who says that she saved our lives. This is her tent." He motioned toward the shimmering walls of the enclosure. "She looks like the messenger, at least, her hair is blaiz, but darker. She is not spotted either, at least I do not think she is, but she, well, *glittered* when she moved around."

"The Naturra have found us then."

"Aryelle, listen to me!" Karril grew exasperated. "They have no wings!"

"Perhaps they are bound like our own," she said, then realized that someone had unbound hers while she slept. "Wait a moment. Let me think-"

"There is no time! We have to leave now, before she comes back! She is out looking for our healer. Come on!" He tried to pull Aryelle to her feet, but she refused to budge.

"Cousin, if she had meant us any harm she could certainly have done so while we slept," she argued logically. "And you say she saved our lives-"

"*She* said so."

"Then we owe her our thanks. I think - no, I remember…we were drowning…but how…? It is all so confusing." She buried her face in her hands and inhaled deeply.

She remembered the pressure building on her body and in her lungs, remembered struggling for her last breath. And then… nothing, until now. Then suddenly she remembered something else. Karril was her responsibility. She raised her head, looked directly into her cousin's frightened eyes, and smiled to reassure him.

"I do not know how we got here, but you should not worry," she said, unknowingly echoing Lureli. "Tell me everything you have seen and heard so far, and I will decide what we should do."

Not long afterward, Aryelle stepped from the tent displaying a confidence she did not feel, Karril following close on her heels. The coming twilight softened the outlines of other tents nearby, bathing them in a rosy glow. Startled, she noticed hulking figures looming on either side of the tent flap, arms crossed, imposing except for the broad smiles that spread across their faces at the sight of them.

Aryelle gaped. Muscles bulged and rippled beneath their smooth, tanned skin. Longish, blond hair fell in windswept waves to their conspicuously wingless shoulders. Her eyes drifted over the well-defined chest of the man nearest her. He seemed to find her assessment amusing, grinning even wider. Hesitantly she returned his smile while Karril eyed the men warily.

"Greetings," said Aryelle in Commonspeak.

The men nodded in return.

"I am Aryelle, of the Kandharra, and this is my cousin Karril. We are in your debt."

The men's eyes followed her movement briefly, returning to her face as though magnetized. Her cheeks flushed scarlet.

"We would like to thank you, but I am afraid we have nothing to offer."

They continued to stare.

"I do not think they understand, Ari," offered Karril. "The woman did all of the talking before."

"Do you understand me?" she asked, tilting her head questioningly to the side. Both men mirrored her gesture.

Doing what came naturally, Aryelle spoke telepathically. *-I am Aryelle.-*

The men's eyes widened in surprise and for the first time their smiles faltered.

-You can speak to me with your thoughts and I will understand.-

They exchanged bewildered glances.

-I am Aryelle- she repeated. *–What are you called?-*

With this form of communication, not so much words but an understanding of what she was asking flooded their minds. But having never heard their own names before, they were unsure how to respond. Tentatively, one of them made a wrist flicking motion with his hand, smallest finger extended. Aryelle understood it to be the sign for his name. She nodded and repeated the movement. Sudden thought detonated through her brain.

-HOW CAN YOU BE IN MY HEAD?-

Aryelle clutched her skull.

-Shhhhh! Think quietly! I can hear your thoughts and you can hear mine. We can speak this way since you do not understand my language.-

-WE CANNOT... we cannot speak- thought the other man, softening his mental tone when she winced.

-And what are you called?-

-I do not know what word our Lady uses, but this is my symbol. - He tapped the tips of his middle finger and thumb together twice. Again, she repeated the gesture and he smiled. This time she returned his smile encouragingly.

-Where is your Lady?-

-In the pavilion with the other of your kind. We will take you to her- he began to lead them toward it.

-Is she your mistress?-

-She is our Duty; we are hers to command.-

-You are bound to her then?-

-Bound by love, not chains.-

Perfect replicas of one another, the men took turns speaking as if they shared one voice.

-Can all of your kind speak in this way, inside your mind? - one of them asked.

-Yes- she responded.

-Even the puny one?-

"I am not puny!" cried Karril indignantly. Though he had spoken aloud, the man seemed to understand that he had caused offence.

-*Humble apologies!*- He bowed low, striking his breast.

-*Accepted*- Karril conceded reluctantly.

-*Ah, young master is generous. And will undoubtedly grow in stature to match his beneficence.*-

Karril beamed. Perhaps they were not so frightening after all.

As they approached the pavilion, the men made it clear that though they were not eager to end their conversation, their mistress might not approve. Belatedly, Aryelle wondered if she had been premature in her conversation with them. Karril had no such qualms.

-*We will just keep it our little secret*- he told them with a wink.

Two more servants, not identical but clearly related, were stationed outside the pavilion's entrance. They stood aside the curtained doorway, looking puzzled when the winged boy winked at them as well. As Karril and Aryelle ducked through the opening, their escorts gestured excitedly to their counterparts.

"I like them," Karril confided to her.

"They seem harmless enough, but I think it is not them we have to worry about," replied Aryelle, shifting her attention to those within. Seated amid plush cushions, the hooded Kandharril across from her, was the stranger matching Karril's description. Her flamboyant appearance and over-abundant jewelry jarred glaringly with the healer's simple white robes. Both stood as Aryelle and Karril came forward.

"Welcome, welcome Princess Aryelle and Lord Karril!" The stranger bowed. "Thy healer hast just begun to tell me of thy quest. How good it was that we stumbled upon thee, else thy quest would be over ere it began!" She laughed a giddy, ingratiating chortle. The Kandharril stood silent, letting them muddle through their own introductions.

Aryelle bristled. "And you find that amusing?"

Lureli was taken aback. "No, of course not. I meant only that thou wouldst-"

"Why does she speak so queerly?" Karril whispered a little too loudly. He had not meant to sound offensive, but instinctively mistrusted her.

"What *doth* thou mean?" asked Lureli through clenched teeth. "How wouldst thou have me address the future El'Kandharre?"

"You may address me as any other," replied Aryelle stiffly, remembering how much she disliked the formality of her father's court. "And how may we address you?"

"My name is Lureli, maiden of the Mer. Forgive my ignorance, but in *our* courts we maintain a certain decorum of language. After all, we are a bit above the rabble now, are we not? But since you prefer to be casual..."

"You are of a ruling class then?" Aryelle asked.

"I, well, you see..." she stammered, color rising in her cheeks, "that is, e-hem... I am."

"You seem unsure of yourself."

Lureli held her head erect. A shimmering, silvery flash streaked across her proud features.

From the shadow of her cowl, Kayanna finally realized why Lureli looked familiar. She had glimpsed someone similar sunning herself on a reef just off the Emerald Shore. Her hair had been raven in color, and she had slipped bashfully into the sea, but not before Kayanna noticed the silvery glint of her skin. How this young woman resembled her! Oh, and how vulnerable she was here! What was she doing so far from home?

Aryelle regarded her hostess' complexion and the arrogant gleam that entered her eyes. Admittedly curious, she had no intention of their acquaintance being a lengthy one. She was on a mission.

"It makes little difference-" they both began.

"-what you think," finished Lureli awkwardly alone.

"What I think is that I owe you an apology and our thanks," said Aryelle with carefully considered diplomacy. "Your tents are most comfortable, though I do not understand how we came to be in them. The last thing I remember was gasping for a dying breath."

"Which it most certainly would have been," Lureli sniffed indignantly, "had I not revived you with a special draught known only to my people. I explained this to your healer earlier."

Aryelle looked back and forth between the two. The Kandharril remained silent, thought shield in place. From the obscurity of her hood, Kayanna nodded.

"And who are the Mer?" Aryelle continued.

"I suppose you've never heard of us. We rarely travel far inland, though we often meet your Naturra near our shores."

"You are from the coast? Chimera Sea? "

"Yes, you might say that."

"That is a long way from here. Even the Kandharra do not usually journey into Wellwood. Now I know why. How is it you are not affected? What is this draught you speak of?"

"The Mer have long depended upon the sea for their...well-being. The draught is made from the bile of a creature that resides on the sea floor. It protects one from the pressure of the depths, both on land and water," Lureli explained. "As I told your healer, we shared this secret with the Naturra many generations ago."

Aryelle frowned. It seemed this stranger was communicating a good deal with the Kandharril, who had so far remained completely aloof with her. Plus, she claimed a connection to her wilder cousins that she herself could not. Jealously reared up in Aryelle's chest.

"The Naturra and the Kandharra are a people divided," she said bitterly.

"Yes, I know. But then how do you come to be traveling through Wellwood? Isn't this their territory?"

"We are on an ambassadorial mission. I come in the name of my father, Elazaryn."

"You will also be attending the Summit on Mt. Cor then?"

Aryelle hesitated, surprised. Should she share her plans? What if this strange woman wanted to go with them? Then again, perhaps it would be better to travel together. She might learn more about the Summit than her father had been willing to share, and about the Naturra as well, it seemed. Besides, they no longer had a guide. Swallowing her irrational resentment toward Lureli, and toward her own people at being kept ignorant of the outside world, she focused instead on the possibilities before her.

"I travel first to the nearest Naturra settlement," she answered truthfully, deciding for the moment to keep her restrictions to herself.

"Surely there's one nearer Ka'Andharra? Oh, yes… your guide. I'd forgotten." Lureli glanced meaningfully toward the silent Kandharril. "I believe you've had a traitor in your midst."

"A traitor?"

"We never found him, but your healer tells me he was Naturra. It seems you've been traveling more northeast than west, but with all this glorious rain how could you tell? You are now in the thumb between the Lifeblood River and Lake Mirth."

Aryelle was stunned. How could her father have sent her out with--- she stopped mid thought. Unless it had not been her father who selected the guide! But then who had? Rachaan? She looked toward the Kandharril, but again met a blank wall.

"He would have known," she murmured.

"Unquestionably," agreed Lureli, thinking she meant the guide.

Aryelle reigned in her thoughts. It was a puzzle she was determined to solve, but now, with this stranger, was not the time.

"Between the Lororil and Lac Ril..." Aryelle wagged her head in dismay. "We are much out of our way."

At that moment, all four servants came blundering in bearing platters of food in one hand, and large vessels balanced precariously on their opposite shoulders. Water sloshed over their backs as they jockeyed for position in the now crowded pavilion.

"Oh, goodie!" gushed Lureli delightedly. "Please," she motioned her guests toward some empty cushions. "Let us eat together and discuss our plans. Perhaps we will have much in common."

As Aryelle and Karril found seats for themselves, Lureli flopped back down and scooped a large handful of green slurry off the nearest platter. Whatever her plans, thought Aryelle, the two of them were as likely to have anything in common as a frog and a butterfly.

Chapter 8 – The Laughing Lake

Dawn birthed a much different day. The sun, having labored through dreary skies for most of the exceptionally wet summer, bore down on them with fierce intensity by midmorning. Though the luminaries were ready to depart long before sunrise, their hostess dawdled abed. Finally, she emerged from her tent in a sleepy stupor, wincing at the brilliant sky. She would have retreated into its shady interior had not her servants efficiently collapsed and stored the tent as soon as she stepped foot outside. Blinking through the glare, she discovered the luminaries waiting expectantly. With a resigned sigh, she joined them.

A short while later they were on their way. Their enigmatic healer hung back as usual. With no guide, and no reason to spread out in the meadow-like spaces between the mammoth trees, Aryelle and Karril followed Lureli's litter enjoying the freedom of marching with wings unbound again. Sunshine lifted their spirits, and the freshening scent of the drying forest no longer seemed heavy and cloying. Up till now they had traveled in relative silence, speaking telepathically when necessary, but once Lureli fully awakened she kept up a steady stream of chatter, commenting on each novel thing along the way. When a hedgehog scuttled by she leapt up, nearly tumbling from her perch. Her bearers lurched to a stop.

"A running urchin!" she squealed with delight. She would've scrambled down after it, but with a nod from the lead bearer, they immediately set out again.

Earlier while waiting for Lureli to rouse herself, Aryelle had spoken with the servants about their need for haste. The big men were eager to oblige. Karril was getting on especially well with them. Aryelle did little to discourage him besides warning that they should not appear too chummy in front Lureli, who now swayed drunkenly back to her seat. She gazed with longing over her shoulder, but did not bid them stop. The aft man glanced back as well, his giant feathery fan brushing her in the face as he turned. Lureli sputtered and glared at him.

Aryelle suppressed a grin, recalling dinner the evening before. Throughout the meal, the servants had repeatedly spilled the contents of the water vessels, each time on their mistress. Expecting her to fly into a rage, Aryelle was astounded that Lureli merely scolded them and returned to the conversation at hand. After the meal they had offered, not tiny fingerbowls, as Aryelle was accustomed to using, but deep, platter-like saucers filled to the brim. Lureli plunged her entire face into the scented water, a blissful sigh accompanying her dripping return to the surface.

Stranger still had been the food they provided. Dishes of raw fish and huge crayfish-like creatures the luminaries declined, revolted by the thought of consuming the flesh of another living thing. There were platters of vegetables and greens, though most were foreign and heavily salted. Accustomed to eating sparsely, Aryelle was content to sit back and watch as their hostess tucked in with abandon. The Kandharril, she noted, ate nothing. Apparently unconcerned about her guests' lack of appetite, Lureli ripped open a shell and regaled them with the story of her journey so far.

She had traveled only half a day inland, but had battled the current of the river from the Lororil's fertile delta for many before that. Why she fought against the river's flow instead of traveling alongside it was a mystery left explained. Aryelle would have raised the question, but Lureli never gave her a chance. They left the river when its rapids became treacherous, miles before its source at Lac Ril - Lake Mirth as she called it. Her intent was to cross the immense natural spring and continue the journey northward via another river at its further shore. Here, she told them, was another Naturra settlement visited by her people long ago. She had sent a runner ahead to make arrangements for her arrival. Obviously, it would be much closer for the luminaries to travel with her to this camp rather than try to backtrack, especially since they were not exactly sure of any other settlement's whereabouts.

Aryelle had listened politely, trying not to stare as Lureli unselfconsciously gorged herself while she talked. *I would swell up like an overripe papaya,* she thought, *and grow too heavy for my wings!* But Lureli, though definitely softer contoured than the luminaries, appeared healthy and fit.

"So, shall we journey together to the Great Summit?" Lureli had asked. "I know a short cut."

Aryelle glanced at Karril, who was refusing the offer of more water from one of the servers, and the hooded Kandharril. Both nodded briefly.

"Yes," she answered, though she still held reservations. Lureli, whose face wore a wide grin and several blobs of dark green food, nodded enthusiastically, continuing her meal and one-sided conversation.

So, today they traveled westward following this strange triangular conveyance, a bizarre little parade through the majestic forest. Karril danced about the feet of the fan bearer like a puppy begging for treats. Aryelle, a few paces back, suddenly longed for his company. A pang of homesickness swept over her. Turning, she searched for the white robes of the healer. If only she could talk to the Kandharril, but she met with stony silence whenever she tried. Why had her father burdened her with such a traveling companion? Feeling petulant, Aryelle indulged in a sulk. A moment later, she bumped into a broad, wingless back, knocking the fan from the servant's grip. It clattered against the litter, which had again come to a halt.

"Why are we stopping?" she asked.

"Midday meal!" piped Karril peeking around one of the twin bearers as he unloaded supplies from a side compartment.

"But it is well past midday."

"And you must be famished- you ate so little last night," added Lureli poking her head through the fan's plumage.

"But surely a quick bite- The tents?" Aryelle queried, as the flapping silk was unfurled. She watched Karril, who was trying to help the men, with a mixture of amusement and concern.

"Of course! You can't expect me to labor all day under the hot sun without a little nap," Lureli answered reproachfully.

Aryelle stood dumbfounded as the tents were erected. The last thing she could imagine was Lureli laboring under the sun all day, or even part of it. Her fan had been propped in a notch on the litter, and Lureli sat unperturbed under its shade. She dipped her fingertips into a water vessel close at hand and flicked moist droplets onto her face as she had done all morning, purposefully ignoring Aryelle. Once her tent was set up, she disappeared quickly inside it.

Karril came over and offered Aryelle a small basket of berries and portion of traveling bread. She thanked him absently. Slowly, she sank to the ground folding her legs beneath her. Her eyes never left Lureli's tent.

Much later Lureli reemerged. Shielding her face with her hand, she stalked past Aryelle without a word. Clearly, her nap had not been that refreshing. Aryelle rose hurried after her as the servants broke camp again.

"Surely we must make haste-," Aryelle began, but gasped as Lureli whirled to face her. Horror and pity mingled in her eyes. The skin across Lureli's bare shoulders and face was blistered and red.

"I'd have been there by now if I hadn't stopped to help you!" she spat, turning on Aryelle accusingly.

"I am so sorry! That must be so painful-"

"What?"

"Your face…"

"What's wrong with my face? Ouch!" She pulled her hand away from her cheek and began flapping her arms, flopping about like a netted salmon. If it had not looked so painful, Aryelle would have thought her comic. Lureli rushed to the litter and searched through her satchel, pulling out a large oyster shell mirror.

"AGGGHHH!" she cried, snapping the shell shut. "Look what you've done!"

"I have done nothing! It was the sun and all that water you kept flicking on yourself. But I can help-"

From out of nowhere, the Kandharril brushed past Aryelle coming to aid the distraught young woman.

Aryelle stiffened, then turned on her heel and stamped away. She could have healed a little sunburn! What did the Kandharril think - that she was a baby? Just like my father, she pouted angrily. She leaned against a giant tree trunk with a huff.

"It does not matter," said Karril a moment later. He came up from behind and rested a reassuring hand on her shoulder. "It matters not the healer, only the health," he quoted from the Book of Illumination. Aryelle did not feel like being illuminated.

"She just barged right in!"

"She who? You mean… our healer is a woman?" asked Karril.

Aryelle realized with a start what she had just said. "I suppose she is. I saw her hands just now, not hidden in her sleeves, and the way she held Lureli like, well, like a mother might." She watched them from the distance. Lureli was smiling now and throwing her arms around the Kandharril in an effusive hug. The healer hugged Lureli in return. A wave of jealousy washed over Aryelle and she turned away from the scene. Tears of self-pity pooled in her emerald eyes. She brushed them angrily as they threatened to spill.

"She is too vain anyway," she tried to console herself.

"Then why does she keep hooded?"

Aryelle heaved an exaggerated sigh. "Not the Kandharril!" she said, glaring at her cousin and then ruffling his hair as he feigned innocence. Thank goodness for Karril. At least he could still make her smile. She favored him with a friendly, one-armed hug.

"Thanks for nothing," she said as he squirmed free of the embrace and jogged off to finish helping the men. Aryelle watched him go.

They arrived at dunes heralding the water's edge shortly before dusk. Having traveled gradually uphill for half a day, they were more than relieved when the shoreline finally came into sight. Lake Mirth - Lac Ril in Empayan, the largest source of freshwater on the continent. Untold flytes above sea level, scooped from a plateau within the giant forest. Streams snaked from it in every direction. Legends of its icy, restorative waters had reached even sheltered Ka'Andharra.

Lureli leapt from the litter onto the sun-soaked sand without waiting for assistance. She tore off the brilliantly colored silk wrapped over her head and shoulders and dove into the water with reckless abandon as the flimsy fabric fluttered to the sand.

For once, the servants did not immediately set to making camp. Instead they stood, like statues of ancient gods, gazing across the red-tinged waves toward the slowly setting sun. Aryelle scanned the lake's choppy surface. Finally she saw Lureli shoot partway out of the water, arms along her sides, wet tresses streaming down her back. Aryelle wondered how she had covered such distance so quickly. Lureli waved toward shore. The statues returned her wave and, like the flip of a switch, promptly attended to their duties. Aryelle turned away as Lureli dove back into the water. Otherwise, she would have seen that what broke next though the waves looked more like a tail than the wet train of the swimmer's gown.

The sun had long set by the time Lureli returned. Aryelle and Karril finished a simple meal of traveling rations and sat poking the fire with long sticks, amusing themselves with the shower of sparks that each jab sent into the air. The Kandharril had retired to her tent, relieving them of her enigmatic silence. Back in Ka'Andharra Aryelle would have shared her concerns with Karril. Now it was her responsibility to protect him. She shielded her thoughts, distracting him with questions about the Mer.

Taking her cue from Lureli's servants Aryelle chose not to worry about her, though she did wonder why they had not joined her in the waves. Perhaps it was too cold for them. The Chimera Sea being farther south would be much warmer. She would have asked them about it, but Jorda, Crispin, Katri and Jaim lie snoring in massive heaps around the fire, exhausted from the day's labor. They had stayed, conversing in their newfound manner, until one by one they nodded off, only their snoring and lingering reek reminding the luminaries of their presence. Jaim, the fan bearer and youngest of the four, had rubbed a smelly concoction of camphor and fish oil onto his brother's achy shoulders. Jorda, the eldest, had returned the favor while the twins took care of themselves. Aryelle suspected it was the ointment that caused their skin to be so bronzed while their mistress was so fair.

Lureli strode noiselessly into the light of the campfire. She perched on Jorda's slumbering bulk as if it were only natural, though by the look of it, her dress was still dripping. He did not stir. She heaved a contented sigh, eyes dreamy as she stared into the dancing flames.

"That water is freezing!" exclaimed Karril. "How could you stand it so long?"

Her smile was radiant. "It was glorious!"

Earlier Aryelle had dipped her toes into the clear, icy water. Karril was right. How could anyone stay in it so long! But not only did Lureli look happier than ever, she was positively radiant. The healer had assumed her blistering sunburn, but it had taken the chilly waters of Lac Ril to restore her glow.

"You must be hungry," Aryelle said remembering her hearty appetite.

"I am content," she replied.

Aryelle could not bring herself to disrupt the peaceful mood. They sat staring into the fire as it died to glowing embers. The lullaby of gently lapping waves and chirruping crickets was punctuated occasionally by a sleepy grunt from one of the men. Finally, Lureli rose and drifted off to her tent. Aryelle and Karril soon followed.

Leaving her tent the next morning, Aryelle discovered that Lureli's servants were building a contraption on the beach. With broken branches dragged from the forest and the partially dismantled litter their creation was taking shape.

They had already lashed several logs together with lengths of sturdy rope dug from a storage compartment. The litter itself was mounted securely toward the front end of the platform, resting on supports a few feet off the sand. One of the bearer poles stood dead upright at its center. Aryelle watched as Crispin and Katri hefted a huge, perfect log into place while Jorda and Jaim tied it quickly on either end.

"They are letting me help!" cried Karril from the far side of contrivance. He was knotting a rope, for what purpose she could not tell. She walked over to where he sat.

"What is it?" she asked.

"A boat, silly!" he explained knowledgeably. "See! The litter is the prow and the mast is there on deck, just like a real ship!"

"I thought you said it was a boat."

"Boat – ship, same thing! We are going to sail it across the lake."

Aryelle had never traveled across water, and had wondered how it would be accomplished. Now she had her answer.

"What makes it move?"

"The wind catches the sail- we will use a tent for that - and pushes us. It will be great!" His eyes shone with anticipation.

Aryelle peered across the lake. She could barely make out the distant shoreline though the day was bright and clear. The breeze was faint against her face. How would it be strong enough to push them that distance?

"Where is the healer?" Aryelle asked.

"The Kandharril is still in *her* tent," he supplied, "and Lureli is swimming."

"Again?"

"She was already out there when I got up. She is like a fish! You would not catch me in that icy water."

Nor me, thought Aryelle. The lapping waves sounded inviting, but Aryelle preferred the tinkling music of forest streams or even the familiar coursing of the Lororil, and swimming was something no luminarie did with great relish.

"Hand me that basket and I will pick some berries for our breakfast," she said.

"I have already eaten with the men," Karril announced proudly. "Sorry, I did not leave any for you."

Aryelle made a feint toward the small basket and flicked him playfully on the end of his nose. She dodged as he made a grab for her, and strolled off to find her morning meal.

A while later she returned to a much different scene. The men, having finished the task of building the boat were laboring to get it into the water. Together they would move a log from under the rear of the boat to the front, inch it forward, and then repeat the process. Lureli supervised from a boulder at the water's edge, brushing her damp tresses with a tortoiseshell comb. Aryelle walked over.

"Why not build it at the water's edge?"

"Oh, they won't touch the water. They don't go into it, only on it," Lureli explained. "Their ancestors were voyagers, but not them. Don't ask why."

"But I thought you were the same people," said Aryelle.

"We are," she replied, "but it's complicated."

Aryelle was about to ask for an explanation when she spied the Kandharril heading straight toward them. In her hand was an adult sized jaboqua. Its color indicated it was freshly woven. The healer walked directly to Lureli with the proffered gift.

"How lovely!" gushed Lureli. "A basket!"

"Not a *kralith*," said Aryelle, laughing at the way Lureli held the floppy brimmed head covering. She had dropped her comb into it. "It is jaboqua - good head flower!" she said, translating. She took the woven bonnet from Lureli's hands, and handing her the comb, deftly placed the jaboqua on Lureli's head, transforming her into a giant jack-in-the-pulpit.

"A sun hat! How lovely!" she repeated, this time with genuine pleasure.

Aryelle nodded. "A mother weaves them for her unborn child, to shield its sensitive eyes from the sun during the child's second revolution."

"Revolution?"

"The movement of the sun across the sky over twelve candles…um, moons time. A child grows within its mother for the first revolution. It is carried for the next two, or until it can ask to be let down. By the fourth revolution they can fly on their own; then there is no stopping them!"

"What child is carried by its mother that long? What if she has another?" asked Lureli peeking out from under the jaboqua's brim.

"That would not happen unless she was of a noble house, and then there are servants. Anyway," said Aryelle, a strange longing in her voice, "it is a very thoughtful gift. It will keep the sun from burning you again." She eyed the healer quizzically, but as usual got no response. Instead, the ever concealed Kandharril bowed to Lureli and walked briskly away.

"Thank you!" Lureli called after her.

The makeshift vessel rocked in the water, its front end floating heavily, the stern still beached a short step offshore. Once the remainder of the camp was packed away, Crispin and Katri helped them step aboard, taking extreme care not to wet so much as a toe. Jorda directed where everyone should sit for balance. Lureli, of course, took up her seat at the prow.

Using sturdy poles, the men pushed off over the water. Then Jorda, who it seemed, had shouldered command lay down his pole and unfurled the sail. The passengers felt a tug as the silk snapped open and pocketed the breeze. Suddenly they were flying over the water, though not directly across to the opposite shore. Aryelle shot a mental question at Jaim, who just smiled and shrugged.

Catching her eye, Karril shouted, "We have to tack against the wind!" He snaked his arm back and forth indicating why they were moving nearly parallel to the shore. Aryelle marveled at how quickly he had absorbed all this new information. Flashing an acknowledging smile, she turned just in time to see the boom come swinging toward her. Reflexes any slower and she would have paid for it with a nasty bump on the head, but she ducked under the arm just in time.

"Look out!" called Karril belatedly, laughing as the cool spray hit his face. The look on his face was positively blissful. He was having the time of his life!

The boat turned and was skimming back the way it came, only slightly further offshore. Now Aryelle understood. In order to move forward they had to zigzag their way across the lake. She glanced at the other passengers. With jaboqua and cowl obscuring their faces, Aryelle could not tell whether Lureli and the Kandharril were enjoying the ride, but she found it exhilarating. Watching the shoreline fly past, she leaned back, keeping an eye out for the shifting boom.

After several criss-crosses, the waves grew rough. Jorda adjusted the angle of the boat. A stiff breeze blew in out of nowhere, and the cerulean sky curdled with ominous clouds. Suddenly crossing Lake Mirth was no laughing matter. The wind began to howl so fiercely that the passengers had to lean into it, searching for handholds to keep from being washed overboard. Icy waves crashed across the craft's surface. As one, the men rushed to drop the sail. The shift in weight unbalanced the crude ship and she tipped heavily to one side. The other rose dangerously high out of the water. Crispin and Katri dove back toward their stations. They seized the ends of the ropes that lashed the logs together. Planting their feet, they leaned their bulk out over the craft's edge. It slammed back into the waves with an enormous splash. Jorda hustled to finish lowering the sail while Jaim quickly made it secure.

Lightning crackled around them. Electricity filled the air. While the rest cowered at the sudden storm's ferocity, Lureli reveled in it. The jaboqua was ripped violently off of her head, flapping behind her like weather beaten wings. She leaned over the prow and drank in the storm's fury, laughing riotously as her tangled tresses danced with abandon. Aryelle raised her head at the sound… and so did the Kandharril. The wind whipped back her hood. She clutched at it, but the gale was too strong, thrashing her silvery-blond hair about her face. Aryelle and Kayanna locked eyes.

The wind, as though born on the breath of an intervening god, died as suddenly as it sprang up. Not a drop of rain had fallen, but the travelers were soaked thru.

"What are *you* doing here?! Spying for Elazaryn? Making sure his precious *baby* does not hurt herself?" spat Aryelle. She rose unsteadily to her feet, wet hair plastered to her head like a hatchling's down. Her breath came out in ragged huffs.

"Aryelle-"

"Or were you afraid I would not take care of Karril? Did you think I would abandon him in the wilderness?"

"No- listen…You, me, all of us – look at what just happened! There are dangers outside Ka'Andharra that none of us could have foreseen!" Kayanna grasped for excuses. "You were still weak from your ordeal. I begged Elazaryn to let me come with you."

"Because you did not trust me-"

"Because I love you! And Karril," she said fervently.

Karril shifted his gaze between Kayanna and Aryelle, but he did not greet his mother. He was just as shocked to find her suddenly in the middle of this adventure and uncertain whether the surprise was a pleasant one.

"I'll just leave you to sort out this little family reunion," said Lureli. Eagerly she dove into the nearly calm water. Her servants shifted on the gently rocking platform, prepared to enjoy the show.

Aryelle ranted on as though no one else had spoken. "Some good you have done us so far!"

She was being unfair, but just now, she did not care. This was more than unfair. This was *her* mission after all, *her* questanna! How dare Father send along a nursemaid! Kayanna was her favorite aunt , and considering what an oppressive stepmother Ladhonna was, the closest thing to a real mother Aryelle had ever known. She had even suckled her when her own first child was stillborn. And now here she was, as if Aryelle was still an infant. The whole journey was a sham.

Despite everything Kayanna was relieved the charade was over. It had been difficult keeping her distance, not only from her son, but also from this woman-child who was just as dear. Better to let her air her feelings than continue with any pretense. Patiently, Kayanna bore the insults Aryelle hurled as she paced angrily back and forth.

Karril avoided the confrontation by climbing onto Lureli's perch in the prow. Beneath the shadow of fast moving clouds, he peered into the crystaline water. From legends that he was forbidden to read, but had of course, he knew that Lac Ril was actually an enormous natural spring, the birthplace of the mighty Lororil, or Lifeblood River. Many thousand *jools* of water bubbled up daily from fissures along its silty floor, sending sand and mineral deposits swirling across it like underwater sprites. Karril reached into a pocket of his robe and drew forth a palm-sized piece of granite he had picked up on shore. He dropped it into the water and watched it sink. It took a surprisingly long time to reach bottom. It must have been several flytes down. Huge fish, larger than the boy who watched them, sliced through the frigid depths.

"She has not surfaced yet," he said matter-of-factly.

Aryelle continued to pace. Her ranting had ceased into stony silence. Kayanna looked up at her son, not quite comprehending.

"She has not surfaced yet," he repeated. "Lureli - she has been under a long time, but I do not see her anywhere."

Aryelle stopped in her tracks. Kayanna teetered toward Karril and peered over the edge. A giant trout swam lazily over the lakebed, but there was no sign of Lureli.

-*QUICKLY!* - Aryelle shouted into the minds of Lureli's servants. -*Your mistress is in trouble! We must help her!*-

"Aryelle, wait," began Kayanna, but Aryelle ignored her.

The men sprang to their feet. The boat pitched erratically. Aryelle lurched sideways into Jorda, barely escaping a plunge over the side. Karril and Kayanna were not so fortunate. They disappeared in an icy splash.

"Do something!" cried Aryelle struggling free of the big man who steadied her. She fell to her knees at the craft's edge as her aunt and cousin returned sputtering to surface. To her surprise, they both burst out laughing.

"What are you doing?" she yelled as Karril splashed her playfully.

"Oh, Ari! It *is* glorious! Come in!" He dove back under the water.

"Wait! Kayanna!" she appealed to her aunt. Her anger was forgotten. "What about Lureli?"

"Oh, she is fine. Look! The lake really is laughing!" Kayanna pointed downward toward the roiling sand.

What was happening? Why were they acting this way? Aryelle turned to Jorda who knelt cautiously beside her.

-*Please*- she asked urgently, -*what is going on? Where is Lureli - and what is wrong them? Luminaries do not like to swim!*-

-You said our mistress was in trouble…-

-She has not surfaced! -

-She cannot drown- he replied, relaxing, *-nor can they. The draught mistress gave you-* he waved to his brothers that all was well *-it will protect you always.*

"But why are *they* acting that way?" She motioned toward the two of them frolicking in the freezing water.

Jorda smiled. *-The laughing lake melts away troubles. They would be happy here until they died. But they would not die from drowning. The water may be too cold for your kind though. Soon they may want to sleep. Their bodies will just stop. Make them come out before it is too late.-*

-Can you go in after them? You are Mer; Lureli said so! Can you not save them?-

-No- he answered, offering no explanation.

Aryelle stared at him in dawning horror. They would die! Standing farther from the side, she called out.

"Karril! Kayanna! Come out at once!"

"You come in!" called Karril.

"No! *You* must come out!"

"You cannot make me!"

Kayanna's head popped up beside the boat. "It really is lovely, Aryelle. Come join us." Her teeth were chattering and the lips around her frozen smile had turned purply-blue.

Aryelle thought fast. The frigid water had obviously addled their brains. "I will join you, but I need to apologize first. Come up so I may offer my wings."

"N-not necessary-"

"I insist!" she said trying to remain calm. "Let it be made well between us first."

Kayanna considered for a moment, and then began to clamber aboard. "I h-h-have already f-f-forgotten it," she stammered as she swung her legs up over the side.

At once Aryelle thrust her toward Jorda. The big man wrapped his arms firmly around the shivering woman, wings and all. Aryelle scanned the water for Karril. He had dived under the moment she grabbed his mother. She spotted him as he surfaced further away, but before Aryelle could call out his name, the rope he himself had knotted earlier shot past her head. Jaim held the other end.

A second too late Karril realized what was happening. As he dove his feet came up where his head had been, and a loop tightened neatly around his ankles. He struggled as, hauled in like the catch of the day, Crispin and Katri fought to keep the boat balanced.

Once landed, Jaim cradled the barely conscious boy as Aryelle loosened the slipknot around her cousin's feet. She patted the big man's shoulder gratefully. His skin felt warm, and she realized the sun had broken through the clouds once more.

Soon the luminaries were wrapped in blankets, held firmly in Jorda's and Jaim's arms to prevent them escaping back into the water. The twins raised the sail, and the boat skimmed across the lake once more. But the pleasure for Aryelle was ruined.

-*What about Lureli?*- she asked Jorda.

-*We will meet her at the further shore*- he replied. –*Do not be concerned.*-

She was beyond concern. In all of her sheltered life, Aryelle had never imagined so many dangers lay outside the city of Ka'Andharra. What else could possibly go wrong?

Chapter 9 – Unexpected Guests

As Jorda predicted, there was Lureli sunning herself on a boulder at the water's edge, radiant and carefree. Aryelle could have gladly strangled her. As they neared shore, she leaped the remaining distance and strode toward her over the pebbly beach.

"What did you mean by dragging us across this miserable lake!" she accused.

Lureli turned calmly toward her. "Lake Mirth is not miserable," she purred, "but you seem to be. Perhaps you should have taken a dip."

"My aunt and cousin almost died in that freezing water! Why did you not warn us?"

"I didn't know," Lureli replied. "My people adore it."

"Your servants knew! Jorda told me!"

"What do you mean, Jorda told you? Jorda can't speak; none of them can."

"Well, they can speak to me, to all of us," retorted Aryelle. The big men were helping Kayanna and Karril ashore. "We can read their thoughts….or any creatures'."

Lureli looked aghast. "You mean you've been reading my thoughts?"

"No, that would be improper."

"Yet you've *spoken* with my men?"

"They wished it."

"They wished it? They're slaves! It doesn't matter what they wish. They'll be punished for this!" Lureli slid down off the rock, but Aryelle caught her by the wrist.

"If not for them, my family would be dead! They have done nothing to deserve punishment."

"But they are mine to deal with as *I* wish!" She wrenched her hand from Aryelle's grip and stalked away.

"They serve you because they love you, not because they have to," she called after her. "Love can be destroyed!"

Lureli ignored her. Aryelle turned in the opposite direction and stormed into the forest.

The sun was heavy on the horizon, casting shadows from the nearby forest onto the camp when Aryelle returned. Her heart was in shadow too. This entire journey was a big mistake. What had her father been thinking? Nothing had gone right from the beginning. People had nearly died, more than once! Their traitorous guide had disappeared, and they had yet to find a Naturra village. A quarter-candle was nearly spent. She should just abandon the quest and return to Ka'Andharra. The hardest part would be admitting defeat to her father. She would almost rather die here in the wilderness. Her impulsiveness had left one man blind, put others in grave danger…and now Lureli's servants had suffered because of her. She was not ready to bear the responsibilities she claimed; she could not even be responsible for herself! As Aryelle slunk miserably toward her tent, Lureli stepped from its shadow.

"I'm glad you're back. We were beginning to worry. Your… um…aunt and cousin are inside."

Aryelle nodded and turned to go in.

"Aryelle?" Lureli waited until she looked at her. "Thank you for telling me - about my men, I mean. I didn't punish them." Her eyes begged understanding. Though Aryelle couldn't know it, her remorse went beyond this incident. "And I'm sorry about the lake. I really didn't know."

"Be at peace," Aryelle answered turning away. Her heart was so heavy it no longer mattered.

Kayanna and Karril were waiting for her. Like the storm, Aryelle's anger had blown itself out in intensity. When Kayanna opened her arms, Aryelle fell into them gratefully. Tears scalded her cheeks as her aunt stroked her hair.

"*Empa dhel an che,*" Kayanna murmured soothingly. "*Zu t'sur, m'yana.*"

"No, I will not see," whispered Aryelle. "It is not well - it is over. I have failed. It is time to return to Ka'Andharra before I get us all killed."

"You own no fault, child. The dangers that befell us were unexpected. How could you have known?"

"If I had waited, had not pushed Father…."

"The world has changed, Aryelle. My own questanna was not so wrought. The *Kra'nochta Empaana*-"

"The Reign of Shadow has nothing to do with it! Wellwood Forest, Lac Ril… they have always been there!"

"The Seal of Silence limits knowledge of them-"

"But I should have been content to seek within the labyrinth."

Kayanna clucked softly. "Our eyes always see more clearly that which has been than that which will be. Yet our hearts long for things unseen. Tell me Aryelle, do you truly wish to return to Ka'Andharra?"

"Not me!" chimed Karril.

"You, dear boy, do not get a vote!" Kayanna ruffled his already tousled hair and drew him into their embrace.

For the first time in days, Aryelle no longer felt alone. Despite her earlier claims, she knew she could not do it on her own, but maybe with Kayanna's help…and Karril's. Instead of frustrating her as it once would have, the thought gave comfort.

-No, I do not want to go home- she thought *-Not yet.-*

They talked long into the night about their plans. They would continue to travel with Lureli in hopes of finding a Naturra village. If they had not found it by nightfall, they would part ways with the Mer, follow the northern shore of Lac Ril to its southernmost point, and head due south through the forest. This should take them directly into Ka'Andharra, *if* they didn't run into the other Naturra camp first. None of them wanted to try their luck crossing the giant spring again. Kayanna and Karril deliberately ignored the sweet call of the waves lapping against shore.

"Kayanna," Aryelle asked, "What did you know about our guide?"

"No more than you, I am afraid, though I will certainly look into it when we get back! I was remiss in not probing his mind."

"I probed, but sensed nothing." This fact weighed heavily upon Aryelle. She should have been able to tell he was deceiving them.

"He may have trained his thoughts to mislead," Kayanna tried to reassure her.

"Why did Elazaryn send me on this quest in the first place? Surely, he had others who could have made the journey and returned by now. Someone who knew what they were getting into."

"He sensed your restlessness. You may not have been ready for *this* journey, but your questanna was past due. Elazaryn finally realized it when you disobeyed him to heal the messenger."

"But why not the labyrinth?" she asked, pushing aside the guilt she felt at mention of the emerald-eyed stranger. "And why send Karril?"

Karril had drifted off to sleep curled up like a kitten amid cushions and silk blankets. Both gazed over at him affectionately.

"Ladhonna and I argued for using the labyrinth, of course. But Elazaryn was right that you should journey outside of Ka'Andharra. Someday you will serve your people as El'Kandharre. You may not be able to hide within the city's gates."

"And Karril?"

"Elazaryn did not want to make the same mistake twice. Better that Karril journey outside the city with you than without, even if he is yet young. He too is of Azadhar's line." *And will rule in your place should you die*, she did not add. "You must understand Aryelle; the Shadow is deepening. Elazaryn knew he must send you before it grew too late."

Aryelle looked at her steadily. The time had come for answers. "My whole life has been lived under the Reign of Shadow, yet no one speaks openly of it. I feel like I know nothing!"

"No one really knows…."

"But *what* exactly is it? Every time I ask the Illuminator, Father, you - all anyone ever says is that it is a great evil! If I am expected to serve my people, I should know what this "great evil" is!"

Kayanna hesitated. How could she explain? The *Kra'nochta Empaana,* though ever present, was still a forbidden subject. The sleepy voice that finally answered Aryelle's question quoted as if from a textbook.

"Something entered Emrysia upsetting the balance of good and evil, an unknowable presence the source of which has never been determined. Unless found, uprooted and destroyed Emrysians will eventually destroy themselves. Together we must discover what that something is."

"Very good, Karril! I see you have been paying attention as you read for Elazaryn. Perhaps he should be more selective in pages," Kayanna said, knowing the words came from her late husband's journal which she had turned over to Elazaryn. "- the ones read *and* those doing the reading!" Karril squirmed uncomfortably and buried his head under a cushion.

"I wish I could tell you more than that," Kayanna's attention returned to her niece, "but Karril is right. No one knows exactly what it is other than a feeling of distrust. The

Kra'nochta Empaana is like a blanket that both dampens the spirit and fans the flame of hatred and anger. At first, we Kandharra thought we alone were afflicted.... because of your mother's passing. But we learned from outsiders who sought healing that the Shadow enshrouds all Emrysia. Fear and mistrust keep the peoples of this land from working together. Everywhere, there is dissention and strife. Those who once lived in harmony are now at war. Most who seek to make peace die in the attempt, including my own husband, Erildhil. His last diplomatic mission-"

Aryelle cut her off. "Father has given up trying!"

"Your father has many concerns."

"But to do nothing about this 'something' that no one seems to know anything about? I do not know if I even believe in it!"

"It is real, Aryelle" Kayanna said ominously. "Your father still seeks to understand, and do not mistake it; to this end he is actively employed. To banish the darkness throughout Emrysia...." she continued guardedly, "well... many candles united shine further into the night, whether one is blind to the darkness or not. That is why Elazaryn's desire is to first unite the Empaya."

"But the Empaya have been divided for generations!" Aryelle argued.

Kayanna sighed. "There has always been some evil in the world. But there is also great good. Whatever caused this imbalance, once corrected, will not take away all that is evil with it. Much is of our own making. We must try to heal this older division ourselves." Almost to herself she continued. "Elazaryn has worked harder than any in that direction, but lately he has lost heart. Rachaan's poison at work! News of a

Summit brought him hope again. He cannot risk attending himself, but perhaps if the others of Emrysia are united it will further the reuniting of the Empaya as well. That is the mission you were sent on," she said meeting Aryelle's gaze. "That is *your* questanna."

"But who am I to begin healing this rift?"

Kayanna smiled at the Aryelle's blossoming humility. "You are no one," she said softly.

Lureli was already out among the waves when the luminaries left their tent the next morning, hers having already been stored away by her industrious servants. While the luminaries foraged for their breakfast, the Mer men finished breaking camp and rebuilding the litter. They were just completing their tasks when Lureli returned, her hands cupped around a secret treasure.

"Could you ask Jorda to fetch me a water jug?" she asked Aryelle. "My hands are full."

Surprised that she would ask, Aryelle obliged. When he brought the vessel, Lureli held her hands above it for a moment, peeking between her thumb and forefinger. Then with a sploosh, she dropped what she held into the half-full container.

"What is it?" asked Karril, brimming with curiosity.

"A reminder of Lake Mirth," she answered. "Come see."

Karril hurried over and peered into the jug. It took a moment for his eyes to find what they sought in its shady interior. There, poking above the surface was a shiny dark head. Two round eyes stared up at him.

"A tadpole!" he exclaimed with delight.

"Why would you want a tadpole?" asked Aryelle.

"For a pet," responded Lureli, gazing fondly down at it. "I found him in the reeds at the water's edge."

"We do not keep pets," said Karril obviously wishing otherwise.

"Creatures have their own lives to lead," Kayanna's tone was matter of fact.

"But he wants to come with us," Karril argued. "He just told me so!"

"I believe he does," said Lureli, smiling at him. "Perhaps I'm learning to read creatures' thoughts as well!"

"We should begin," said Aryelle. "Which direction to the Naturra camp?"

"We follow the shoreline to the south. The Naturra are at the base of the falls on the other side of the river."

"The other side? I thought we were already south of the river. Why not come ashore closer to their camp?"

"There are sandbars further along. We would've been unable to get close enough to shore. Don't worry - it shouldn't take long to reach it," Lureli said confidently. She headed toward her refashioned litter. Jorda hoisted the jug and followed her.

"At least we are headed in the right direction for home," murmured Aryelle under her breath.

The hike was a pleasant one. For ease of travel they moved slightly inland, keeping the water in sight. Lureli was uncharacteristically quiet, gazing thoughtfully into her makeshift aquarium. The luminaries chatted amongst themselves, often including the men in their telepathic conversations. To an observer they would seem like a silent troupe, except for the occasional bark of laughter from one of the Mer. When that happened Lureli would look up in surprise, then wistfully back toward shore.

By mid-afternoon, they caught a whiff of cook-fire smoke. They quickened their pace, weaving deftly between the giant redwoods. Already they had lost their overwhelming sense of wonder at the majestic forest. Eventually they encountered the ion-charged air marking their approach toward the falls. The shoreline curved inward, and rocky outcroppings became more frequent down ever-steeper terrain. They veered further inland in search of an easier path, the thunderous music of rushing water just off to their left.

The hillside was strewn with granite boulders and areas of wet, loose scree, making their descent a difficult one, especially for the litter bearers. Slipping and lurching, they caused several small avalanches as they inched their way downward. Lureli clutched her water jug tightly, its contents sloshing between the fingers of her hand. Finally, they reached the bottom of a wide ravine and stopped for to rest a moment before continuing.

Kayanna was distracted. Something was not right. They had not been quiet coming down that slope. Surely the Naturra would have sentries posted and their approach been noticed by now. She was about to mention her unease when the magnificent falls came into view.

Unlike the Lororil, this river caressed the landscape instead of barging through it. The waterfall started with a sheer drop over the cliff face. Then, flowing over bedrock into patiently carved basins, it cascaded into a series of frothy pools and shimmering fountains. These ruptured into numerous smaller flumes that leapt musically step by rocky step. Rainbow mists rose in breathtaking beauty against the moss-shouldered granite. A deep pool recollected the river at its basin. At last, here was a waterway the luminaries could appreciate.

The breeze shifted. Kayanna noticed the smell first. Instead of freshened air purified by the falling water, it grew heavy with the stench of charred flesh. She looked for the source. Across the river in a clearing stood several dozen shelters crudely fashioned from branches and mud. At their center, a smoldering fire burned and off to one side, a horrific vision. A pile of lifeless bodies haphazardly stacked in a jumble of emaciated arms, legs and torsos. Kayanna gagged and seized Karril to her, quickly turning away.

Aryelle glanced from the falls to her aunt, and then to the scene of devastation across the river. Her brain made no sense of what her eyes told her she was seeing.

"Stay back!" called a hoarse voice. A bedraggled man stepped into view. "Stay where you are- don't come any closer! There is only death here."

"What are you do- Oh, by Japhra! It's Fransi!" cried Lureli. "Fransi!" She jumped from her seat, almost falling off the litter. The bearers lowered it unevenly in their haste.

Across the river stood another large, though thinner blond man, similar in features to the four traveling with them. A mangy, ripped blanket draped over his shoulders, sashed at his waist like a tunic. In his arms, he held a corpse.

"I beg you! Please, come no further! The plague," he said unnecessarily. Turning, he threw the body onto the smoldering heap.

"No!" screamed Lureli leaping from the platform. Jorda caught her in his strong arms. He had not heard the man's words, but he still had eyes, and the air was rank with the smell of death. He held his mistress tightly, protecting her from her own rash behavior. She pounded her fists against his chest.

"Let go, you fool! Fransi! Jorda, its Fransi!" Her struggle against him was useless. The big man's eyes glassed over. Emotion drained from his face. The other men appeared carved in stone as well.

"Was Fransi your runner?" Kayanna asked gently.

"Not *was*, is! That's him right there! Fransi! Come over here!"

"Do not come!" countered Kayanna firmly.

Lureli whipped her head toward her. "What do you mean? Even if he's been infected, you can heal, can't you?"

Kayanna shook her head. "This is *Dru'noch*, Black Death. The Naturra are empaths as well, yet look! Not one lives. I am afraid I cannot help this man. He will soon die like the rest."

Lureli strangled a cry as she turned back toward the horrible scene. Fransi moved around the pile and tried to lift another body. When he couldn't disentangle it, he resorted to grabbing a pair of legs and dragging a corpse forward from the rest. He stopped and wiped his brow with a sweaty forearm, leaving a streak of soot across it. He continued wearily on. The rest looked on helplessly.

"Can we do nothing at all? We cannot just leave him here like this." Aryelle sobbed in a strangled voice.

"To survive ourselves- that is our only choice."

"That is no choice! You sound like just like Elazaryn! We must save him, we must!"

"Aryelle-"

"No!"

"Aryelle," pled Lureli, her tone now one of reason. "Kayanna's right. You can't risk your lives to save his."

"Yes, I can!" she cried defiantly, and waded into the river.

"Come back!"

"Stop!" Fransi held up a filthy hand. With the other, he pulled a dagger from the folds of his stained tunic. He held it high… and then plunged it deep into his own chest.

"NO!" they all shouted. The silent screams of the four bearers reverberated through their heads.

"Don't…come….any furth-………." Blood bubbled from Fransi's lips as he staggered backward and fell onto the smoking pyre.

Kayanna wrapped herself around Karril. Lureli buried her face deep into Jorda's shoulder. Aryelle stumbled backward, falling heavily on the rocky bank, where she sat in stunned silence. Only the bearers - big, blond, beautiful and eyes full of pain - were fortunate enough not to hear his agonized screams.

"He was their brother, three years younger than Jaim, the only one of them able to speak. I can't believe he's dead."

Lureli and the others sat staring into their campfire. No one wanted to leave its warmth for the haunted silence of the tents. The day's work had been gruesome. The horrible stench of burning corpses still filled their nostrils even though they had made camp far downstream.

The luminaries were in a state of near shock. It was not their way to burn the bodies of the dead. It was customary to preserve them with herbs, cocooning them in silk wrappings. They would then pass the funereal chrysalis hand-over-hand all the way to the Gate - the large, arched doorway that edged the steep bank of the Lororil. There the deceased were passed a final time through the hands of their relatives and members of the Kandharril. Through the Gate, they were deposited into the river to drift downstream toward the Chimera Sea. What became of them then was part of the Great Unknown. This burning seemed barbaric, but Lureli insisted it was the custom of the Mer. The ashes that remained were sprinkled across the water. The result was the same; both were given to the sea.

None of them knew what the Naturra custom had been, though the luminaries suspected it would have been similar to their own. But the bodies were too numerous, time for gathering herbs and preparing the dead too short. In the end, they decided to build up the fire and finish what Fransi had started. But first, they called out to make sure no one was left alive in the camp. Black Death, though highly contagious, was borne only on the breath of the living. Usually it killed its victims within a day. Dead bodies posed no threat. The runner must have reached the village very soon after the epidemic began. They all realized how narrowly they had avoided the same fate.

Had not one of her own been among the dead, Aryelle felt certain Lureli would have passed by. For Aryelle, Karril and Kayanna, leaving the camp as they found it was not an option. These *were* their people, even if they had not considered themselves as such. They could not leave without helping family find their way to the afterlife.

While Aryelle and Karril gathered kindling and small branches, the brothers hauled larger branches and bodies over to the fire, averting their eyes from Fransi's still smoldering corpse. Lureli and Kayanna carefully checked through each of the small huts for additional bodies. By the time their grisly work was finished it was late in the day.

Now, in shared silence, they sat mesmerized by the dancing flame of their own cook fire. Karril snuggled close to his mother, head in her lap as she stroked his unruly blond hair. Lureli sat across from them, two big men on either side, sorrow etched in their faces. Aryelle sat alone, deep in thought.

"All of them bound…,"she murmured.

"What did you say?" asked Kayanna startled.

"Their wings, the children- all of them were bound."

"To keep them from flying off once they were exposed, I expect," Kayanna mused.

"But the adults-"

"…would not have left. They would know better."

"I do not know whether I would have," said Aryelle in a small voice.

Kayanna gazed at her thoughtfully. She had been through so much in these last few days; they all had. But clearly the time had come. Reaching into a deep pocket in her robe, Kayanna withdrew a rolled parchment and handed it across to her niece. Elazaryn's seal was upon it. Confusion clouded Aryelle's brow.

"A message from your father," Kayanna explained. -*Go….you should be alone.*-

Aryelle rose hesitantly.

"We'll give you some time before we retire," she whispered, squeezing her hand in reassurance as Aryelle walked past her.

"Should I send someone with her?" asked Lureli watching her disappear into the night.

"Not necessary," Kayanna answered. "She will need space to think.

They fell silent once more. Finally, Kayanna could bear it no longer. "Tell me," she asked, "How is it that Fransi could speak when the others cannot?"

"It's complicated" Lureli answered evasively.

"I have time."

"Little sponges soak up whatever gets spilled nearby," she said, indicating Karril.

Kayanna looked down at him. He was nearly asleep.

"Then tell me, how is it that all five brothers came to be your servants?"

"Six brothers actually, the youngest remains at home. They were… um, captured by my mother and given to me as a gift. I've had them for years."

"Captured?"

"Well, yes, that's complicated too." She looked frustrated.

"So they really are slaves."

"More like pets that work."

Kayanna regarded her curiously. "But you said they were Mer. Do you make pets of your own people?"

Lureli blew out a big breath. She was tired. "Why don't you just ask them" she said, exasperated, "in that way you have?"

Kayanna looked at the brothers, her eyes full of compassion. Each seemed lost in his own bittersweet memories. "Now is not the time; their grief is too fresh and I too am tired. I would offer to assume it otherwise. But I may ask them… when the time is right." Searching for a more congenial topic she asked, "What about yourself? How old are you, Lureli?"

"My! Full of questions suddenly, aren't we?"

"You do not have to tell me. I was merely curious. Usually I can tell how many revolutions someone has passed…."

"How old do you think I am?" Lureli tossed her auburn mane.

"I would guess about twenty revolutions." She actually looked much older, but Kayanna had seen beneath her façade.

"That would be nineteen years, right? Aryelle said you counted the time before birth too," she added knowledgeably. "Well actually, I'm only eighteen of your revolutions, or about that."

"Ah - so just two more than Aryelle."

"What? I thought she was older than me!"

"You are very alike, both trying to seem much older than you are."

Lureli huffed and crossed her arms. Kayanna just smiled indulgently and quoted:

"Not spending your youth in youthful pursuits,

Will someday, forsooth, see you long for your youth
And pursue youthful truths when it just does not suit
For truthfully using youth only suits youth-"

"And nary a soul who is long in the tooth," murmured Karril in his sleep.

"What's that supposed to mean?" asked Lureli.

"Only nonsense, a poem I learned as a child. It does not even come from my own people." Her smile grew melancholy. "My sister Leandhra, Aryelle's mother, taught it to me. She was always interested in the lore and customs of other races."

"And you're not?"

"Never as much as she was."

"Isn't she still?"

"She passed through the Gate just after Aryelle was born."

"She's dead you mean? Then Aryelle and I have even more in common."

Suddenly, a brilliant star-like orb came shooting thru the night, dodging trees and dipping madly. It circled each person, zipping out of the way to escape the frenzied swatting of the startled Mer.

"What is it?" cried Lureli, batting it away from her face.

Kayanna laughed, a tinkling golden sound. Karril sat up, his eyes alight with wonder. Miraculously the Mer felt their cares lifted as the orb zigzagged high into the air. Then it shot off toward the tents.

"It seems Aryelle has a visitor!" Kayanna answered.

Chapter 10 – Pain

Aryelle, m'yana,

That you are reading this at all means three things; that you have not yet delivered your message to the Naturra; that you now know that it is Kayanna who travels with you; and that she feels you have reached a point in your personal journey where you might be willing to accept a little fatherly advice.

I know you have long chaffed under my over-protective wing, just as I did under my father's before me. It is our loss that we cannot see with eyes of wisdom such as come only with age while we are still young enough to believe fully in the clarity of our own vision. Such has been my mistake, thinking that only I could bring about the reuniting of the Empaya. But my vision was too narrow, my pride too great.

Therefore, I am offering you a choice, and the decision is yours alone. It is my wish that you deliver your message, and after staying with our brethren for the prearranged time, you return to Ka'Andharra to prepare yourself as my permanent ambassador to the Naturra until such a time as you succeed me as El'Kandharre, thus rekindling my dream of a reborn Empaya. (Your talents as healer have not gone unnoticed, though perhaps your judgment in using the gift has disinclined the Kandharril from accepting you as an acolyte, as I know you hoped.) This option will fall to Karril should you refuse, though the delay until he is ready to assume the position could cost our people greatly.

One other path lies presently before you, one that even with the T'sura I cannot see thru to its end. The Summit on Mount Cor will draw people of good will from across the continent of Emrysia, those determined to uncover and fight the evil that has infected this land. Though often misdirected, I know you to be such a person as this. While it would serve me to have you follow a more familiar path, I would no longer limit your vision. The way may be fraught with dangers unknown, and I may yet live to regret lifting the shield of my wings, but the decision to continue or return must not be forced upon you. I will know which path you have chosen if Kayanna returns alone with Karril, for you must not take him with you. One of you must someday serve as Brightest Candle to our people after me. I would not see both flames extinguished at once.

Choose well, m'yana. My light is dimmer in your absence.

- Dadher

Aryelle startled as the bel darted into the tent. The parchment she was holding slipped thru her fingers, fluttering to the ground. It pinned the curious sphere of light carelessly beneath it. Cautiously, Aryelle raised one corner of the parchment and peeked under it. Out shot the bel like a glowing cinder from a crackling fire. It circled the tent's interior, and then sped back to Aryelle, bobbing in the air as if reprimanding her for such disrespectfulness. Unable to control herself, she giggled girlishly.

She had read thru her father's letter several times, but for the moment it lay forgotten. Here was a piece of Elazaryn himself sent as only the most gifted of luminaries were able. His bel was the merest sliver of himself, part of his own inner light. Given to aid and encourage, she knew the bel would stay with her until either she sent it back, or Elazaryn died. Until it returned to him, her father's light would indeed burn dimmer, but unnoticeably so. Aryelle smiled and was grateful.

"*Dhe din zu, Dadher,*" she whispered, warmed by his intended embrace. She retrieved the fallen parchment and scanned its contents again.

It was incredible that he would give her this choice, entrust her with this responsibility at a time when she trusted her own judgment the least. If he hoped that the last week had matured her, his wish had been granted. But she felt no confidence in her ability to decide wisely in this matter. She guessed by her aunt's tone when she delivered the letter that she would offer no council.

Aryelle was unused to this feeling of indecision. Her interior world was largely black and white. Right and wrong had always had distinct lines. Now the edges were blurring. Both choices held promise and danger. A week ago, she would have thrilled for the opportunity to live among the Naturra, whose ways she longed to learn. But that was before she had watched their lifeless bodies thrown one by one into a smoldering fire. It was before she had met the Mer, whose customs and lifestyle were intriguingly mysterious. There was so much of the world yet to see, so many people to meet…and so many unknown perils waiting. To do as her father wished would mean the security of returning with Kayanna and Karril. But what if there were no Naturra left? What if the plague had infected their other settlements? And if not, it was possible that when Elazaryn learned the fate of this village he would change his mind about letting her become an emissary to the others. To return to Ka'Andharra might mean entering a gilded cage once more. But given how fraught with misadventure their journey had been so far, it was entirely likely that she would never return. Did her father sense this as well? She did not fear death, but there was so much more of life she yearned to experience. Sixteen revolutions, a mere fifteen out of the womb, were not nearly enough time to see all there was to see, do all she knew she must do.

-*What do I do Dadher?* - She stared directly at the bel hovering inches from her face.

Without warning, intense pain like an explosion at the back of her head struck Aryelle so hard that she fell to the ground. She clutched her temples between her palms and squeezed her eyes shut. Her mouth opened in a silent scream. She could make no sound, no cry for help. Hot tears bathed her face. Never had she felt such agony, nor would she ever again. This moment must be her last for who could survive such an onslaught? But death did not take her, nor unconsciousness, though she prayed for either to put an end to her pain.

The bel darted nervously around the room, bouncing like a surreal strobe light. Aryelle staggered to her feet only to collapse once more, unable to stand for the throbbing between her temples. She knew she must get Kayanna, but she could not move. An eternity passed as she lay there, curled into a ball, and still there was only hot, searing pain. No longer a girl, just a vessel filled with suffering.

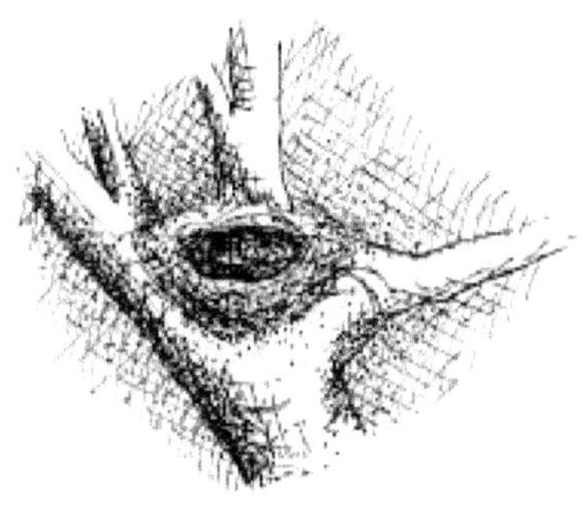

Chapter 11 - Disappearance

She awoke surprised to find herself alive, equally surprised that she had ever slept. Certain that she would never see morning, Aryelle had simply allowed the pain to envelop her. She had no idea how she ended up on her sleeping mat. And yet here she was, feeling rested if a little shaky, and totally free of pain. Karril was across the tent, breathing evenly. Kayanna was not. Perhaps she had risen earlier. Aryelle was anxious to tell her what happened. She sat up and stretched, carefully fingering her scalp for any sign of last night's affliction, but her head felt as it always had. She gathered her necessities and stepped quietly from the tent, careful not to wake Karril. Yesterday had been a long, hard day for him as well.

Once more skies were overcast and the air felt heavy and damp. Knowing Lureli preferred this weather, Aryelle looked toward her tent just in time to see the other young woman emerge. Aryelle felt an unexpected rush of fondness for her. She began to walk over, but just then the bel zipped thru the open tent flap, its light less pronounced though still glowing in the gray morning light.

"I see that… that… thingy found you last night! I thought it was a giant firefly at first." Lureli eyed it warily as it darted back and forth between them.

"The bel is a gift from my father." Aryelle peered at the bobbing ball of light as if she were suddenly seeing it for the first time. It had appeared just before her head felt split open last night.

"Bel – cute name. Does Bel always dance around like that?"

In answer, Aryelle held out her hand and the tiny sparkling orb alighted on her opened palm. She closed her fingers around it, placing it carefully in the silken pouch she always carried slung over her shoulder.

"It is enough to know that he is with me," she said. "I was about to look for my aunt. I need to discuss something with her."

"Maybe she's down by the river. I was just going there myself. I think I'll go a little further downstream and see if there's a pool deep enough for a swim." Lureli seemed anxious to be off by herself, and called over her shoulder, "Watch out for the mossy stones on the bank – they're really slippery!"

"Meet back here soon," said Aryelle. She did not want Lureli to disappear for hours again.

When Aryelle returned to camp alone. She found Karril and Jaim stirring up last night's fire. The others were nowhere to be seen.

"Have you seen your mother?" she asked.

Karril looked up. "I thought she was with you. I have not seen her since my eyes grew weights last night. She must have put me to bed. I do not remember getting there myself."

"Has Lureli come back yet?"

"I have not seen her either."

Aryelle frowned. Where was Kayanna? She needed to talk to her. She still had not decided what she was going to do, although she knew for certain which direction she wanted to take. She sat down on a log the Mer had dragged over to the fire. There was nothing to do but wait.

Lureli returned eventually borne on the backs of her men. Crispin unfolded the litter's supports and they sat it down gingerly. Aryelle had never seen her dismount it in her usual manner. She would have found it amusing if she were not so concerned.

"What took you so long? Did you see Kayanna?" she asked.

"No. Isn't she back yet? Oh well, she's always kept to herself," said Lureli dismissively.

"Only because we were not supposed to know who she was," said Aryelle.

"Why not? She never did say…"

"It is not important now. I just hope she comes back soon. There are decisions to be made. We should be on our way."

"Oh, not today! Surely you don't expect them to go on without a chance to mourn their brother?"

"But we must!" Aryelle said emphatically. "They carried you just now-"

"I forgot something and they brought it to me, that's all."

Remembering their lost expressions last night, she conceded. "I am sorry. Of course, they should mourn. That is why they have not broken camp," she observed.

The brothers looked back and forth between the two young women. Though excluded from the conversation, they seemed to understand it was them being discussed. Then Aryelle realized Karril was translating for them. Rising to her feet, she motioned for Lureli to join her in her tent.

"Come. I would have a word with you in private." She looked directly into Karril's eyes. "You will let us know the moment Kayanna returns?" she half asked, half commanded.

All of the men nodded.

Kayanna had still failed to return by midday, and by then even Lureli was concerned. She sent the brothers, mourning or no, into the surrounding forest in search of her. As the day wore on toward late afternoon, they straggled back one by one, alone.

Only Karril seemed unperturbed. "It is probably another test - part of your questanna," he told Aryelle nonchalantly.

"Kayanna would not do that," said Aryelle, trying to convince herself.

"Maybe, maybe not. She might be trying to force your decision," said Karril.

"My deci- You read my letter from Elazaryn!" cried Aryelle.

"Well, you left it lying right there on the floor of the tent where anybody could step all over it. I did not think it would matter," he said defensively.

"It does matter! Ohhhh! What are we going to do?" As always when she was agitated, she paced back and forth.

"Go after her," said Karril. His tone was matter-of-fact.

Aryelle stopped in her tracks. He was right of course. There was no other choice. Kayanna had indeed forced her hand. After all, the letter had been lying there for her to find as well. But which direction to go in?

"Follow the river, of course," answered Karril reading her thoughts. "That is the way Lureli plans to travel. Kayanna would assume you will stay with her."

"You are right again, O Knowledgeable One" Aryelle snapped, "but we will not leave until nightfall. We have to wait that long at least, in case she comes back."

But Kayanna did not come back. What's more, Lureli refused to set off that evening. She claimed it was for her men's benefit, their being unable to see well enough to travel at night. Aryelle suspected she had her own selfish motives. She explained that Bel, as Lureli dubbed her father's light, could light their way, but still she declined. Lureli and Karril went to their separate tents while Aryelle fumed by the campfire, impatient to be doing something, anything. She was still frustrated when a while later Lureli poked her head out of her tent. She withdrew it again without a word. When it happened a second time, Aryelle got up and headed off to bed, though she knew it would be impossible to sleep. Lying awake, she heard the quiet rustle of a silken flap as Lureli stole from her tent. Probably off for a midnight swim, thought Aryelle. Lureli certainly did love the water. Did it help her overcome waves of homesickness like the ones that occasionally swept over Aryelle? She longed right now for the familiar scent of home, for the valleo branches that wove in and out of her room, the fragrance of Ladhonna's herb garden that wafted up to her. Lying awake, the night sounds of the forest amplified against the backdrop of the rushing river, Aryelle missed the silence of the polished halls of Ka'Andharra, the echoing stillness of the Galleries, the tranquil fountains and softly tinkling chimes that usually lulled her to sleep. She was so tired! Hopefully before the morning her aunt would be back. Or better still, she would wake up to find that the last few days were just part of a bizarre dream…that tomorrow she would wake to find herself snug in her own suspended bed.

Instead, she awoke to the uneven drip of water from Lureli's hair as she bent over her.

"Good, you're up! I'll wake Karril."

"But it is still dark out," said Aryelle sleepily. "Did you just get back from your swim?"

"Swim? No, it's raining outside. The sky looks murderous, blacker than I've ever seen it. But it's definitely morning."

"Any sign of Kayanna?" Aryelle asked hopefully.

"No, but I know where we should check first. And luckily, it's right on our way."

Karril got up and quickly joined the men.

Yesterday in the privacy of her tent, Aryelle had confided in Lureli sharing the contents of Elazaryn's letter and her indecision, but she had neglected to mention her pain. Because of it, Aryelle was less anxious to go her own way. Staying together seemed logical at least until they found Kayanna. Lureli had maps of all of the waterways on the continent, and Aryelle felt safer with her servants around.

As soon as they stepped out into the pouring rain, the men descended, stowing the tent into the waiting compartment on the litter. Lureli climbed up over the backs of her servants and the sodden caravan struck out. For once Jaim did not hold the fan above his mistress. Instead, he walked side-by-side with the luminaries. Rain poured down their backs, soaking them to the skin. The luminaries shivered with the chill, but the Mer seemed oblivious, and Lureli practically blissful. They came to a widening of the river and crossed over easily, its shallow, rocky bottom obscured by the dance of raindrops across its surface. They followed the river as it wound its way steadily northward.

"Where are we going?" Aryelle called after a time.

Lureli turned around in her seat. "Thru the Swamps of Dire" she called back, "to see the Omniscients."

I had to ask, thought Aryelle.

Chapter 12 – The Omniscients

The Swamps of Dire were dire indeed. Leery of what might lurk in the fabled swamp, Aryelle would have preferred not to enter them at all. She was given no option. Careening down a muddy hillside in the blinding downpour, her only choice was whether or not to remain on her backside. She clutched at a swiftly passing tree root, and managed to turn over - just in time to save her wings from being ripped loose from their bindings.

She had been foolish to insist on scouting ahead alone. One misstep was all it took. When Lureli and Karril heard Aryelle's rapidly descending scream they warned the bearers to watch their steps. It was a miracle that any of them reached the bottom in one piece, even more miraculous that they found her so quickly. It was dark and, except for her wings, Aryelle was covered head to foot in foul, brackish slime. Jaim and Karril were the first to reach her. Finding her unhurt, they pulled her from the muck with expressions determined to be serious. Lureli, on the other hand, laughed out loud when she saw Aryelle's mud-streaked face.

The caravan regrouped. Lureli gestured broadly, shouting directions above the pounding rain. Aryelle stayed in the rear with Karril as Jaim took up the position of point man, scouting cautiously just ahead of the others. They hadn't gone far when he disappeared into a sinkhole. Luckily, they were able to pull him free using the feathered fan staff before he was completely sucked into the thick ooze.

They decided it would be safer to travel through the murky water than around it. Though dense with clinging vegetation, the water would probably hold fewer pitfalls than the semi-firm landscape. They might step into unexpected drop-offs, but what was that compared to well-disguised patches of quick-mire. Aryelle questioned why the men could wade here since at Lac Ril they had not even stuck a toe into the water. Lureli mumbled something about likely habitats and qualifying depths, and reached into the container to tickle her pet tadpole. For once, she preferred not to experience the water for herself and remained comfortably on her litter.

She was certainly being evasive thought Aryelle. The men themselves were even less forthcoming, as if their mistress had instructed them to keep the matter hushed. Aryelle did not think to question Karril. Wading through nearly waist-deep swamp water the only parts of her still dry were her wings. She was glad she had thought to wrap them. Wet wings were heavy. The spider-silk bindings repelled the water as effectively as a duck's feathers.

The Mer cast several anxious glances at a passing water-adder and were constantly swatting away huge, biting mosquitoes; snakes and insects did not bother the luminaries, who simply thought-messaged them away. It was too far north for the enormous lizards that haunted the southern wetlands. Soon everyone relaxed, if not enough to enjoy this part of the journey, at least enough to stop constantly looking over their shoulders.

Aryelle ducked under a curtain of draping moss, brushing it aside with her arm. As she did, dozens of tiny red spiders scurried over her shoulder and back. She shuddered and ordered them firmly off with her mind. The spiders immediately jumped to the water, scuttling across its surface in every direction, dodging raindrops and the ever-widening ripples they caused. She realized then that the rain was beginning to let up. For the first time that day, she could see more than a few feet in front of her face. She looked ahead just in time to see Karril disappear beneath the oily black surface of the swamp.

"Karril!" she cried lunging forward. Before she could reach him, strong tentacles wrapped around her legs and torso and dragged her under.

Lureli waved her bearers to a halt. Leaping from her seat, she rushed to the platform's edge, poised to dive into the murky, churning water. A long, twisting tentacle shot out, encircling her legs and pulling her off her feet. She clutched at Crispin, screaming into unhearing ears as she was wrenched from his grasp.

The Mer were frantic. Crispin and Katri had both seen her go under. They beat the water with their hands, out-stretched fingers searching below the surface. Jorda and Jaim waded back to them through the waist deep water, but by then Lureli's thrashing had ceased. Jorda held up a hand to make them stop, and they peered across the opaque surface for some larger ripple of movement. There was none.

Through root-filled channels and underwater passages, Aryelle was dragged like bait on a line. Occasionally her head broke above the surface where she gasped for breath, until somehow her mind registered the fact that Lureli's anti-drowning potion was keeping her lungs from filling with the brackish liquid. Struggling was hopeless. As one tightly wound tendril spiraled around her body, the last would slither off, part of a vast network. She passed from tentacle to tentacle. Eventually it dawned that her captor was not some mammoth swamp monster but the swamp itself, the very roots and vines of the miserable bog. She could only hope that Karril was enduring the trip.

The water grew shallower. She was dragged across the slimy bottom, then hoisted roughly into the air and tossed onto a spongy, moss-covered bank. There sat Karril, scratched and streaked with muck, pulling strands of swamp weed from his hair. She clambered over to him and they hugged each other tightly.

"Karril! Are you alright?"

He nodded. "I just wish your hair was not so smelly," he said, pulling himself away. "That was some ride! Where do you think we are?"

Before she could answer, Lureli sailed thru the air and landed with a squishy thump nearby. The writhing roots slipped beneath the water's surface. Lureli's hair hung in mud-streaked tangles over her face, what remained of her necklaces and baubles hopelessly snarled with weeds. She sat sputtering and panting, unaware that she was not alone. The poor thing nearly jumped out of her skin when Aryelle spoke her name.

"Aaaaaah!" She flung her hair away from her face and skittered backwards like a crayfish. "Don't do that! You scared me!" she glared. "E-yhew! Do I look as awful as you do?"

"Yes," Aryelle was truthful. She waited expectantly. "Where are the others?"

"I don't know," answered Lureli, raking her fingers through her hair. "I was pulled under by that… that whatever it was. I didn't see what happened to them."

"It was the swamp."

"Yes Karril, I *know* we're in a swamp!" she bit sarcastically. Being dragged through brackish water had put her in a very foul mood.

"It does not want them, the Mer men," explained Karril. "It just wants us."

"What do you mean, '*it just wants us*'? What wants us?"

"The swamp."

"The swamp wants us? How do you know?" asked Lureli peevishly. "Oh, wait- don't tell me! You can read plants' minds now!"

"Of course!"

"What do you mean, 'of course'?" her voice grew shrill.

"Karril is right," said Aryelle. "But it is not saying why it wants us."

"Oh, jiggling jellyfish! Has the world gone crazy? First I find out mute slaves can talk; I just can't understand them.

Then I'm abducted by vegetation, with which *you* can hold a conversation. I'm losing my mind!"

"Losing or lost, at such a great cost!"

"What did you say?" asked Lureli.

"Nothing," said Aryelle.

"Looks *and* mind going, and now temper showing!"

"Enough!" shouted Lureli bad humouredly.

"It was not me!" cried Aryelle and Karril at the same time.

"Tsk! What a pity; she could be so pretty."

The disembodied voice hung in the air around them, not echoing, but lingering like a bad taste in their mouths. Lureli blanched.

"Who said that?" demanded Aryelle.

"Bossy, bossy! Youth is so saucy!"

"Who are you?" she asked looking around.

"We are."

"We be."

"We sisters three," came three hollow voices in unison.

"What do you want with us?" asked Karril, more bravely than he felt. "Why did the swamp bring us here?"

"Brings us presents!"

"Brings us toys!"

"Brings tasty-licious girls and boys!"

Lureli gulped. "You mean to eat us?" She scrambled over to the luminaries.

"What of the others, the men traveling with us?" insisted Aryelle.

"Too ripe!"

"Too tough!"

"Not sweet enough!"

"Where are you? Show yourselves!" she demanded.

Suddenly the air around them began to shimmer, like heat waves off a desert. Three indistinct figures gradually took shape, floating closer as they grew more defined. Their hair was stringy, hanging in limp greenish-gray strands about their hollow-cheeked faces. Their eyes, colorless and protruding, rolled and blinked eerily. They were clothed in dingy rags, yet each sported a brightly colored jewel brooch clasped at her throat, the gaudy gems set in ornately carved gold. As they materialized, they chanted in turn;

"Three souls seeking-"

"Three shall find-"

"Sisters selfless-"

"Heart-"

"Soul-"

"Mind!"

Now Aryelle and the others could see clearly who the voices belonged to. Standing side by side just a few paces away was a trio of dumpy little women no more than three feet tall. Unable to help herself, Aryelle smiled. There was nothing to fear here. The women smiled back, huge gap-toothed grins.

"I am Aryelle of the Kandharra. This is Lureli of the Mer, and my cousin Karril. Greetings!"

"We know who you are; we saw from afar," said the three.

"And w-who are you?" stammered Lureli.

"Meetings and greetings! What we wants is eatings!" complained the first hag. Her smile twisted into a sneer.

"Yes- scrunching and crunching-"

"-and tender grub-munching," drooled the second and third. They smacked their lips repulsively.

Aryelle grimaced. "We would know whom we are feeding," she said, though she knew.

"We're Suess-"

"-and Giesel-"

"-and Theodora-"

"Keepers of the Dire flora," they said by way of introduction.

"But, what… are you?" asked Lureli.

"Never changing."

"Ever growing."

"Wisdom ranging, knowledge knowing."

"*You* are the Omniscients? Well, I guess appearance isn't everything."

"We come in search of you," said Aryelle. "But how do we know you are who you say?"

"We see all, know all, tell all, it's true," they answered indignantly in unison. "Pose-posit a question and we'll answer you."

Though their knowledge of the outside world was censored, every Kandharra child had heard tales about the Omniscients, three ancient sisters of unknown race, keepers of all the secrets of Emrysia. It was said that nothing, future, past or present was beyond their knowing. Looking at them, Aryelle had her doubts.

"I have many questions, but one of great importance. Before I ask it though tell me, how do you come by your knowledge?" She saw immediately that the sisters possessed a streak of vanity. So far, they had been unable to resist answering any question they posed. Perhaps she could use this to their advantage.

"Pondering purpose," answered Suess.

"Positing thought," added Giesel.

"Seeking inside wherein conscience is wrought," finished Theodora.

"Why do you always speak in rhyme?"

"Riddles and rhyme to pass the time!" said all three.

"Are your answers always truthful?"

"Some foolish-"

"Some wise-"

"Some truth in disguise!" they cackled.

Aryelle thought. She was not exactly afraid of the grubby little women. But if they made a break for it, she was certain the swamp would just carry them back. Somehow, she must get the Omniscients to set them free unharmed. But how?

"Waiting, waiting, hesitating- let us eat, pang-hunger sating," growled the first and fattest old hag.

"Head-whomping, limb-chomping!" said the middle one, pulling a long, thick bone from beneath her tattered robes.

"Beat-neatly, completely," the third whispered over-loudly into her sister's ear. She grabbed the gruesome club and smacked against the palm of her hand.

"Wait! We're royalty! Diplomats! Emissaries to the Great Summit on Mt. Cor. You must let us pass!" cried Lureli.

"Gnaw their bones and suck their meat. Royal children are especially sweet!" The Omniscients began to float closer. As they did, they started to swell, inflating like balloons.

While small in stature they had seemed laughable, but now they transformed menacingly until they loomed over the three cringing youths. Saliva dripped down their wrinkled and warty chins.

"Eat us then, but you will not learn our secret!" Aryelle thrust herself in front of the others.

"What's this?" they cried, deflating to their original size. In their surprise, they had forgotten to speak in rhyme.

"Yes, we have a great secret. Eat us now and you will never know it," declared Aryelle. "You will be omniscient no longer!"

"Tell us!"

"Show us!"

"We must know this!"

"Ooooh- you grow smaller and even your rhymes grow weaker!" she taunted them.

The shrunken sisters huddled together whispering, oblivious to the fact that they were still speaking loud enough for the young people to hear.

"Know we must, this secret keeping!"

"Know we must or, boo-hoo, be weeping."

"Tell us all if they are sleeping," said Theodora in a sly drawl. They bobbed their heads gleefully.

Lureli and Karril exchanged anxious glances, but Aryelle remained calm. Carrying Elazaryn's light boosted her confidence. She cleared her throat to get the sisters' attention.

"We will tell you our secret if you answer three more questions, and answer them truthfully" she said, a plan formulating in her mind, "-and you must promise not to eat us before you have answered all three."

"Hard bargain!" squealed Suess.

"Galoobrious jargon!" complained Giesel.

"Real deal," Theodora said with a wink to the others.

Ignoring the other two, Aryelle posed her question to the third hag. "Where is Kayanna of the Kandharra?"

Theodora was the smallest Omniscient. As they watched, her strange bulgy eyes rolled backward in her head. She stretched out her arms, exposing the bony limbs as her ragged sleeves fell away from them. Fingers splayed, she flexed her hands and brought together the tips of her index fingers and thumbs forming two perfectly round circles, which she held out before her. With a quick twist of her wrists, she flipped her hands over and brought them to her face, creating a bizarre mask. She peered through her fingers searching for a distant vision. In a scratchy singsong voice, she began to chant:

"Wandering through the forest towering
Vision blurring, pain overpowering
Stumbling, falling, strained from healing
Into arms from shock still reeling
Brother, sister, ancient kin
Help her homeward once again."

Aryelle listened closely. Puzzling the words out in her mind, she thought she understood part of the message. If she was not mistaken, some wandering Naturra from the plague-scarred village had found Kayanna and were helping her to return to Ka'Andharra. But strained from healing? She could not remember Kayanna expending any light on their journey. At least, none that would leave her drained and in pain as the Omniscient's rhyme suggested. Then she remembered the unexplainable pain in her head, just two nights before – the pain she was sure she would not survive. She had woken the next morning to find it but a surreal memory, and Kayanna gone. Shaken, she turned toward the others.

Lureli looked dazed. The hag's message had gone completely over her head. But Karril was sympathetic.

"She will be alright. It is not your fault."

Warmed by his compassion and understanding, she nodded. After all, it was his mother that had gone missing. She thanked him and made a mental note to tell him just what Kayanna had done for her, and to treat him with a little more respect in the future – should they have one.

"Quickly ask - next task, next task!" said the little Omniscient elbowing her sisters.

"Yes, yes! Two left – one less," they rejoined.

Pulling herself together again, Aryelle considered for a moment. Before she could speak, Lureli blurted out "Where are my servants?"

"My turn! My turn!"

Aryelle looked at her aghast. She waved her hand, but it was too late. Suess had gone into *her* eerie trance routine, even more bizarre than her sister's had been. She turned her back to them, suddenly reaching up and popping off her head. Aryelle and Karril gasped. Lureli's hands flew over her eyes. Spinning toward them, the headless body gently placed her head - eyes roving wildly side-to-side - on the ground in front of her. She then proceeded to stand on top of it. Her eyes shot straight up and her mouth, almost buried in the springy moss, chanted:

"Secret, silhouette,
Shadows fleeing waters wet.
Shiny fishy, glitter golden,
Siren singing. Slaves beholden
Waiting, wondering on a stage
Till their mistress turns the page!"

"W-what's that supposed to mean?" asked Lureli peeking through her fingers. Suess' frumpy, headless body jumped down with a flourish, did a perfect pirouette and scooped up its head. She bowed to her sisters' enthusiastic applause.

Quickly Aryelle jumped in to answer before the Omniscients could take this to be their last question. "It means they are back at the litter waiting for us to return! Now do not say another word; you have cost us dearly already!"

Lureli was offended. She sniffed dramatically and shuffled closer to Karril.

"I just wanted to know," she pouted.

"Now Giesel! Now Giesel! We bargained- don't weasel!" panted the middle Omniscient, anxiously awaiting her turn. The three hags fairly danced in place, eager to complete their part of the deal.

Aryelle's mind churned frantically. Her plan, hastily improvised, required *her* to be the one to ask the questions! Now she was at a loss. If she were not careful, they would lose any chance of continuing. She knew she must hurry. Weighing her options, she decided just to ask how they could free themselves. But then Karril spoke up in bold voice, belying his tender age.

"How did the Reign of Shadow enter Emrysia and how may we defeat it?"

Aryelle stared at him horrified. How could he! As much as all of Emrysia yearned for that answer, what good would the knowledge do them if they never made it out of the Swamps of Dire alive?

"A pair- no fair!"

"No fair, not fun! That's two, not one!"

"Stop!" demanded Aryelle before the third hag had a chance to protest. She might be able to turn this to their advantage. "You made no rules before we asked. Each of us has had a turn, now each of you must also answer," she said. "That is his question. What say you?"

The Omniscients mumbled and grumbled, but finally Giesel stepped forward. Without any fanfare other than her emerald jewel glowing as she spoke, she blandly intoned:

Scales tip unbalanced
Hatred and fear
Evil is winning
End times are near.

Three royal children
Siblings fair
Serving one master
Land, sea and air

Sing now, ye sisters
Color, form, light

Gifts freely given
Conquer the night.

"But what does it mean?" asked Lureli again. This time Aryelle was puzzled as well.

"No more questions! Now you're telling-"

"Secret sharing, shadows felling-"

"Knowledge giving, dark dispelling!" The Omniscients wrung their hands together and greedily licked their lips, hungering as much for this tidbit of information as for their prisoner's flesh.

"Wait!" shouted Aryelle as the Omniscients loomed forward. "Your answer is not good enough! How may *we* defeat the Kra'nochta Empaana if *we* are not able to leave here? Our bargain was for the truth. You lie!"

"Trick and cheat! You'll pay; we'll eat!" cried the Omniscients, enraged.

"No!" cried Aryelle as swamp tendrils slithered swiftly from every direction to wrap around the three young people. They thrashed helplessly. The little hags cackled with glee. Agilely they dodged the writhing roots as they danced around their struggling captives. They chanted:

"Murky, miry, slimy bog
Fill with friendly fumey-ous fog.
Swirling, twirling, maddening mist
Drinking deeply, poison kissed,
Sleepy-eyed children, sweetly slumber
Burdens borne now unencumber.
Questions asked us; 1 – 2 – 3
Questions answering - she, me, thee

Future, present, unknown past
Answers to your questions asked.
Tell us now as you are sleeping
What's the secret you've been keeping?"

As their song ended a foul, swirling fog did indeed appear, snaking its way through the twisted, moss-draped trees. The fog swirled cloyingly around the prisoners, and despite their efforts to avoid it, breathe they must. Vision blurred and heads nodded as they succumbed to its drug-like effects.

The Omniscients were impervious to their nasty pet poison. They wrapped themselves in foggy cloaks, twirling and whirling in a grotesque victory dance around the slumped figures. Suddenly, with a loud snap of Theodora's fingers, they came to an abrupt halt. Without a word, they floated forward. Each faced one of the bound youngsters. Leaning wrinkled brows against smooth foreheads, they siphoned off every thought each had ever had, both conscious and unconscious. The sisters gave a running commentary as stolen memories flooded through their minds.

"Ahhh! Death and dying-"

"Bodies burning-"

"Silence speaking-"

"Not worth trying-"

"Secrets learning-"

"Bed is leaking?"

They all looked up at this, and then returned to the reel playing in their heads. Their rhyming observations hung heavy in the deadened air. On it went, through the travelers' journeys and beyond. When all of the information locked inside their captives' brains had been exhausted, the Omniscients leaned back, pondering. The children slept on.

Theodora spoke up. "It could be them."

"Not all, a-hem!" said Giesel, irritated at having to remind her sister of their never-ending game.

"Should we, shan't we, shall we eat them?" asked Suess, worried that a tasty meal was about to slip through her fingers. "Could we? Can't we? Awww- we beat them!" She complained as Theodora wagged a finger at her.

"One is missing; one out of keeping. But two are present, right here sleeping. Send them, must we on their travels or destiny for all unravels," she explained.

"But-"

"No ifs, no buts, no candy, no nuts! Suck it up sister! Show us some guts!" barked Theodora.

Giesel had another idea.

"What if we only the odd one eat? The others set free, while we still get meat?"

Theodora deliberated. Giesel and Suess waited anxiously, drooling and clicking the tips of their ragged nails together. Then Theodora shook her head. "Destiny is sometimes fickle, changing with death's swinging sickle. All must live, them we be sending, we here to await whatever ending."

With that, she clapped a staccato beat. Both vines and fog responded immediately. As the swamp carried their prospective meal away, the sisters hungered after them.

Chapter 13 – Parting Ways

The swamp hefted the hapless travelers in the direction they had come from, sometimes through the fetid water, but just as often now over the pocked and root-veined bog. Foul-smelling mist swirled along with them, a corrupt companion designated to keep them asleep. Nearing where they were originally abducted the vapor drifted ahead, wrapping its poisonous cloak around the unsuspecting Mer. By the time the last tendril uncoiled to deposit its load onto the litter, the platform was already crowded with huge slumbering men. Powerful creepers hoisted the entire thing into the air. The vessel holding Lureli's new pet tumbled over, spilling its contents into the murky waters of the swamp until a vine snaked around the neck of the jug and returned it to its place. Then the litter was borne away by the creepy shoulder-less servant.

****

Aryelle was convinced she was still dreaming. A jumble of bodies surrounded her. Ghastly visions of dead Naturra floated through her brain. She screamed, waking herself the rest of the way. Panting, she heaved an unfamiliar leg off of her own. Lureli sat up and turned a bleary eye toward her. They stared at one another.

"Where are we?" croaked Lureli finally.

Karril moaned. Crispin's legs and one of Jaim's arms were draped across his slender body, pinning it to the wooden platform.

"Am I dead?" he whispered.

"I am here Karril-is-alright," Aryelle slurred. Her tongue felt thick and furry.

"Help me!" he said panicking.

Aryelle staggered to her feet, stepping clumsily over Crispin's broad chest. Abruptly he sat up, knocking her off balance, but catching her awkwardly as she fell. Aryelle patted him on the shoulder. Her mind was too fuzzy to formulate an explanation as his unfocused gaze reflected her confusion. He helped her to stand and, wobbling, she pointed to his legs. He peered at them as if trying to figure out if they actually belonged to him. Finally deciding they must, he lifted them off Karril. Jaim rolled over, still asleep, removing his bulky arm.

Karril stood up too quickly. Blood drained from his head into circulation-starved limbs…and he promptly collapsed in a faint. There was no one to catch him. He hit the deck with a thunk.

Jaim rolled over a second time and fell with a thud to the solid ground beneath the litter. On the other side of the platform, Jorda and Katri scuffled over who was crowding the other more. Lureli began to giggle uncontrollably until finally her laughter became hiccoughing sobs.

-*What a mess!* - thought Aryelle slumping into Lureli's vacant chair.

It took a while for everyone to feel normal again. Eventually, they were able to rouse themselves enough to build a fire. Lureli and Karril hunkered down beside it while Aryelle paced nearby. The Mer men were taking far longer than usual setting up camp.

"You two almost got us killed!" said Aryelle, still fuming as she came to sit by the fire.

"And you were saving us?" spat Lureli.

"I had a plan!"

"Well, you could've let us in on it! Next time we may not-"

"There will be no next time," said Aryelle. "We part company here."

"No! We need to stay together!"

"I will ask for your opinion when I want it, Karril!" Aryelle snapped. "I know what is best for us." Actually, she wondered if she did. Her plan of escape had proven full of holes. Yet somehow here they were, away from the Omniscient's greedy little clutches and not only out of the Swamps of Dire, but out of the forest, poised on the very edge of a great plain. No thanks to her, she admitted to herself.

"I agree, Karril. You should stay with me..." Lureli fixed Aryelle with a look that was a mixture of distaste and envy. "…both of you," she added grudgingly, getting to her feet. She stalked away.

"We are no safer with you, that much is clear," Aryelle called to her retreating back. "Besides" she added turning back to Karril, suddenly apologetic, "we still need to find your mother."

"She is with the Naturra - I know it! They will help her back to Ka'Andharra."

"Karril," Aryelle said softly, "Kayanna is missing because of me."

"No she is not! She did not have to come along!"

"That is not what I mean."

She sighed. How could she explain the events of…could it be only two nights before? Whatever had happened to Kayanna was her fault. She would have to make him understand that. Hopefully he could forgive her since he would still have to trust her to get him home. Aryelle sank to the ground beside him and described every excruciating detail, including how she thought she would surely die.

"You heard what the Omniscients said, 'strained from healing'? She was bearing *my* pain. She must have assumed it after I lost consciousness."

"But what was it? Where did it come from?"

"I do not know," she answered carefully. "I was hoping that Kayanna would."

"My mother is strong, Aryelle. She is most skilled of all the Kandharril. Only Elazaryn is more powerful."

Aryelle wanted to believe that Karril was right, that Kayanna was fine wherever she was. But how could he know? He had not felt the intense onslaught. Would Kayanna have been able to dispel her pain? Would she have been strong enough alone? A week ago, Aryelle had flaunted her own capabilities. Now she knew better.

"The Omniscients said she was heading homeward. We must turn back-"

"Please, Aryelle. This may be our only chance-"

"We have already used up more than our share of chances cousin."

"Then do it for the future!" he implored. "*Di suip!*"

"*We* may be our only chance-"

"- to meet with other Emrysians…to try and overcome the darkness…"

"If Rachaan keeps tickling Father's ear-"

"Your father's ears are tickled only as much as he allows," said Karril in defense of his favorite uncle.

"I know, but Rachaan despises the other races. You know it was by his council that father ordered the Seal of Silence. And we now know nothing! He will do everything he can to keep us from joining the other races, let alone reuniting the Empaya."

"I am sure Elazaryn knows that. He probably has someone else he could send to the Summit too."

"But it should be me!" Aryelle argued with herself, still struggling with old resentments. "I am blood of his blood, bone of his bone!"

"But we are just children…"

"I am not a child! And…I will go to the Great Summit! I will represent Ka'Andharra." She looked Karril squarely in the eye. "I am sorry about Kayanna, but I must do this. And I suppose you will have to come with me."

"If you think it is the right thing…."

"I do."

"*Ho'kay dhe bo'and;* Then we stay together," Karril said in agreement.

Aryelle blinked. How had the conversation taken this turn? Her cousin looked up at her innocently. But before Aryelle could comment, the air was filled with Lureli's piercing scream. They sprang to their feet and rushed to her. Lureli's head was bent over the empty water vessel.

"He's gone!" she cried.

"Who is gone?" Aryelle took a head count of the Mer.

"Tad! My poor Taddy is gone! He must've fallen out in that nasty swamp!"

"Your pet? He is better off there than in that cramped pot."

Lureli scowled at her. "He *wanted* to be with me I told you! Besides, his legs were growing in really fast. Pretty soon he wouldn't have had to stay in it."

"Well, if he was smart enough to escape he earned his freedom."

"You don't know what you're talking about!" Lureli pouted. "He loves me!"

"I am glad someone does," said Aryelle shaking her head. She turned and walked way.

"I am sorry about Tad," Karril said peering into the empty jug. Then he brightened. "But I do have some good news! We are going to stay with you!"

"Wonderful" murmured Lureli as she glared after Aryelle's departing back.

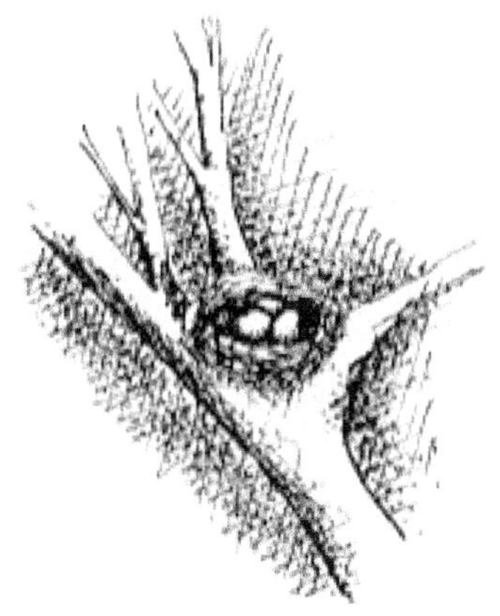

Chapter 14 – Council Grounds

The remainder of the journey to Mt. Cor was uneventful. They traveled for the most part in uneasy silence. Tension between the two young women increased with each step. Karril tried to joke with Aryelle, but she seemed too intent on her mission to exchange pleasant conversation. The few comments Lureli made were biting and sarcastic, making both of them glad when she lapsed into a brooding sulk. The Mer were subdued.

Aryelle knew they missed their brother. She considered the events of the last few days; so much had happened in such a short time! She would never be the same, and doubted the others would either. She missed Kayanna too, but believing she was on her way home helped. She tried not to think about what Elazaryn would say when she showed up without them.

Despite everything, Aryelle was still fond of her new freedom. Since leaving home she had experienced more than she ever dreamed possible. Back at Ka'Andharra, someone was always hovering. She could tell the monotony of this endless plain, however, was boring Karril to distraction. The poor boy! If mischief could be found, he was sure to be in the middle of it – this adventure had emphasized that! - but there was no excitement here. It felt like they were crossing a rustling, golden ocean at a snail's pace. For Aryelle it came as a relief.

At her urging, they had veered west cutting across the northern corner of the prairie rather than following the river's many twists and turns. Lureli's reluctance to leave the river was secondary to their need to make up time. Mt. Cor loomed in the distance, the nearest and largest of the entire Aurrac range. They fixed their sights on the mountain and headed directly for it. But after a day and a half of travel, they seemed no closer than before. Had it not been for constantly overcast skies, Aryelle knew Lureli would have pressed them to turn back to the river. As it was, though she complained bitterly about the heat, she ordered her men to hold their course.

Aryelle wiped her brow and scanned the horizon. The far-off cry of a raptor reached her ears. She searched amid the gray backdrop for its outspread wings. Tilting her head farther back she spotted a distant speck circling directly overhead. It turned and wheeled far above them. Spreading her fingertips since her wings were bound, Aryelle raised her slender arms in imitation, skimming the tasseled tops of the waist-high prairie grasses. *This is what it is like to fly free*, she thought, enjoying the sensation. Karril smiled blandly at her. She returned it with a satisfied grin.

The clouds thinned as evening approached and it promised to be a clear and starlit night. They stopped for their evening meal. To the luminaries' surprise, Lureli demanded they continue on after only a brief rest. Aryelle knew without reading her mind that she was thinking of the bright sun they might have to travel under the next day. She readily agreed, though Lureli's manner was irksome. She had not exerted herself in the least, having ridden the entire way on her litter. Aryelle would be glad when they finally parted company.

As the sun sank behind the Aurracs and the first stars appeared in the eastern sky, they set off once more. Crispin and Katri switched places to give their weary shoulders a rest. Jaim offered to take Jorda's position, but his older brother refused. The heavy poles of the litter balanced evenly on both of his shoulders. Karril stayed in the rear of the caravan with Aryelle, leaving Jaim to lead their way.

Aryelle loved the burgeoning evening across the wide-open spaces. The chirrup of crickets and clicking shower of grasshoppers disturbed by their passing was subtle background music. But all around them, a symphony of singing insects lifted their voices to greet the rising moon. Silva Kandharra, the Great Silver Candle. Tonight she would be nearly full, a pool of luminous silver against a black velvet sky. Her mirrored light outlined the departing clouds along the horizon, casting their shadows across the undulating grass.

Aryelle unfastened the clasp on the silken pouch hanging at her side. Instantly Bel shot into the air, twinkling and circling to greet his heavenly sister. As if knowing what was expected, he hovered directly above the litter. For the luminaries there was no need, but the radiance he emitted brightened the path for the Mer. The bearers offered their silent thanks. In response Bel bobbed above them and held steady with their pace. They trekked on thru the night, the peaceful journey punctuated by the occasional far-off howl of wolves.

With the first rays of sunlight warming their backs, they discovered how much ground they had covered during the night. Mt. Cor no longer loomed in the distance; it stood practically before them. Its great height rose from the prairie as a towering pyramid, and they could make out a village on the slope at its base. They proceeded with caution, though they were invited guests. Suddenly, speaking into everyone's mind at once, Aryelle called a halt. Lureli looked around in surprise. It was the first time she had heard the other girl's thoughts inside her head. Aryelle could tell she did not like it, and she certainly wasn't used to taking orders. Lureli started to complain, but Aryelle shook her head. She held a finger to her lips, her look of watchfulness warning that she was serious. Bel zipped down from the sky and Aryelle quickly tucked him away. Lureli allowed Jorda to lift her gently from the platform once he and the others had set it down.

A suspicious rustle sounded at their right. Aryelle motioned to Karril and Lureli to stay put. She instructed the bearers to circle wide and come in behind whatever might be approaching. For all their great bulk and inability to hear, the men moved almost silently. Eyes alert, the youngsters continued to whisper together. They were not surprised when they noticed an unnatural ripple in the tall prairie grass. Crispin's sharp eyes saw it too, just a few yards from where the caravan had halted. He tiptoed toward the spot. A woman's head and torso appeared, popping over the tops of the golden grasses like a rabbit out of its hole. Out shot Crispin's strong arms engulfing her in a not-so-gentle embrace.

"Let go of me, you stinking low-lander!" The woman struggled, cursing, and butted her head hard against Crispin's throat. He dropped her, gasping for breath. Katri, Jorda and Jaim hurried to him, surrounding her. She turned on them like a cornered beast. Brandishing a short blade, she held them at arm's length.

"Touch me again, you pretty pagans and I'll slit your throats and leave you for the buzzards!" A whitish-blond strand of hair escaped her thick braid. She shoved it behind her ear, never taking her eyes off the circling Mer.

-*Let her come*- Aryelle told them.

To the woman's surprise, the men stopped trying to approach her. They stood erect, folding beefy arms across their chests. Her own chest heaving, she eyed them warily and straightened to her full height. She was no taller than Karril.

"These men are servants and will do you no harm….unless I wish it," said Aryelle with authority.

"They're *my* servants, not yours!" hissed Lureli under her breath.

The stranger strode fearlessly forward. Arrogance marked her strong features. Her sun-bleached hair and leathery, tanned skin had aged her from a distance. But as she drew near, Aryelle saw that she was hardly older than herself. A creamy tan halter of pounded chamois covered her upper body leaving her shoulders bare. A quiver of arrows and a bow were slung across her back. As she stepped from the tall grass, she switched her blade to the opposite hand and thumped her breastbone with a closed fist.

"I am Eleanor," she announced, "Aurracan huntress and protector. You are nearing Holy Ground. State your business or die!"

More than the unfriendly greeting caused the luminaries to stare in shock. Though Aryelle had gleaned snatches of information from the Illuminator, and knew that the races of Emrysia varied like the flowers in Ladhonna's garden, nothing had prepared her for this. Standing before her, from the waist up, was a perfectly proportioned young woman. But where her hips curved outward, curly white wool covered her lower body, which was full and round and ended in two stubby legs with cloven-hoofed feet. She was - the Aurrac were… *fauen*!

"State your business quickly, or feel my blade!"

Regaining her composure Aryelle took charge. "I am Aryelle of the Kandharra, daughter of Elazaryn, El'Kandhar, and heir to the Seat of Ka'Andharra." She gestured broadly toward her cousin. "I present my cousin Karril, Son of Erildhil, who follows me in succession to the throne."

Karril bowed, never taking his eyes off the bizarre stranger.

"And the glittery one?" Eleanor asked brusquely.

"I'm Lureli of the Mer, and I don't like your tone! You smell, and you have the manners of a stupid goat as well-"

"Please excuse our companion," Aryelle apologized, glaring at Lureli. She had gotten used to the other's strange complexion, but not her rude remarks. "She suffers from the heat and is not feeling well. I see it has affected her judgment as well."

Eleanor snorted and stamped an impatient hoof. "Were that not so I'd challenge her to combat. Advise her to take caution - I'm in a testy mood myself! Goat indeed!" To emphasize her point, she hawked up a great wad of phlegm and spat forcefully. Lureli wrinkled her nose in disgust, but fortunately held her tongue.

"We come," continued Aryelle, as if talking to a fauen was an everyday occurrence, "to attend the Great Summit. We represent our peoples in the name of peace to those who would fight to overcome the Shadow which has blighted the land these many years." She was surprised at how easily the despised formality rolled off her tongue.

"What's this Summit? The only summit I know of is the top of Mt. Cor."

"You mean, *on top* of Mt. Cor."

"I mean the mountain peak."

"No, no - Summit… a Great Council. A gathering-" Aryelle tried to explain.

"Hmph!" Eleanor snorted. "I've heard nothing of it. It's a hoax!"

There had to be a mistake. Had they come all this way for nothing? "A messenger….an other-worlder, arrived at Ka'Andharra just less than a candle past. He carried a scroll bearing tidings of a Great Summit, inviting all of the races of Emrysia to come together-"

"A runner came to the Mer too," said Lureli. "He was awfully handsome, though I suppose he wasn't the same one that came to you," she nudged Karril.

Aryelle ignored the interruption. "-and together we will seek to identify and overcome this common threat. Perhaps you have not heard of these tidings as a mere huntress?"

"Maybe not" Eleanor sneered, "and maybe *you* speak lies to save yourself. The Aurrac use no messengers save their own."

"I do not know how he came to bear this invitation, only that we are responding to it."

Eleanor's eyes narrowed. "You say you're Empaya," she said circling behind Aryelle, "yet all I see here is a pack. Where are your wings?"

With a flash, her blade sliced through Aryelle's bindings as though they were nothing but air. Aryelle's wings, ready to escape after their long confinement, unfurled with a crisp snap. Eleanor jumped back with a start, dropping her blade. Karril darted in and scooped it up.

"I said Kandharra, not Empaya," Aryelle corrected. She nodded at Karril and he handed the knife back to its owner, handle first.

Eleanor took it and regarded them. "Same difference."

If the Aurrac saw them as one and the same, then how much longer before they were. Aryelle took it as a good sign. "Take us to your elders and we will see about this hoax," she said.

"Aurrac chieftains are spread throughout these mountains," Eleanor elaborated with a broad sweep of her arm, "and do not meet often. It's courting disaster to call them together without grave purpose. But tomorrow I journey to the Upper Village of Mt. Cor, home of Borrac, Chief among Chieftains. You may come with me - if you can keep up - and present yourselves to him at your own risk."

"Why risk? As you see, we have come in truth."

"There's always risk with Borrac," she said, stuffing her blade into a sheath at her side. "He is….unpredictable."

"Then how should we approach him? I assume he was the one to invite us."

"It pays to approach him carefully. And watch your back."

"I can see that is a good idea around here."

Eleanor shrugged. "*I* won't kill you for sport. Come! You can stay in the house of Nodd until we leave."

"But why not leave right now?" asked Lureli impatiently.

Eleanor stared at her coldly. "I must prepare."

With that, she turned her back on them and began walking toward the village at the foot of the mountain. For a moment no one else moved. Then Aryelle and Karril hurried after her, leaving Lureli to mount her litter and order her men to follow, which she did with a wave and a flurry.

They had almost reached their destination when they heard a familiar screech, no longer far-off, but just overhead. Something fell from the sky like a stone, landing just in front of Eleanor. She bent to retrieve it, holding up a dead rabbit, its long ears dangling, and no trace of blood on it. Quickly Eleanor strode a few paces ahead, picked up three more, and tied the double brace together.

"You're off by a few paces, Hornet!" she hollered with a grin, holding the conies high.

"Skreeeeeah!"

A peregrine falcon, its striped breast thrust forward and wings tipped back to reduce lift, circled once, and then came to land on the leather wristband covering Eleanor's outstretched forearm. She attached a slender, leather thong to one of its legs with her free hand. Slinging the rabbits across her shoulder, she reached up to stroke the bird's dark head. It pecked at her fingers searching for a treat.

"Tsk, tsk, tsk! You bring back conies, but I bring back fairies and mermaids! I should be getting a treat, not you!" She smiled at the falcon as if sharing a joke, then proceeded to enter the Aurrac village.

Karril looked at Aryelle. "What is a fairy?" he asked.

"I think we are," she answered.

If meeting Eleanor was unexpected, it was nothing compared to their introduction to the villagers. As they moved between the grass huts of the village, a boisterous herd of half-sheep children swarmed around them, some speaking, some bleating, all of them decorated with tattoos and beads. Grass tassels and feathers adorned their hair and fleece. Some had budding horns either high on their foreheads or curling above their ears. Several were missing limbs on either their beastly or human halves, a few on both. One poor youngster had no arms or legs at all, and was carried on the wooly hip of an older child, whose one good arm supported it. Surprisingly, all of the children looked cheerful, though somewhat undernourished. Eleanor patted each one kindly as they skipped and danced around her. She held up her quarry to the children's cheers, and then tossed them to an older boy. His body was intact but his face disfigured by a huge purple tumor that spread thickly across his forehead. He trotted off with his prize, the dozen or so other children parading after him.

"What happened here?" asked Aryelle with concern. "What happened to those children?"

"Nothing," answered Eleanor stonily, "except that they were born." Her eyes tracked their carefree movement across the compound. "That's just how it is in the lower village."

The color drained from Lureli's face and she swayed woozily in her seat. Aryelle and Karril exchanged glances. A full-grown male fauen was approaching them. A thick shock of unkempt gray hair surrounded his face, hair and beard tumbling in a shaggy mane over his bare shoulders and chest. Like the boy who had just left, a protuberant crimson stain splashed across the fore of his skull. Unlike him, the rams' horns curling out of either side of his head were thick and scarred. The wool of his lower body was matted with dirt and blood.

"Peace be, Nodd" Eleanor greeted him.

"This is not your usual peace offering Eleanor," he growled with a nod in the travelers' direction.

"I don't think even hollow stomachs could stomach *them*," Eleanor grinned knowingly.

Nodd looked at her askance, and then swept her up in a bone-crushing embrace. Hornet squawked noisily. When at last he set her down, Eleanor squeezed the ram's arm with affection.

"I've given Jode a double brace, scrawny - but young enough to keep your teeth in your head, old man! And I've brought you visitors from across the prairie, perhaps with stories to tease your deaf ears."

"Yes, you know how I like stories," his chuckle was baritone. "Practically the only pleasure left me now!"

"And thank goodness for that, you old goat!" she quipped with a wink.

Nodd turned his attention to the newcomers.

"Peace be," he said through a nearly-toothless smile.

"I bid you peace also," responded Aryelle, still assuming leadership for the group. She forced her tone to remain calm though her heart raced within her chest. Her eyes drifted between the fauen's formidable horns and his bloodied torso.

Noticing her discomfort, he glanced down at himself and bellowed with laughter. "It's slaughtering day, but not for guests, don't worry."

Eleanor smirked as Aryelle forced a smile and made their introductions.

When she got to Lureli, Nodd interrupted. "Does this one think she's better than everyone else? Why doesn't she walk like the rest of you?"

Panic filled Lureli's eyes as he moved around the litter. Without warning Nodd slapped a hand against the platform causing the mechanism to release its supports, startling everyone including the Mer. Aryelle cautioned them to hold their ground, sensing Lureli was in no real danger. She started to explain about Lureli, but Eleanor beat her to it.

"That one's sickly. You can always tell a fish that's been out of the water too long."

"Yes, she is a little green around the gills" Nodd observed. "Let's get her down to the river before she starts to stink!"

To Aryelle's surprise, the old fauen signaled to the Mer in the same manner Lureli used. The bearers seemed nonplussed, and then nodded in agreement. They picked up the litter and headed off carting Lureli, white-knuckled, in the direction Nodd indicated.

"Now, don't you fret; she'll be just fine," said Nodd, leaving the luminaries to stare after them. A few moments later, Aryelle realized that Nodd and Eleanor were deep in conversation. At the mention of Borrac, Nodd glanced up in alarm. He shook his dappled mane at Aryelle.

"These were the Council Grounds in days past, missy. I haven't heard about this council you're looking for. But then, I've been out of favor with Borrac for a long time. You'd be wise to be cautious where the Chieftain's concerned. Stay here as long as you like; in the lower village, all are welcome. Don't expect them to be as cordial at the summit unless, as you say, you've been summoned by Borrac himself."

"I do not know for certain it was Borrac who sent the messenger. But we have come too far to turn back without discovering the truth. We will go with Eleanor tomorrow as she offered."

"Tomorrow? But you just arrived!" Nodd looked Eleanor squarely in the face. "Child, I'd rather feast my eyes on you than my stomach on those conies you brought! I thought we'd have you with us for a few days at least."

"I'm sorry Nodd. Perhaps next time," Her eyes took on a far-away look. Aryelle could tell there was more to her story than she was willing to share.

"Then there's much to be done if I'm to have any time with you at all - or any time to hear *your* stories!" he told the luminaries. "Take them to Althea, Eleanor, and I'll join you when the slaughtering is finished."

With a nod of his head he took his leave, disappearing around the side of one of the huts.

"Come" said Eleanor. "The house of Nodd is this way."

"What about our friend?" asked Karril. "We should find her. She did not look well."

"Are you sure that one is your friend?"

Aryelle answered for him. "She is our companion on this journey. We must see that she is safe."

Eleanor considered them thoughtfully. "Well," she said at last, "at least you're *her* friend."

She turned to go, but the luminaries stayed rooted in place. Realizing they hadn't moved, she called over her shoulder, "Come on! The river is this way as well. You can see for yourself how she's doing," and left them to follow in her wake.

The river as it turned out, surged down the mountain and over the prairie to the confluence of Leaping Falls River. Along the way, it snaked around the perimeter of the lower village creating a natural boundary between the lowlands and southeastern slope of Mt. Cor. Since during the night the caravan had veered slightly off course, their approach had been from the southwest. It also meant they arrived with dry feet.

Along the way, they passed several villagers going happily about their business. They spared little attention for the newcomers save a friendly wave, though each greeted Eleanor heartily. Like the children, many were disabled or disfigured in some way, some grotesquely so.

A separate cluster of grass huts interconnected by flat stone walkways and a common thatched roof marked the edge of the village. Through openings in the largest, central structure, Aryelle and Karril could see the riverbank beyond. A broad figure darkened the doorway before stepping into the light.

She was easily the fattest creature either of them had ever seen. Great folds of flab swung under each arm. Multiple chins were stacked above an abundant, drooping bosom held aloft in a woolen halter that was bursting at its seams. The halter's straps buried deep into the flesh of her shoulders. Over it, she wore a plain, white apron. Her wooly hindquarters were incredibly broad, barely clearing the lintels of the doorway, and her hair, which was white, streaked with gray, hung pleated into two long braids. Two smallish horns curled out of her head at her temples. She wore no other ornamentation and aside from her girth, seemed normal to the undiscerning eyes of the luminaries.

"Althea."

Eleanor inched forward on less than eager hooves to be engulfed in her embrace. Noisy tears escaped the older woman. Then she held Eleanor at arms' length. With a mother's scrutiny, Althea turned her chin and clucked her disapproval.

"You're not eating well child; you're all wool and bones! We're not sending you up that mountain for them to starve ya to death, you know! It's a good thing you come on slaughtering day. We'll have a feast tonight! A celebration! Ho! And who do we have here? More visitors? The more the merrier! You're always welcome at Nodd's table, provided you can spin a good yarn. The old bugger likes a good story, ya know. Well, come in! Come in! Don't just stand there all day. Eleanor, leave that pesky bird of yours outside; I don't want droppings all over my clean house again! Yep, it's gonna be a hot one, I can always tell. If I could reach all the way 'round the bulk of me, I'd give myself a good shearing, that I would! I should wade right into that river," she said gesturing toward it as she led the way into the dwelling's shady interior, "like your mermaid friend out there. Course, then I'd be damp all over and need me a good wringing out. What's the matter? Glory! Did ya ever see such wings! Bend down a little lower girlie, or you'll never get 'em through the doorway! And aren't you a scrawny fairy lad! I'm just set to do a washing out back there. Take a load off and I'll fetch ya something cool to drink. The other fellows they didn't want any. Quiet types aren't they. But I got some nice fine hops perking - mercy! - if I can find clean horns enough!"

Still bleating away, she waddled through the back door toward the river, leaving her guests in stunned silence. The house was rich with the warm, spicy aroma of simmering herbs. Eleanor ambled over to a grass mat near the outer wall of the room. Folding her legs beneath her, she half sat, half lay down. She closed her eyes, effectively cutting off any interaction between them. Unsure of what to expect in these unfamiliar surroundings, the luminaries remained standing self-consciously in the center of the room.

From where she stood, Aryelle could see Lureli's bearers posted like sentries on the bank of the river. Lureli had to be in the water. Aryelle knew she must be safe; otherwise her servants would not just stand there. Eleanor had said something about her being a fish out of water. Lureli sure swam like one, but how could Eleanor have known that? Then again, Nodd had easily made himself understood by the deaf bearers. He did say that this used to be the council grounds. The Aurrac and Mer must be on familiar terms, she surmised. They probably knew much more about each other than Aryelle had been able to learn in just a few days of travel.

She had so many questions. The Aurrac were like something straight from her imagination. She could hardly believe such strange creatures existed, let alone that she was a guest in one's home. And what about the fact that almost everyone they had seen so far seemed deformed in some way? The world was getting bigger at an alarming rate. Aryelle did not know if her perceptions of it could keep up. Karril on the other hand seemed to be taking it all in stride, adapting marvelously well for someone just as sheltered. For one who had never labored harder than bearing a cup or reading a missive for his El'Kandhar, he seemed to be enjoying the menial tasks the Mer set for him, and had learned quickly to shoulder whatever responsibility he was given without complaint. His mistrust of Lureli had blossomed into open admiration. And, it seemed, he had sized up their new situation, realizing that holding his tongue with these strange people was the better course. Aryelle hoped Lureli would discover the same.

She looked over at Eleanor, whose eyes were still closed. Aryelle took the opportunity to study her tanned face. It was beautiful in an angular way, with a strong jaw and high cheekbones. Her hair, streaked many shades from the sun, was woven into a loose plait. She had no horns that Aryelle could see, nor was she deformed. Before they entered Nodd's house, she had tethered the falcon to a post that appeared to be meant for that purpose. After hanging up quiver and bow, she had removed the simple leather wristband that protected her from the falcon's talons. Aryelle had noticed then the tattoo on her upper arm; three curved lines rising and falling, the lowest broken in the middle, the others mirror images. She studied it now, but made no sense of the strange markings. Her eyes drifted to the wooly half of Eleanor's body. It looked so soft that she was tempted to reach over and stroke it, burying her fingers deep into its fluffy white curls. Aryelle looked up, startled to find Eleanor staring scornfully back at her. She shuddered all the way to her wingtips.

Althea returned and caught the two young women glaring at one another. "Wings are great if you like flyin', but they sure don't keep you warm at night, my mother always said. Flimsy lookin' things - are fairies wings even good for flyin'?"

Before Aryelle could answer, she launched into another rambling monologue.

"Yep, my mother loved that saying. That, and the grass is always greener on the other side of the bridge. Oh, and knit one, purl two, though I don't know what that has to do with why the whey won't curdle! Heh! She was full of 'em, and I dare say I inherited a bit of her wit, don't cha know. But mercy, what a talker! She could talk the ears off a cornstalk! Cor, whee! Glad I missed that one! Now where was I going? Oh yes, goodness sakes, me alive! I'd forget my horns if they weren't growing out of my own head! Just into the pantry to fetch an oatcake or two to go with that hops. It's nigh about time for a nip and a tuck, don't cha think? Best call that friend of yourn from the river." She breezed out of the room again, surprisingly agile for her great bulk, leaving everyone in the room feeling breathless.

****

Aryelle groaned inwardly, imagining Althea and Lureli squaring off for debate, the one type of warfare luminaries relished. But she wasn't enjoying this. Both seemed determined to comment about every topic under the sun. Whenever one paused for breath, the other jumped in, oblivious to whether anyone was listening or not. Between them, Aryelle, Karril and Eleanor had barely spoken a word. At least, thought Aryelle, I am learning more than I ever wanted to know.

What she learned most vividly, sorting through all the trivial dribble and inane sayings, was how alike two totally different creatures could be. They agreed on absolutely nothing, yet race aside and barring the fact that Lureli was totally self-absorbed and Althea practically selfless, they seemed to get along like oatcakes and honey, to borrow one of Althea's pet phrases. Their instant friendship left Aryelle feeling even more an outsider. So did the fact that they seemed to know so much about one another's people. If ever she regretted Kandharran insularity, the feeling intensified now that she was actually face to face with Emrysia's other races. While the conversation centered on their everyday lives and habits, their common knowledge left little room for explanation to the very questions Aryelle wanted to ask. Recipes and gossip meant nothing to her; she wanted to know these people! Who were they and where did they come from? How did they come to be so different from her kind? Would they all be able to overcome their differences to build a united Emrysia?

"What's the matter girlie? Did ya fall asleep over there? Cor, ya barely touched your beer and cakes. No wonder you're thin enough to see through! I was askin' if ya wanted some more, but I can see both you and the little fellow aren't much for eating. I know it's not the cooking; ain't never had a complaint!"

"Forgive me," Aryelle blurted, interrupting, "but then why are the children all but starving?"

All eyes fixed on her. Althea looked as though she had stopped breathing, and Aryelle could practically hear their heartbeats echoing around the room. She had shocked herself with the question, asked with neither diplomacy nor forethought. But now that she had their attention, Aryelle did not back down. "That they are all deformed is obvious. Is it too big of a burden to feed them properly? Have they not suffered enough already?"

Eleanor finally spoke. "I know your people are empaths, otherwise I would consider that insult a lack of good breeding instead of just ignorance, and be obliged to defend our honor."

"I did not mean…I do not know…."

"That's right! You know nothing!"

"Then teach me!"

"The welfare of our children is not your concern!"

Again, Aryelle and Eleanor glared at each other. Althea broke the uncomfortable silence.

"There's one oatcake left. Lureli, how about you…"

Lureli looked from face to face around the low table, the last crumbs of her snack still tumbling down her chin. Then unexpectedly, her eyes rolled skyward and she slumped forward.

"...Mercy! Cor, I knew it was too hot! Quickly now, let's get her back into the river."

Later that evening, Nodd raised his cup signaling the feast to begin. Villagers and guests reclined in a large circle on the bare earth, this time in the open air in the center of the village. The entire population, about forty souls, had turned out for the celebration, with the travelers and Eleanor bringing the number to nearly fifty. Children and elders alike sat or lay with no apparent order or hierarchy, though Nodd was clearly leader among them.

Any concerns over the children's treatment were soon laid to rest as Aryelle observed how the adults doted on them. The more severely handicapped were lavished with the most attention. The girls' hair had been pleated into elaborate braids, decorated with colorful beads and brilliant feathers. Boys and girls alike wore circlets of ivy like crowns, and bracelets of wildflowers around their wrists. It seemed the arrival of newcomers was cause for celebration. Aryelle could hardly believe all of this was in their honor.

As platters of food were brought forward by the women, she was proven correct. The men took turns standing, ceremoniously offering thanks to the gods for the bounty now provided. Platters of fish accompanied prayers to Argo, god of flowing waters. Roc, the sun god was honored along with Sheala, goddess of the hunt, for bread and game. Earth, harvest, rain, fire; the Aurrac had deities for every aspect of their lives. After the lesser gods were acknowledged, Nodd stood and praised Cor, god of the mountain, worshipped and feared above the rest. Then the feasting began.

The children were served first. Beer and wine flowed freely, and as they feasted, the revelers grew louder and more boisterous with each cup. Aryelle and Karril, unaccustomed to strong drink, limited themselves to water, passing as well on platters laden with animal flesh. They watched with some concern as Lureli, now completely recovered from her fainting spell, ate and drank with reckless abandon. The Mer men, seated as equals among the people of the village, dug in as well. They chatted in sign with many of the adults nearby, and made funny faces to the delight of the Aurrac children.

As the sun passed behind the mountain and shrouded the village in shadow, a bonfire was lit in the center of the circle. A few hours remained until nightfall, but the pall of the mountain was stronger now that it blocked the evening sunlight. Aryelle shivered though she was not cold. The light-loving luminaries felt the gloom more intensely than those used to living in its shade.

Plates emptied and sweets were passed around. Flutes, horns and drums of all sizes appeared. Soon the strains of a lively jig were enticing the revelers to dance. Aryelle's heart lightened as she watched a train of children twirl and leap around the dancing flames. A few of the adults joined in, occasionally tossing a laughing youngster high into the air. The love and goodwill the fauen felt for each other was stronger than any despair cast by the shadow of the mountain. She watched the boy Jode make a daring half-twist leap over the fire to land exultant on the other side.

"Did'cha get enough girlie? Hate to see ya wasting away. Here, I'll take that for you."

"Your son dances well" Aryelle complimented Althea, careful not to revisit touchier subjects as the older woman gathered her plate. Althea seemed to have forgotten the incident.

"Wha', Jode? The showoff!" She smiled and gazed at him affectionately. "He's Nodd's, not mine."

"But I thought you and Nodd-"

"Sure, yer right there, but Jode's mother is Lavina, my sister. She lives up at the summit with the rest of Borrac's ewes. 'Cept me, of course. I come down here to Nodd when Jode was born. Brung him down so's Borrac wouldn't run him through. Lavina couldn't; she was too sick after birthing him. My own young'un that spring didn't make it, and I was just plain sick of Borrac, so I switched 'em, and me and Eleanor high-tailed it. Course when he figured out I left, Borrac come down the mountain hisself for the first time ever. No honest fightin' fer that one, no! He come in the middle of the night with a sharp blade and went after Nodd and the other rams while they was in their beds! Stole their manhood, that what he done. Worse than killed 'em, if ya ask me. Killed all the children in the village too, except Eleanor, who survived by the wool of her teeth, and Jode who I was a-nursin'."

Aryelle looked at her in horror.

"But there are children here" she said.

"Yep, how could we live without 'em? Our hearts were broken, that's for sure. But then, the babies started a comin'. Jest floatin' down the river, sure as sunrise, every spring a new crop. Not the regular children mind, but the less than perfect ones. Eleanor found the first one come spring melt. Pulled a basket right out of the water and there was Silene -

she's the one over there with the baby on her hip - crying fer her mama's tit, and no one here but me able to suckle her. I've nursed every one of these young'uns, and more besides seeing as some didn't make it. But at least they all had a fighting chance. Better'n they'd a had up on the mountain. I figure that's what their mammas musta thought too. They float 'em down and we keep 'em and mark 'em as our own. Nodd, he's real handy at tattooin'. Guess I'll nurse any more what come along, long as these jugs don't run dry. They shouldn't, least not afore these young'uns start breeding kids of their own."

She paused for breath. Aryelle was too stunned to speak. Finally, she was discovering something of importance about the Aurrac, but what shocking things to learn. It made sense now why all of the children here were deformed; they were rejects from further up the mountain. Since several adults were afflicted as well, Aryelle could only assume that they had banded together, exiles from the summit, fortunate to even be alive. In turn, they had given these poor children a chance at life. But why? Why had they all become outcasts? And what was the answer to her indelicate question this afternoon? After they had helped Lureli back into the water, Althea had muttered excuses about needing to 'air her washin'. She left Eleanor to show them to one of the side dwellings. Aryelle and Karril had rested there until called for the feast.

"...been hiding 'em every autumn since," Althea was saying, breaking through Aryelle's reverie. "There's a cave 'round the other side of the mountain that Borrac ain't never found out about. This year being such a wet one and all, we had a harder time of it than usual, stock dying and crops not takin'. That's why the young'uns look like they do. Should'a jest told ya that earlier. Didn't have much t' spare, and when the Chieftain sends for his due, it don't pay to cut him short. He jest collected a few days ago, and the young'uns got back yesterday. That's why it was slaughtering day today- so's we can fatten 'em up again right off. Now that Borrac's men have been here and gone-"

"You mean Borrac sends someone to collect a portion of your food?" Aryelle was learning that to participate in a conversation with Althea she had to jump right in.

"Portion? Hah! He robs us blind! Sends his patrol; there's barely enough to make it through the winter after they've been here. Course, we hide what we can with the children, mostly livestock. Sheep and goats, you know. But still, we can't hide much or they'd suspect."

"Sheep and goats? You are…shepherds? Forgive me, but are they not your cousins?" Aryelle was afraid she had overstepped the boundaries again, but Althea seemed to take it without insult, probably because she had tipped a few cups herself.

"Right tasty ones! Hee-hee!"

"Where are they?" Aryelle asked, repulsed. "I have not seen or heard them anywhere."

"Most is up the mountain, of course. Borrac likes to see the whole herd so's he can take his pick. He'll set the few he doesn't keep loose, and when they wander this way again, we'll herd 'em in for the winter. They'll breed and we'll have a whole new flock come spring. See, the grazing gets tough further up, 'specially come snowfall. Borrac needs us. We see to the livestock and crops here below, and he sits up on his mountain gettin' fat!"

"Now Althea," said Nodd, stretching his arms around her girth as he came up behind her. Aryelle wondered how much of their conversation he had heard. "It's time for stories, but let's hear theirs first."

"Ah, get off with ya, you horny old ram! Don't be lightin' fires ya can't put out!" She grabbed a handful of his hoary beard and gave it a good-natured shake. Nodd retaliated with a playful smack on the rump as she carted off the plates she'd collected. Looking back over her shoulder, Althea gave him a knowing wink.

"Mother of Cor, would that I'd have had my way with that ewe back when I had the chance!" Nodd looked after her with longing.

"Excuse me?"

"Just the ramblings of an old fauen, dearie. Never you mind." He shook his head wistfully. Then, with unexpected enthusiasm, he clapped his hands together. "Now, how about a tale?"

"I am not particularly good at stories. Perhaps Lureli…"

"Asleep in her beer, I'm afraid. I see she drinks like a fish too!" he said with a chuckle.

Aryelle did not know what to say. Though usually outspoken, she was shy when it came to putting herself on display. They had imposed on these people's hospitality and she wanted to do something for them in return, but getting up in front of everyone and telling a story? She was not sure she could. Thankfully, Karril, who had been silent and watchful most of the evening, came promptly to her rescue.

"I know a good story," he said getting to his feet.

"That's a good boy!" Nodd smiled broadly and clapped him on the shoulder. With a grand gesture, he gave him leave and walked around the circle back to his place. Aryelle sighed in relief.

Karril winked at her and turned to face the gathered villagers. The womenfolk stopped their bustling and returned to where they were sitting. An expectant hush fell over the crowd. Children who had not already drifted off to sleep looked up at Karril with wide-eyed wonder. Clearing his throat, in a high, sweet tenor he began:

EPIC OF A BUTTERFLY

(Tales of Wings)

Vainly in a puddle spied
A Butterfly his grandeur
So flitted he from lofty height
To get a closer gander.

He rested at the puddle's edge
And leaned webbed-wings way o'er
And saw upon the surface smooth
Great pinions numb'ring four.

"My wings!" he cried. "How glorious!"
(They were indeed divine)
"Majestic! No - Imperial!
There are none so fair as mine!

Oh, King of Butterflies, Thy beauty
Doth eclipse Thine minions
Whose drab, pathetic little wings

Compare not with Thy pinions!"

And as he gazed upon his grace
The bashful breezes blew
And pushed him tenderly 'til he
His mirror tumbled thru.

He sputtered and floundered and splashed about
As the weight of his wings drew him down,
Then bobbed toward the surface and gave a loud shout
For he did not care to drown.

Then butterflies other, and none the lesser
In beauty, with wings of lace,
Came fluttering there from everywhere,
And gathering at that place.

"Save the Beauteous!" pleaded the Vain,
To those who hovered near,
But off they flew quite hurriedly
As if they did not hear.

"Come back!" cried he, and sank for deuce,
And rose, filling his lungs for a third
Knowing this time would be his last-
When this was what he heard.

"Stay calm, Your Highness!" piped a voice
From somewhere far behind.
"I'll save you, but tis only fair
That payment shall be mine."

Then shot a rope like gossamer
From puddle's distant shore
"Hold fast, and quickly now, Your Grace,"
He heard the voice implore.

So clinging to the lifeline
Like a fisherman's prize lure
He let himself be pulled out from
This peril to one newer.

For posted on the water's edge
His rescuer so bold
Had five feet firmly planted
With three more the tow to hold."

The adults and older children gasped. Aryelle hid her smile of amusement from youngsters yet to grasp the rescuer's identity. Anxious whispers broke out and Karril paused dramatically. He was giving a masterful performance, adjusting pitch and intonation, using posture and gestures to enhance the tale. As elders shushed children in breathless anticipation, Aryelle noticed the spellbound faces of the Mer. She gently probed their minds and found that so far at least, the story for them had been merely a pantomime. Too bad, she thought, for they were missing much. Softly into their consciousness', so softly that at first they were unaware of it, Aryelle began to translate, gifting the Mer with their first poetry purely for pleasure's sake. Her eyes glittered when, moments later, they turned delighted faces toward her.

Karril's gaze raked the crowd as he took up the tale.

Soon heaving sodden plumage toward
The puddle's pebbly shore,
The Butterfly his savior sought
To thank him for his chore.

"Ah, bless you sir" the Butterfly
His victor gaily met
For stumbling shoreward could not see
To whom he was in debt.

"G-good Sir, I owe to you m-my life!"
He stuttered, wet and trembling
"Come, show yourself! For now I fear
My brain is disassembling...."

But as his misted vision cleared
He gasped in sheer surprise
For creeping from the shadows
Was a beast nigh thrice his size.

Another rustle from the crowd, this time as children snuggled nervously beneath protective arms. Those left wondering about the villain were about to find out.

"It is not sir, but Madame,"
Drawled the Spider slivedly.
"There now, good friend, shake out your wings.
You must come in for tea."

And though the Butterfly had thought
To flee, t'would seem ungracious.
(Besides, his wings must dry before
He sought the sky so spacious.)

So hoisting him upon her back
As easily as could be,
She hauled him to her domicile
Within an ancient tree.

And there her children greeted them
With unexpected zest
All ninety circling 'round her feet,
Though one could be a pest!

"Patience dears!" their mother cried
Above the thunderous din.
"If you're to have a treat with tea
You must first let us in."

Then crossing o'er the threshold dark
Into her humble lair
The Spider soon deposited
Her load onto a chair.

A comfy chair, the Butterfly
Was grateful to admire,
Beside a hearth within whose grate
There burned a cheery fire.

At first their guest sat anxiously
As tea was put to boil
But room's dim light and fire's warmth
Hence bade his nerves uncoil.

And soon, though not the guest's intent,
He drifted off to sleep.
(The children had been warned, you see,
To not let out a peep.)

When he awoke, the kettle's piping
Cutting through his slumber,
He found that he was tightly wound
With strands of silk past number.

And all the spider children,
Ninety creeping, crawling squibs
Were standing 'round him drooling
Spoons in hand, and wearing bibs.

"Cor-whee! That were yesterday!" Althea hooted pinching the rosy cheek of the child cuddled next to her. The adults chuckled good-naturedly while the recently returned youngsters feigned offence. Jode jumped to his feet and waggled his tongue, pretending to be famished. Silene shifted with embarrassment and pulled him back to his place. He nudged her playfully.

"Jest you wait!" warned Althea winking. With a dramatic sweep of his arm, Karril drew them onward.

As comprehension dawned and fear

Spread quickly 'crossed his face,
The Butterfly had but one thought-
He must vacate this place!

"Ah, Lady," croaked the Butterfly,
His voice a nervous quiver,
"Please spare my wretched life! In turn
A gift I will deliver!"

Now, the Spider liked to bargain
For she felt herself adept
At coming out the winner
Once the promised deal was kept.

And so she listened to the plan
The Butterfly now offered
And eagerly accepted lest rescinding,
He un-proffered.

Then with the blade whose purpose sure
Had been to slit his throat
The spider slit instead the threads
Which formed his silken coat.

The children whined, they wailed, they pouted
Tantrums threw galore
As Mother helped the visitor rise,
And showed him to the door.

But then, to them, behind his back,
The Butterfly heard her utter

"Crisp wings a tasty morsel make
When they are spread with butter!"

And to his horror a fist shot out
Hard, giving him the shove
Whilst quick! Another grabbed his wings
And tore them from above.

He gasped in pain, yet bolted
Making good on his escape,
And through the doorway stumbled blind
With countenance agape.

And falling from the Spider's doorstep
Far up in the tree,
The Butterfly hit every branch,
Abrading nose and knee.

He would have splattered on the ground
But for a well placed web
On which he rested for a time
In hope his pain would ebb.

And when the wingless wonder
Finally dared to look around
With gaping eyes, to his surprise,
Imagine what he found.

He amongst the bodies of
A thousand flies did lay,
Some were fresh and some were…well,

Beginning to decay.

But one fly near the middle of
The webby insect graveyard,
Was still buzzing, buzzing, buzzing-
For to live he clearly favored.

Then noticing the Butterfly
(Now less his glorious wings)
The Fly, a bright metallic green,
Bawled, "Help me with these things!

Come here you ugly, hairy beast
With coiled proboscis bending,
And lend to me a helping hand
Or witness soon my ending!"

Laying his chin along his shoulder, Karril flicked out his arm, imitating a fly in search of food. There were squeals of laughter as he plucked the feathers from a young girl's hair, and even more when he pretended to find a morsel of food in Nodd's beard.

"Go on with you now, finish the telling," Nodd shooed him away, as anxious as the rest to learn the Butterfly's fate, and now the fly's as well.

The Butterfly looked round to see
Whom he addressed so meanly.
"Am I" thought he, "to whom he speaks?"
And felt his loss more keenly.

Through waves of pain came now a thought,
To him, and came it clearly,
That self-same attitude of his
Had cost him ever dearly.

Though to show mercy could have meant
Both healing and redemption,
The fly's insulting words earned not
The Butterfly's exemption.

So taking now his turn to jape
One weaker and in trouble,
The Butterfly called "Sure, I'll help!
I'll be there on the double!"

And crawling over carcasses
He reached the struggling creature
And freed him using hand and nose,
Which was a useful feature.

And as the final sticky strand
Was broken by his tearing
The Fly looked at him wond'ring
At the grin that he was wearing.

"I am just happy you are free!"

Then pointing, he did gush,
"A lovely tea's been poured for you
Up there. Now better rush!"

And so, true to his word,
The crafty creature, bargain keeping,
Sent forth the fly to certain death,
Which no one would be weeping.

For in dealing with the Spider
Thought his cunning upper shelf,
He had promised and delivered,
One more beauteous than himself.

And though he would have never dreamed
It possible, the Vain One,
Had found of value as he fell,
His life to be the main one.

And now this tale must draw to end
For though more lies awaiting,
Your hunger wanes for tales so long,
And soon will be abating.

But lest you think that, moral told,
You are wiser now and knowing,
Remember, like the Butterfly
There is always room for growing.

A pregnant pause followed Karril's humble bow, and then the Aurrac burst into applause. Stamping and beating the ground with the flats of their hands, they acknowledged Karril's skill as a masterful storyteller. Blushing, he quickly sat down.

"Wonderfully done, Kay," exclaimed Aryelle, leaning toward him. She knew her cousin was quite the scholar, but of poetry? Though she had often heard the tale, she could never have memorized it.

"I had to make up odd bits," he admitted self-consciously. "Look, Nodd is going to tell a story next."

Aryelle gazed across the circle. Nodd had risen to his feet. A hush fell once more and he began to speak.

"Many harvests ago, when the red moon hung heavy in the sky, Argo, River God danced his way down the mountain. Mighty Cor looked on in anger. He did not like that the river should flow like blood from His Mountain. He did not like that the river played and laughed to a music that he could not make. And he did not like the caresses given to his bride Echinacea, Goddess of the prairie, by this interloper. And so Cor demanded that Argo change course. When Argo resisted, Mighty Cor grew furious! He grumbled and growled and bared his teeth. He shook and threw boulders down the mountain to frighten Argo. But Argo danced over them. Cor, enraged, exploded! Great clouds of smoke and liquid fire poured from his open mouth, coursing down the mountainside, swallowing everything in its path. Argo was frightened and died in his bed. But Echinacea gathered Argo in her golden arms, covered him with her green and purple flowered cloak, and breathed life back into his body. Now Argo is wiser. He still dances and plays, but only sings loudly in the spring while Cor is still asleep. He no longer runs his many fingers through Echinacea's golden hair, but hugs her shoulder gently, like a brother. And when the moon is full and red, he offers Cor back the blood that the God thought stolen. And Cor is appeased."

Aryelle noticed several villagers nodding and glancing toward the waxing moon as the ancient legend was retold. At the end of the tale, the Aurrac applauded enthusiastically once more. Aryelle sat absorbing the story's message.

When the applause died down, Nodd asked Eleanor for news from the Upper Village. Borrac's patrol, it seemed, had little inclination to share information with the despised lowlanders. Nodd sat down and Eleanor rose to her feet. Her voice was strong and matter-of-fact.

"Borrac, High Chieftain is taking yet another wife. The marriage will be held during the Autumn Blood Festival. Because of this, and in honor of his virgin bride, Borrac has invited the other Aurrac chieftains to come and participate in this season's blood sport. All have accepted. Over the next few days, they will be journeying up the north side of Mount Cor. I come with these tidings bidding you to remain close. Do not leave the south slope. It will be a very dangerous time at the summit."

"Then stay here with us" said Nodd. Around the circle, there were murmurs of agreement.

Eleanor shook her head. "I must return immediately; I am expected. If I did not return, you would all be in great danger."

"What of yourself? Borrac's blood sport is always dangerous, but with the other chieftains who knows? It may get out of control!" The villager who spoke was an older, one-eyed ram whose left arm hung limply at his side. Scars crisscrossed his upper body, battle wounds from his younger days. His words held weight.

Eleanor drew herself up proudly. "I am Eleanor, Aurracan huntress and protector, daughter of Althea the Bountiful and right arm of Sheala, Goddess of the Hunt, who has spared me to her service. My knife is sharp and my mind clear. I will not be harmed!"

Staring at her blade, held high and glistening in the flickering firelight, Aryelle was struck by the power of her words. In the silence that followed, Althea's muffled weeping and consoling whispers from the ewe beside her could be heard.

Across the circle, Nodd and Eleanor's gaze locked together like rams' horns. When Nodd finally looked away, there were tears in his eyes. He struggled to his feet as if achy and tired from the day's hard labor. Perhaps he was, thought Aryelle, but more likely it was a heavy heart that weighed him down. He shuffled away and one by one, the other fauen did likewise, carrying the youngest in their arms. Jorda picked up Lureli, who was snoring like a hibernating *slobear*, and hoisted her unceremoniously over his shoulder. The other Mer looked as if they had drunk a few too many cups of the strong Aurracan ale. They staggered off toward Nodd's house.

Soon only Eleanor, Karril, and Aryelle remained by the fire. Eleanor stared into the glowing embers oblivious of their presence. Eventually she looked up. "We leave at daybreak, if you're still set on your course." Her voice was softer than they had ever heard it.

"Like Argo? Yes, we are still coming with you," confirmed Aryelle despite her reservations.

Eleanor nodded. "Then you must promise me this: I will speak first to Borrac on your behalf while you remain hidden in the Upper Village. If I don't send for you within a day's time, you will return down the mountain. Agreed?"

Earlier in the day, Aryelle would not have conceded willingly, but after learning what she had about Borrac, she thought it only wise. "Agreed. But answer this: it sounds as if they *are* forming a council. Why did you not tell us earlier that Borrac had already called the chieftains together?"

Eleanor looked at her fiercely, skepticism showing in her eyes.

"Because…I know Borrac."

Chapter 15 – Entrance Denied

The next day dawned crisp and cool, a perfect harvest morn, the first of the season. The prairie stretching south and east of the mountain was aflame in golden light. Soon the little village at the mountain's base was awash in its first cheery rays.

Aryelle awoke with a start, afraid she had overslept. She had gotten used to the comfortable Mer sponge, and this woven-grass sleeping mat was no better than sleeping directly on the ground. It was one thing for the Aurrac, with all of their soft wool for cushion. Last night it had taken her forever to get comfortable and her dreams had been restless. She stumbled to her feet and shook Karril awake. He sat up groggily, rubbing his eyes, but as his brain registered his whereabouts they popped wide open. He jumped to his feet and followed Aryelle down the walkway into the main portion of the house. There they found Althea hovering over Eleanor as the fierce young woman bolted her breakfast.

"Finally - you're awake. I'll go wake the others," Eleanor greeted them brusquely.

She shoveled in a final bite and pushed her plate aside. Without another word, she brushed past them. Althea stared after her, lifting the corner of her apron to dab her leaky eyes.

Aryelle and Karril did not know if they should help themselves to what was on the low stone table or get something from their own dwindling travel provisions. Althea finally turned toward them.

"Oh here, sit down, the both of you. Goodness, how're ya ever gonna make it up that mountain! A good stiff wind would blow ya over! There's porridge dears, and plenty of honey and cool goat's milk, lessen ya'd rather have a warm squirt of fresh. No, I s'pose not! Well then, gracious me, I guess you'll probably be running low on provisions fer yer satchels too. I'll jest go round ya up those leftover oatcakes, and maybe some hard cheese. No? No cheese? Cor! Nodd told me he noticed ya didn't eat any meat last night at the feast, but I'd a bet my horns everybody liked cheese! Well, I don't have much else ready. If ya were to stay an extra day or two....but I don't s'pose Eleanor would be willing to wait. Headstrong, that she is, jest like her father...Oh!" At the mention of Eleanor's father, Althea broke into noisy sobs and hurried from the room, leaving the luminaries to fend for themselves.

They had just finished small portions of porridge when Eleanor returned alone.

"Seems your friend won't be making the journey up the mountain with us. Says she feels like she's grown another head and both of them are throbbing. Her boys are still out too."

"We cannot just leave without them!" Karril said, devastated.

The look in Eleanor's eye told them she would gladly leave them all behind.

"She will be better off here, Kay. Eleanor knows she has come for the Council, and we can always send for her once we know that it is happening - when she feels better," Aryelle said reassuringly. She shot a questioning look at Eleanor, who shrugged indifferently. "You know how much she likes the water. We're saving her a difficult trip."

This logic seemed to satisfy him though Aryelle could tell he felt nervous about continuing without the Mer. She felt a little nervous herself as they followed Eleanor out the back door of the dwelling.

"The river wraps around the other side and disappears into the mountain part way up" Eleanor commented, "but we won't be following it anyway." She pointed straight up the craggy face of the mountain. "That's our route."

Their eyes followed her outstretched arm, and their jaws dropped in disbelief. A narrow, barely discernible trail zigzagged back and forth directly up the steep southern face of Mount Cor. Jagged boulders and brambles, like serpent's teeth, surrounded the lower portion of the trail, which was all they could make out from their vantage point.

"Sure you want to come along?" asked Eleanor with a definite challenge in her voice. Aryelle could only nod.

"Then gather your things. It's time to go." With one eyebrow raised, Eleanor again lifted her gaze to the summit.

Her expression grew stony. Then she went inside to say her goodbyes.

The luminaries went to collect their few belongings, making sure to borrow a couple of sleeping sponges, which rolled up nicely. Then Althea loaded them down with as much food as they could possibly carry. She checked Aryelle's makeshift wing bindings making sure they would hold since Aryelle's original bindings were damaged beyond repair. Attempting to avoid one last, smothering embrace, Eleanor dodged out the front door to un-tether Hornet. Althea tucked an extra water skin into Aryelle's shoulder pouch and sniffled.

"She's a good girl, that 'un. It's a struggle lettin' her go, but she'll be alright - she's a survivor. You take care now, and don't let them up the mountain scare ya. They's jest folks like us, only they don't always know it yet. But watch out fer Borrac. He's a nasty piece of- well….never mind. Jest don't get on his bad side if'n you can help it."

Aryelle appreciated the advice. She hoped Eleanor would also be willing to coach them on how best to approach the Aurrac chieftain, but thought she had better to wait to ask her. Nodd did not come to see them off, and Eleanor seemed put out by his absence. Althea whispered excuses for him into Aryelle's ear.

"The old goat's got a tender spot fer that girl. Child of his heart, if not his loins. Don't think he could bear to see her leave again."

Aryelle eyed Eleanor, framed in the doorway, whose figure testified to the fact that she was female though her behavior more befitted an arrogant young ram. She spat. She cursed. She hunted and fought. She had joked so easily with

Nodd, yet scorned Althea's attention. Even her self-assurance as she readied to ascend the mountain. Aryelle was sure her eyes deceived her. Then she remembered Eleanor's tenderness toward the children of the village. Perhaps her bravado was only for show.

The sun's heat increased with the incline. The luminaries helped one another scrabble up the steepest sections hour after dreary hour, and Aryelle wished she had turned down Althea's offer of additional provisions assuming they would find food at the summit. Accepting her generosity had been her gift to Althea since Eleanor so despised her coddling. To Aryelle, who never knew her own mother, it was incomprehensible. But then, not much about Eleanor made sense.

Striding several paces ahead of them, Eleanor appeared lost in thoughts of her own. She carried very little besides her bow and quiver, making Aryelle wonder about the preparations she had said she must make. She was upwind so Aryelle could smell that she had not bathed. A plain leather armband now covered the tattoo on her upper arm; other than that, she looked no different. Hornet was soaring on the air currents high overhead, so the wristband further down Eleanor's arm was unoccupied, leaving her free to pump her arms as she traversed the rocky slope. Her sturdy sheep's hooves carried her surely over the rough terrain. Aryelle wished Eleanor still carried the falcon. Perhaps then she and Karril would be able to keep pace. Just as the thought entered her head, Eleanor turned and waited for them to catch up.

"We'll rest here a bit. You're not Aurrac, so you'll need to adjust to the altitude gradually or you might become sick."

"Thank you" puffed Aryelle, slightly out of breath.

"I just don't want you to slow me down," she said dismissively. She pulled bow and quiver over her head, squatting beside a neatly piled pyramid of stones.

Karril drew out a canteen made of tightly woven grasses and sealed with resin. He took a long swig and passed it to Aryelle. She offered it first to Eleanor, who refused.

"We'll make two more stops before we reach the Upper Village. Conserve your water; it gets steeper from here. But when we reach the ridge it will level out for a stretch."

"And then the summit?" Karril asked as Aryelle took a sip and returned his canteen.

Eleanor shook her head. "The Upper Village sits just below the summit. Tomorrow I will go on up to Borrac's compound from there, but you will come only after I send for you." She glanced toward the peak and quickly back. "Come. We need to get there before nightfall."

And though they had barely caught their breath, Aryelle and Karril fell into step behind her.

Later when they stopped for a second time, the luminaries pulled open the pouches of food Althea provided and ate hungrily. After days of travel their bodies were becoming conditioned to it, but this hike was proving far more demanding.

"Today we should have begun our return to Ka'Andharra," Aryelle mused. It seemed that a lifetime had passed since she left its safety.

"They will be worried-" said Karril surprising her; she had not realized she spoke aloud. "-but Kayanna will tell them where we have gone."

Aryelle looked at him earnestly. "Do you think so?"

"She is alive," he said with confidence. "I know it."

Aryelle felt certain as well. "But Father will still worry. He may send someone after us."

"Then you'd better get moving!" said Eleanor coming back down the mountain toward them, having scouted a little further up the trail. "I know all about keeping a step ahead of overbearing fathers."

"Nodd is overbearing?" asked Karril innocently.

Eleanor snorted and started to climb. Karril felt Aryelle's hand on his shoulder.

-Nodd is not her father- she said silently, *-Borrac is.-*

-But I heard Althea tell you Borrac tried to kill her along with the rest!- Karril fell into step beside her. *-His own daughter?-*

Aryelle could see him struggling with the possibility. Luminaries numbered their days from the moment of their conception. It was the parents' joy and duty to love their children, just as they had loved them into being. She knew Karril was old enough to know how that happened, but realized how naïve they both had been to believe everyone in Emrysia would feel the same way. Borrac was a monster if what she had learned was true. But his own flesh and blood? It made her shudder.

-Aryelle, we should turn back.-

"What?" she exclaimed.

Eleanor glanced over her shoulder at them. Aryelle dragged Karril alongside.

-What do mean, turn back? It is too late!-

He looked at her miserably, his thirst for adventure suddenly vanished. "I want to go home!" he whined.

Aryelle gaped at him in disbelief. Then she remembered how young, how vulnerable he really was. Intelligence often masked the fact that he was still a boy. The few revolutions difference between them had been time enough for her to discover that adults were not the images of perfection they portrayed themselves to be. Kayanna was right. There had always been evil in the world, evil that lurked in the heart of each one. But… the shadow was growing, and the only way they could do anything about it was to keep going.

Karril planted his feet. *-Aryelle, please-*

-You are just tired Kay.-

"I am not! I want to go home!" he demanded loudly.

Further uphill, Eleanor stopped climbing. Exasperation showed on her face.

"Look Karril," Aryelle whispered, "We will go back as soon as we find out about the council."

"You will not," he argued stubbornly. "If there is a council you will want to stay and be part of it!"

"Well, so did you a few minutes ago!"

"That was before."

"Before what? Before you realized what kind of people we were dealing with? Wake up, cousin!" she hissed, hating what she was about to do. "Do you think the Aurrac alone have secrets?"

He eyed her warily. "What do you mean?"

Aryelle heaved a sigh. "I mean that the Kandharra are not as innocent as they seem."

"The Kandharra do not kill - they heal!"

"They heal only when it is convenient. Only when it suits their purposes. They cannot even heal the rift between themselves!"

"I know that!" he said throwing up his hands. "It is why the Empaya are still divided."

"We live longer than the Naturra, did you know that?"

"We are more enlightened. We live longer by keeping more healing power to ourselves, spreading it throughout the Circle-"

"Do you know why it is that only the royal houses of Ka'Andharra have more than one child?" she interrupted.

"Of course. I learned that in first level over two summers ago. It is because a woman's chanzu only lasts till her nineteenth revolution, then she cannot bear any more children. Since only royals marry before their eighteenth revolution, everyone else only has time for one child." Aryelle knew this better than he did. It was exactly why she was expected to marry later this winter, except a consort had yet to be chosen for her. There was a shortage of suitable young men. Karril eyed at her strangely. "What does that have to do with it?"

"It ends only because the Kandharril wish it to."

"What do you mean?"

"Chanzu ends-"

"No, the Kandharril; whatever they wish happens?"

"In a sense Kay" Aryelle sighed, suddenly tired and wishing she did not have to be the one to tell him the truth. "They make it so. Why do you think every young woman in the city is presented before them in the Ceremony of Illumination? Not because her chanzu has ended, but because the Kandharril make it so."

"Why would they do that?"

"Because we *are* living longer, partly because of the extra *cha'kra,* the life force they drain from each fertile young woman that stands before them."

"But-"

"But nothing, Kay! Do you not see?"

"What am I supposed to see? Tell me?"

"That the Kandharril are part of the evil. They deny life to others for the sake of their own."

"But the Kandharril are healers…my mother…. Elazaryn-"

"The Kandharril of old were healers alone, but now? Now they have become the dictators of our present *and* future. And the future they have chosen holds no future for us."

"But," he argued, "you will eventually be presented to the Circle as well."

"Not until my twenty-second revolution, and then only if an heir has already been produced. Royalty, it seems, gets extra time to replace themselves.

"How do you know?"

"Because Ladhonna did. Her chanzu ended on her twenty-first naming day. That was when she was presented before the Kandharril. It did not matter that she had not had a child because there were already two heirs from the line of Azadhar. You and I had already been born. The Kandharril would postpone it no longer."

"Who told you that?"

"Gaelen's daughter, Laellen. She should know. Their family was common before Gaelen was appointed councilor to Elazaryn. Her mother was just days from her Ceremony of Illumination but they had not yet conceived. Because of Gaelen's appointment, the ceremony was postponed. Three revolutions later Laellen was born. Her mother's ceremony was held the next day."

Karril knew that Laellen's naming day was the day after his own. "Do the people not suspect?" he asked.

Aryelle shrugged. "Some do. Special privileges have always been awarded royalty, even those made and not born to it. Of those who do know, most do not care. They consider it their duty."

Karril fell silent. He looked up the hillside. Eleanor was picking at the dirt under her nails, waiting for the luminaries to work it out among themselves. She glanced at him, one eyebrow raised in question, but as he turned his attention back to Aryelle, she threw up her hands in disgust, and resumed climbing.

"Why are you telling me this now?" he asked.

"So that you will come with me. We need to do this, Kay. We need to see beyond ourselves. In a few more generations, there will be no Kandharra. You know we are fewer; we have begun to die out. Which is also why we need the Naturra. That little village back there was not their only settlement. If there is a council, they will be there."

"And if not?"

"If not" she shrugged, "we go home. If we are lucky we will find them on the way."

"And the Kra'nochta Empaana? I thought we came to fight the shadow with the rest of Emrysia."

"We must fight it first in our own hearts. The Kandharril cannot see the evil in what they do because they are only looking at the good they perceive."

"Gazing only into the light one cannot see his own shadow. The Book of Illumination is right." Karril thought hard. "So Borrac could be both good and evil, just like the Kandharril? He could have called a Summit to fight the growing darkness without even realizing that he is part of it?"

"You are wise beyond your years, Karril, son of Erildhil." Aryelle started up the path, certain that she had won him over. He watched her go.

"Aryelle?"

"Yes?" she said without turning.

"I will come on one condition."

"What is it?" she asked, still not looking back. He waited until she stopped and turned to meet his gaze.

"That we see it to the finish. That we save our people from themselves."

"We can only try," said Aryelle.

"Then so we shall," Karril answered.

The trail turned sharply. Aryelle thought she saw a flash of hoof further ahead, but when they reached the spot, Eleanor was still nowhere in sight. The thin mountain air took on the chill of late afternoon as the luminaries plodded onward. Meanwhile, the altitude factored in and their breathing grew labored. Minds began to slowly drift, conscious thought evaporating like mist.

Aryelle leaned heavily against a rocky outcrop. Karril caught up and leaned next to her. When a tumble of loose gravel showered toward them they rolled out of the way, narrowly escaping a miniature landslide.

"Nodd!" they cried in unison when the old fauen's birth-marked face appeared over the outcrop.

"Sorry about that!" he apologized, grinning and in far better spirits than the last time they had seen him. He sprang from the overhang with an agility that surprised them all. "Haven't been that nimble since the last time I hoofed it up this mountain, and that was too many summers ago to remember," he said.

"What are you doing here? We thought you were Eleanor," said Aryelle.

"Do you think she is alright?" asked Karril.

"Eleanor? Sure, she can take care of herself. But she shouldn't have left you alone."

"I think we were slowing her down," admitted Aryelle.

Nodd frowned and looked them over critically. "Look at you! You'd be easy prey for Borrac's patrol," he said voicing his disapproval. Both were breathing hard and were covered with scratches from brambles along the trail.

"Why you are here," asked Aryelle, noting his appraisal. She jutted out her chin in perfect imitation of Eleanor.

"That's my concern," he said slinging off his pack, "but since I am here, I guess it's my job to take care of you. This is as good a place as any to catch your breath. I might even have some salve for those scratches." He rummaged through his provisions. "I'm sure Althea tucked some in here somewhere."

"These are nothing," said Aryelle. She closed her eyes for a moment and concentrated. In an instant, she and Karril were surrounded by a soft, incandescent glow. When Aryelle opened her eyes, both the light and scratches were gone. Their breathing had returned to normal.

"Cor! It amazes me the way you empaths can do that!" Nodd exclaimed. "But don't let Borrac see it. He's suspicious of anything he can't understand, which is just about everything, if you ask me."

"You have known other empaths?" asked Aryelle.

Nodd nodded. "The forest ones, what you call Naturra. They've come to council before, but not for many, many years. You're the first of the fairer folk I've met."

"Fairer folk?" Having never met any Naturra other than their former guide, Aryelle could make little comparison. "So that is why Eleanor called us 'fairies'."

"We call the others Brownies because of their clothes."

Aryelle glanced down at her own robe. The silky fabric was now dirty and frayed, but still held its opalescent sheen. She winced at the memory of the filthy rags covering the plague-decimated bodies in the Naturra camp. Yes, she and Karril would seem like fairer folk, even in their present state. "Tell me more," she asked.

Nodd was, for once, not in the mood for stories. He shook his head. "Since you're able, we'd better try to catch up with Eleanor. I thought I'd meet up with this trail earlier and be well ahead of her. Guess my memory is faulty. "

"So you are coming with us?"

Nodd's shaggy brow furrowed. "Against my better judgment, yes! The chieftains all coming down off their own mountains spells trouble. And for a wedding – hah! Borrac's planning something, and I'm going to find out what."

"Perhaps they are coming for the Summit."

He snorted. "Like I am!"

"But Borrac will be angry when he sees you. Althea told me-"

"Told you everything I suppose. Words flow out of her like glacier melt; once you get her warmed up there's no stopping her!" His eyes twinkled with fondness as he spoke of her. "Well, what Borrac don't know won't hurt him! I'll hole up in the Upper Village; there's still a few folks I trust there. He won't come down from the summit complex till festival day. And that's all you youngsters need to know. In fact, the less you know the better! We'd better keep quiet now. I don't fancy a run-in with the patrol."

Aryelle agreed. But what would they find when they reached the Upper Village? She knew they were walking into a potentially dangerous situation. Yet her instincts told her that they must continue. Had they not come through safely so far? They followed Nodd's lead as he scrambled nimbly over the outcropping, trying to be as quiet as possible. At least his pace was easier to keep up with than Eleanor's was.

When they reached the third resting point marked by another cairn of stones, Eleanor was still nowhere to be seen. Nodd grew frustrated.

"It's not like Eleanor to not wait – she should be here!"

"Maybe the patrol-"

"She's part of the patrol!" he admitted grumpily. "That's why she's able to come down to the lower village."

"But I thought she was one of you" said Aryelle.

"Eleanor was born in the Upper Village, but she's one of us, alright." Aryelle could see him deciding just how much to explain. "Several years back she was found by the patrol. She's always been headstrong that one - the fool girl wouldn't stay hidden in the caves with the others. Borrac's men took her as a foundling to the Upper Village thinking she'd come off one of the other mountains. They meant to make sport of her during the festival, but I had taught her how to fight and hunt and take care of herself. When she bested Borrac's top rams, he placed her in their ranks to shame them. No ewe since Sheala, Goddess of the Hunt, has carried a weapon. Eleanor wields hers proudly. The rest of the patrol resent the wool off her, but they fear Borrac more. And evidently she's found his favor."

"Does he know she is his daughter?"

He looked at her sharply. "Borrac thinks she's dead." Karril blanched. Althea must have spilt the whole bag, Nodd thought regretfully. "I've paid dearly for my mistakes, but I've also learnt from them. I will not trust Borrac again."

"How can she stand to work for him?" asked Karril. "She must hate him-"

"Love is stronger than hate. See, serving him is the only way she can leave the Upper Village to see us. She may hate him, but she loves us more."

"It must be hard to grow up hating your father," Aryelle mused.

"She doesn't know."

Aryelle looked quizzically at Nodd. "She does not know he tried to kill her?"

He shook his head. "She doesn't know he's her father."

When they reached the high, stone wall surrounding the Upper Village they were nearly spent. They had not caught up with Eleanor. Presumably, she was already within the enclosure. Nodd was less worried about her than about how *they* would be received. Afraid of leaving the luminaries to face the guards alone, he had taken time at their last rest stop to wind a crude turban around his head using a length of coarse white fabric that he pulled from his pack. It concealed his distinctive purple birthmark adequately enough now that it was twilight, but in broad daylight, his disguise would be less effective. As they approached the gate, he cautioned them to hold their tongues and let him speak for them.

"Halt! State your business!" The sentry that peered down from the wall's height was less intimidating than his tone implied.

"I'll tell my business to no-one!" retorted Nodd brusquely. His booming baritone trumped the young guard's tenor.

"By order of Borrac, Chieftain of Cor, I demand that you state your business before you enter these walls," he said a little less surely.

"Since when does Borrac send rams still wet behind the ears with mother's milk to guard his gates?" Nodd demanded. "What's your name boy?"

"Nashor" the young ram answered hesitantly.

"Nashor, aye? Well Nashor, you never give your name to a stranger when you're on guard duty, didn't you know that?"

"No, I mean, yes sir."

"I should report you, Nashor!"

"Yes sir. No sir!"

"Well which is it?"

"No sir!

"No, I shouldn't report you?"

"Yes sir."

"Then open this gate, Nashor, and let me pass!" thundered Nodd.

The guard glanced over his shoulder and then shook his head. "State your name and your business!"

"So you want my name now too, aye? You didn't ask for it before. How come?"

He stared down mutely at Nodd.

"Who do you think I am, Nashor?"

"One of the other… chieftains?" he said haltingly.

"Of course I'm one of the other chieftains, you idiot! Why else would a stranger come to Borrac's mountain, inviting death, unless he was chieftain of his own clan and had no need to challenge Borrac of Cor?"

The flustered sentry shook his head.

"I am Rogar of Rewol!" roared Nodd. "Now let me pass!"

Jumping practically out of his fleece, Nashor hurried to unfasten the latch at the top of the heavy wooden gate. Nodd squared his shoulders and straightened his turban, waiting for it to swing open. It had barely moved when a beefy, callused hand pushed it shut again. Nashor backed away, slinking into the shadows. An older, battle-scarred ram with one jaggedly broken horn stepped forward. He leaned over the edge of the wall, sizing them up.

"Rogar, aye? Trying to bully my greenhorn, are ya? He's got his orders, and I'll deal with him later fer breaking 'em," he drawled menacingly, "but fer now let's find out a bit more about yerself, shall we? You look familiar, but it's kinda hard to see ya in this light."

"Well, at least Borrac's got one ram worth his horns," countered Nodd. This new turn of events seemed not to bother him in the least. "The last I heard he had completely surrounded himself with fools. Oh, but what's that? In this light it looks like you've only got one good one."

The guard's swift intake of breath hissed through clenched and rotted teeth. "I'm no fool, Rogar of Rewol, *if* that's who ya are. Neither is Borrac of Cor. You'd be wise to remember that!"

"You would be wise to open the gate before Borrac hears of your-"

"My what? Loyalty? You can't trick me so easily, old goat!"

"I was going to say insubordination, but I think I prefer 'stupidity'."

"Why, you- entrance denied!"

"Wait! What about us?" blurted Karril as the guard huffed and turned away.

"Yer with him aren't ya?" he growled.

The luminaries glanced nervously at Nodd and one another. Nodd inclined his head and gave them a subtle wink. Shaking his fist at the guard, he stomped off grumbling.

"We met on the trail," explained Aryelle hastily as Nodd retreated into the twilight.

"Well, yer not Aurrac that's fer certain! State yer names and business then!"

"This is Karril, and I am Aryelle of the Kandharra Empaya-"

"Empire, ya say? Ain't no empire here 'ceptin' Borrac's. Be off with ya!"

"Not empire, Empaya… the family of people. We are here at Borrac's invitation."

"Oh, yer one 'o them what's been called to the council, aye? Little young, aren't ya?" Then the guard's tone changed. "Yeh, yeh, alright. I thought a few more might be a comin'."

"Others are here?" Aryelle could not keep the excitement from entering her voice.

"Heh! Yeh, they're here alright! Jest a'waitin' fer the…er, festivities to get under way," he sneered. "You can come on in and join 'em." He swung the gate wide, leering down at them as they entered the enclosure.

The wall surrounding the village was wider than they imagined. Half a dozen of the Mer could have easily stood side by side on its raised walkway. Of layered stone and mortar, it formed an impenetrable fortress though what the Aurrac needed protection from was a mystery. Aryelle spotted several skulls with and without horns imbedded in the thick wall, positioned to face those entering. She shuddered. Perhaps what the Aurrac needed protection from lay within these walls.

"Nashor! Make yerself useful, ya spineless slug! Take our *guests* to the Shattered Horn and see's they gets settled." He gave the younger ram a painful kick in the hindquarters as he attempted to slink past.

"That's enough, Torc! You have no authority here."

Eleanor, now wearing a heavy leather jerkin similar to the sentry's stepped forward from a alcove. The older ram backed down, scowling at her with his heavy brow.

"So you finally made it," observed Eleanor.

"Yes, thanks to…..yes, we did." Aryelle could have kicked herself for her near slip-up.

"You know them?" asked Torc, jerking his thumb toward the luminaries.

"We met on the road."

"You too, aye? What about the old fella with the turban – did ya meet him too?"

"What old fella?" demanded Eleanor. "There's no one else here."

"I sent 'im packin,'" bragged Torc puffing out his barrel chest. "Word is no outside Aurrac gets in 'less here by invite."

"Fool! He should have been detained for questioning! Borrac won't like knowing strange rams are lurking about on his mountain."

"Claimed he was a chieftain, Rogar of Rewol-"

"There is no Mt. Rewol! Don't you know anything?"

"I didn't let him pass, like your pretty boy here would have," Torc sneered mockingly.

Meanwhile, Nashor had climbed down a crude ladder and approached the luminaries. He was tall by Aurrac standards and broad across the chest, but appeared even younger up close, his dark features lacking the chiseled edge maturity would eventually give them.

"Better to have the stranger in our grasp within these walls- Nashor!" she called, as he attempted to lead the luminaries away. "Bring them to Lavina's. I want to question them further."

"But- Borrac's orders!" Torc complained as Nashor led Aryelle and Karril out of sight.

"Borrac's orders are not made to line your pockets alone! The Shattered Horn is fine for other chieftains, but not for children."

"So what if they are? Borrac said there'd be-"

"We'll discuss what Borrac said or didn't say some other time, Torc. The gate is my jurisdiction now, not yours. I know what racket you run down at that dump you call an inn. You can forget it."

He leered at her greedily. "Ya know, you kin have piece of it anytime ya want. There's them that'd pay their weight in silver fer a chance at a ewe with a little fight in 'er!"

Eleanor spat on the ground at his feet. His lecherous smile only broadened.

"Keep it to yourself!" she commanded, "and leave those fairies alone! I've got work to do." She stormed off through the doorway she'd come out of, sending out another guard to take over Nashor's watch.

Chapter 16 – Truth Be Told

Unlike the haphazard cluster of grass huts making up the lower village, the walled mountaintop city known only as the Upper Village was built almost exclusively of weathered stone. Low buildings sprawled and abutted one another, interconnecting as properties changed hands or families intermarried. Winding streets and alleyways, cobbled and hard packed, snaked narrowly between dwellings, and with the exception of the occasional peddler's handcart, were navigated solely by hoof.

The Upper Village of Mt. Cor, oldest mountain settlement of the Aurrac, was also the largest. After Borrac's rise to power he rid the city of undesirables, or at least his idea of them, and expanded his patrol. Of course, a certain criminal element still remained, due in large to "contributions" that regularly poured into the Chieftain's coffers. Those driven out, the weaker or less than perfect, made homes for themselves elsewhere within the vast mountain range, avoiding established clan-herds, shunned as outsiders. Nodd's lower villagers had chosen to remain at the old council grounds as a permanent subclass, lives spared in exchange for their labor as shepherds. The Upper Village dwellers vacillated between admiration of Borrac's policies, and fear of what their unpredictable chieftain would do next.

Aryelle had drilled Nodd for information as they ascended the mountain. Now that they were actually here, the mass of stone buildings made her feel caged in. The Aurrac they passed eyed them suspiciously, in sharp contrast to the lower villager's hospitality. Cobbled streets and quaint shops appeared clean and orderly, but an underlying stench assailed the luminaries' delicate senses. There were absolutely no trees.

But one oasis of hominess existed - Lavina's boarding house.

Lavina was exactly as Aryelle had imagined she would be after meeting Althea, though her figure proved even more abundant. Besides size, they shared the same generous nature and loquaciousness. Lavina, as it turned out, was also the young guard's mother. She welcomed the luminaries like long lost kin, fussing and fretting over them, making sure they had plenty to eat and drink before shooing them off to bed.

Aryelle and Karril for their part felt their journey up the mountain had been but a dream. Had they been any less tired, they might have noticed the worried glances exchanged between Nashor and their hostess. Settled into adjoining rooms, they collapsed in exhausted heaps, not even bothering to wash or remove their wing bindings. Back in the common room, Nashor and Lavina spoke in hushed tones as they waited for Eleanor to join them.

Eleanor slipped through the night, nimble hooves carrying her swiftly toward her destination outside the wall. She pressed herself against the textured rock, sifting through the music of nocturnal creatures as they came to life. There, to her left, the one call she strained to hear - a falcon's swallowed skreeah, misplaced in the early evening hours. She whistled back, imitating it perfectly. A shadow stepped from behind a low boulder and she breathed a sigh of relief.

"What took you so long?" asked Nodd, drawing closer. "My bones are too old to be out in this cold." A lilt in his voice belied the chastisement.

"What are you doing here? Borrac would kill you in an instant if he knew." Clearly, she wasn't pleased to see him.

"And are you going to tell him?"

"Even Torc, dense as he is, could figure out that Rogar of Rewol is really Ragor of lower. Just because Borrac stripped you of your Aurrac name doesn't mean that everyone has forgotten it! Torc is dangerous-"

"Beaten by a ewe in even competition and you still consider him a threat?"

"Beaten by Eleanor, trained by Nodd - excuse me, Ragor of lower."

"Actually I prefer *Rogar*."

"You crazy old coot!" She grinned despite her misgivings. "So you don't care if you get yourself killed - what about the fairies?"

"It wasn't me that left them alone on the trail," he scolded now serious.

"I knew they would make it; they're stronger than they look. I came ahead to make sure Nashor would be waiting for them at the gate, and he was. You threw him off. He wasn't expecting them to arrive with one of the chieftains."

Her lengthy explanation was evidence enough for Nodd that she felt his reprimand. She always tried to justify her reckless actions by shifting the blame. He was pleased with himself that he could still read her so well.

"Well, this chieftain is cold and hungry and looking forward to sitting in Lavina's warm kitchen. So do your duty, Guard, and take me in!"

Eleanor was not so easily cajoled. Circumstances had changed since she'd left to patrol the base of the mountain at the last full moon. While keenly aware of Borrac's plans to take another wife, there were other campaigns afoot that she was not privy to. Torc's renewed confidence with their chieftain didn't comfort her.

Nodd understood her hesitation having experienced Borrac's capriciousness on more than one occasion. If he were to find them together there was no telling how disastrous the result might be. But it was a chance they would have to take.

"I'll take you to Lavina's," said Eleanor finally, "but you have to promise me that you won't let yourself be seen by anyone other than me."

"And the fairies?"

"And the fairies."

"And Lavina, of course."

"Of course."

"And what about that strapping lad, Nashor? He'd make you a sturdy mate," Nodd teased.

Eleanor blushed. She wasn't blind to Nashor's impressive physique, but as his superior she found him a little too pliable. It didn't matter that they were cousins; everyone was related in these mountains. The Aurrac had few taboos; only identical bloodlines like full siblings, or parent-child couplings were forbidden. But though many young rams had pleased her eye, she hadn't found any yet worthy of her respect.

"And Nashor too" she conceded, "but no more."

The next day dawned cold and clear on the summit of Mt. Cor. A light frost coated the rocky ground. The ewe responsible for warming Borrac's bed last night had slipped away unnoticed as soon as the chieftain fell into his usual drunken stupor. The timid, young servant who delivered his breakfast tried to back out of his chambers without waking him, but in her haste she upset the platter of fresh meat, sending it clattering to the floor. She stood frozen to the spot, goats' blood dripping down her apron as the bleary-eyed leader shook himself awake. He raked an arm across the empty bed. His eyes came to focus on the trembling ewe standing near the door. With a sudden lunge, he grabbed her by the hair and pulled her close.

"You'll do," he said.

"She's back, Chief. Chief – I said she's back!"

The insistent voice finally penetrated his fuzzy brain. Borrac looked up to find Gorron, his limp-wristed steward, hovering over the bed and waving a crumpled note in his hand. He sat up, snatched the note, releasing the wide-eyed ewe he had pinned beneath his arm. He looked at her without recognition. "Get out," he ordered.

She bolted from the bed, clutching her bloodied apron to her budding bosom as she fled the room. Borrac's steward watched her go disinterestedly.

"*She* returned to the village last night. Torc said she went back outside the wall briefly. *He* didn't actually witness her return, but *she* was seen entering Lavina's boarding house." Gorron passed on the information as if tattling on naughty playmates.

"Torc, what an incompetent fool!" Borrac raked manicured fingers through his coarse dark hair, which matched the fleece of his lower half but for the starkly contrasting silver at his temples. Gorron crossed the room and drew a tankard of ale for him from a half-empty keg. Borrac downed it in a single gulp, tossing the empty mug back at the steward, who quickly refilled it.

"Is everything ready? Everyone here?" the chieftain asked, daring the steward to answer in anything but the affirmative.

"Of course" Gorron replied, tugging at his lace collar, knowing full well as he did so that a few of the other chieftains had yet to arrive. His reputation, possibly his life, depended on the hope that they would find the head chieftain's summons irresistible.

"Good! See to it that they're kept entertained until the games begin tomorrow. That shouldn't be too hard at the Shattered Horn." He belched, pausing to savor it. "Send that wench who just left down there. She needs a little breaking in."

"She's still a lamb-"

"And that matters to me?"

"Yes, of course Borrac," he said avoiding his master's eye. He backed toward the door, sidestepping around the overturned platter. "Right away."

"And send my regards to Eleanor" Borrac called after him. Gorron nodded pursing his lips, and closed the door firmly behind him.

"To Eleanor" Borrac raised his cup in salute, "my future wife."

At Lavina's table in the wee morning hours, Nodd sat spellbound as she related tale after tale of Borrac's increasing depravity. Lucky for her, the chieftain had lost interest years ago, leaving the once favored ewe free to run her boarding house in peace. She no longer had to visit the summit, but she still worried about those that did.

"He's takin' to beddin' ever'thing! Thinks he can breed hisself a pure race, like he's a god or somethin'. Ever since we started sendin' those babies down the mountain to ya…" She told Nodd what he had already surmised, that any misshapen or unwanted child had been floated down the mountain stream, swollen each year with the spring melt. Since Borrac impregnated too many ewes to keep track of, he never noticed any decline in his herd's numbers. But he did notice there were no more abnormalities, which he attributed to the gods' pleasure. "…their acceptance of him among their ranks," Lavina told Nodd. "Thinks he made a name fer hisself when he followed Althea down and raided ya at the lower village-"

"Because of you and me-"

"Hoo-ee! Is that what you been thinkin' all this time?" She hooted with laughter, her jowls a-wobble. "You was fun, Ragor, but I knew you was keener on Althea than me. She jest weren't willin' ta let ya in her bed while Borrac was layin' claim to it. And Borrac knowed it too," she said, growing serious. "That's why he was so fearsome mad when she left him and come down to you. He didn't even know 'bout no baby of mine that looked……. like you." Her eyes strayed toward the purple birthmark that peeked out from under the makeshift turban. "But he would'a killed him fer sure if he had."

Nodd's voice held no condemnation. "His name is Jode," he said.

She met his gaze with a melancholy smile. Jode, an outcast's name. But outcast or not, she owed Nodd their son's life, the lives of all those children they had sent down the mountain.

Just then the kitchen door opened. In walked the handsome young guard, coming off duty. He ducked to avoid striking his head on the doorframe.

Lavina's smile brightened. "Ho, Nashor, come and meet our guest."

Nashor was stunned to see the old ram from the gate sitting calmly at his mother's table. Almost as stunned as both rams were at what she next said.

"Ragor, this is Nashor…Jode's twin."

It took plenty of explanation to set the record straight. Nashor knew he had been born a twin like his mother, though she had told him his twin died at birth. He never dreamed his brother was an outcast of the lower village, nor that his real father was their leader. He had always believed Borrac was his sire. At least now he was free of that burden. He craved no relationship with the chieftain… nor with this ugly, old goat for that matter. Muttering excuses, he stumbled off to his room to think and to sleep. Nodd, on the other hand, wanted every detail, prying Lavina with questions whenever she stopped to take a breath.

The sun was high in the sky by the time Aryelle and Karril awoke. They made their way to Lavina's kitchen and found Nodd, rocking back on his chair and twiddling his thumbs thoughtfully. They greeted him with questions as Lavina jumped up and began bustling around the kitchen.

"There ya are dearies, mercy me! Is it as late as that already? And not even a decent meal on the table!" She scolded herself. "Well, sit down, sit down! We'll remedy that soon enough. Ragor- I mean, Nodd," she said trying the name for the first time, "get yer lazy feet off'a my table and make yerself useful. Yer the one kept me jawin' all mornin'! Cor!"

"Where is Eleanor?" asked Aryelle.

"On up to the summit by now I s'pose," answered Lavina. "Leastways, she left pretty early this mornin'. Borrac's complex overlooks the city. You kin see it if'n ya look out that window."

Eleanor had left, in fact, shortly after letting Nodd into the village by a secret door and making sure that she was seen entering Lavina's house alone. She had witnessed too many of Borrac's nefarious escapades up close, and had no desire to hear them repeated over again.

"Did she say-"

"Said she'd be back by tonight, gettin' ready fer the games tomorrow. If she ain't, yer s'posed to head back down the mountain with…Nodd here. Guess she wants to make sure ya steer clear of any trouble. I got a feelin' Nashor might be askin' fer a wide patrol so's he kin come with ya. I'd come myself if'n ya could just roll me down, but I don't s'pose ya could. Sure would like to see Althea agin though. And Jode."

Aryelle and Karril exchanged a look, and Lavina nudged Nodd.

"Well, go ahead an' tell 'em. I gotta git some grub on!" She waddled over to a pantry and began pulling food down from the shelves, pausing occasionally to wipe her eyes.

"Well," said Nodd "seems I've got another son….."

While Lavina was laying out a meal for her guests, Eleanor sat rigidly in a sunlit room of Borrac's summit complex, ignoring the polished slate that reflected her unfamiliar image darkly back to her. She scowled at the ewe who was raking a comb across her scalp, tugging and braiding her hair into two long braids. Next, the stylist coiled each thick rope around an actual ram's horn, and then slathered it with a thick, shiny paste effectively cementing the two together. Eleanor's head felt leaden with the extra weight.

"Is this really necessary?" she asked through gritted teeth.

The other ewe began jamming eagle feathers into the arrangement, forming a crown across the top of Eleanor's head. "Better you than me!" she answered brightly. "I wouldn't go near Borrac if I didn't have to, if you catch my meaning. But he was specific- he wanted you to look like a ram, or as close to it as I could get'cha."

"But I've competed in the games before without all this!" Eleanor complained.

The hairdresser shrugged and jammed another feather into Eleanor's scalp. When she was finished she stood back to survey her handiwork.

"I s'pose that'll do," she said, "but you should get rid of that armband. It ruins the balance." She reached toward her arm, but Eleanor slapped her hand away.

"It stays!" she barked, tugging the armband back into place.

"Please yourself," said the ewe, gathering her supplies and making a hasty exit.

"I will," Eleanor grumbled. And one by one, she began plucking the feathers from her paste-stiffened hair.

Gorron announced her arrival. Borrac turned expectantly from the window where he stood gazing out over his city below. His face fell as she entered the room.

"That stupid ninny! I'm surrounded by imbeciles! Didn't I make myself clear?" he hammered his fist against the sill.

"Not exactly the greeting I expected," said Eleanor. Her hair hung loose over her back, shiny and dripping. She strode toward the chieftain, stopping directly in front of him. Eleanor tilted her chin upward, her dark eyes challenging his.

Borrac quivered with rage, fists clenched at his sides. His lip curled into a sneer and his nostrils flared as he fought for control. "You are so like me!"

"More than you know," she responded dangerously.

His sneer twisted into a wicked grin. Grabbing a fistful of wet hair, he crushed her lips in a bruising kiss. When he lifted his head, she glared at him.

"I would kill a lesser ram for taking such liberties before our wedding night," she said icily.

"Then it's good that I'm not a lesser ram isn't it?"

"Nor I a lesser fighter for being female."

"Indeed!" His fingertip traced her jaw as he moved around her to sit on a low bench. "I'll enjoy taming you." A fire blazed in the hearth nearby. He patted the space next to him, but she shook her head.

"I'm not staying. I came before the games to ask about some visitors who are here."

"We have guests?" he asked in mock innocence. "Do tell."

"I understand they've come for a council of some kind?"

"Hmmm….. Don't concern yourself with politics, my dear. Fighting suits you better."

The gears in Eleanor's head whirred. "I'm just curious. The Shattered Horn hardly seems the place for diplomats, and Lavina's was practically empty when I got back last night….."

"The other chieftains are used to worse. As I said, don't concern yourself. You must be in top form for the games tomorrow. I can hardly wait for them to witness your skill. They already acknowledge *my* supremacy, of course. But after you win the games and I claim you for my own, they'll want to declare me a living god, greater even than the mighty Cor! And together we'll create a superior race- a *divine* race of Aurrac!" He leered hungrily. "Perhaps we could start early," he said reaching for her.

She pulled away moving coyly toward the door.

"Perhaps not" she threw over her shoulder. "I must be in top form for the games, remember?"

"Then I shall see you there, my warrior bride."

He refilled his cup as she left. Gorron stood outside waiting, and slunk into the room in Eleanor's place. Seeing him Borrac snarled, his face turning livid, "She found out! How could she have found out?"

"I don't know-"

"Are all of the ambassadors accounted for? Did any escape? Or did some fool break silence? I want answers!" With a bellow of rage, he grabbed the heavy curtains that draped the window and ripped them from their hangings. Like a matador he swung them, overturning tables and chairs in a maelstrom of impotent fury.

"Yes, Borrac," said Gorron cringing away.

"Don't 'yes, Borrac' me!" the Chieftain roared. He charged toward the steward, grabbing him by his scraggly beard. His spittle sprayed Gorron's face. "Do you know how long I have planned for this? How carefully I've plotted?" He pulled him closer, close enough that Gorron could feel the tip of his chieftain's thick, curling horn and smell his hot, foul breath. Then Borrac tossed him aside like a rag into the nearest chair. "When Eleanor was captured she fought like a wildcat. The patrol said she gutted one of them on the spot!" He began to pace. "Oh yes, she'll make fine sport at the Blood Festival, I thought. And she did, but not how I expected. One after another of my most promising rams fell to her, even Torc - the coward! She should've finished him off! But no- it's been harsher punishment than death, him bested at every turn by a mere ewe! And since his profit at the Shattered Horn lines our coffers as well…but he has failed me again! If Eleanor knows of my little surprise ahead of time, she'll avoid the games. I'll be made a fool in front of the other chieftains!" He whipped around to face his audience of one. "The herd believes I am favored of the gods, do they not?"

Gorron nodded mutely. Borrac continued pacing.

"My plan must work! She *is* a goddess! They must all be made to see that. When she proves herself once more in the games, she must then slaughter the ambassadors of the other races for all to see, confirming our superiority over the rest of Emrysia. Aurrac from every mountain will beg for blood to flow throughout the land!"

"But Eleanor has always declined her share of blood sport. Why don't you slay the ambassadors yourself?" Gorron dared to ask.

"The gods have already given me a sign of their approval. Our race has been purified, the fruit of my loins made perfect, unblemished. Eleanor must offer her final proof that she is worthy to be the vessel through which I will sire an invincible generation! She *will* accept the privilege earned when she wins the games. She will partake of blood sport! And when the blood of all the races of Emrysia flow together, together we will fulfill the prophesies of our people!"

"And if she declines?"

"Then she'll be a fitting sacrifice to the people's newest god - me!"

Chapter 17 –Captive

Eleanor stopped more than once on her way down from the summit to heave the contents of her churning stomach onto the ground. Bile scorched the back of her throat. She was playing a dangerous game. The thought of Borrac's lips on hers filled her with revulsion, but still she vowed to see her charade through to the end. There was only one way to overcome an adversary as vile and twisted as Borrac - to beat him at his own game. When all of his defenses were down, when she'd proven herself to the other chieftains, that's when she would humble him. Yes, she would allow him take her as his bride… and then she would bring him to his knees. He would beg for mercy, the kind of mercy he had never shown. A divine race indeed! When she was done with him, he would be incapable of siring anything. She would not kill him as he had tried to kill her – no! She would extract like payment for what he'd done to Nodd. Her revenge would be just and sweet.

There were only two problems. The first was the luminaries. If she had read Borrac right, there *were* other foreigners here expecting to attend a council. Had Borrac really planned such a thing? She couldn't believe it possible. But if other ambassadors had come, she'd have to find out where they were staying and how much they knew. The luminaries could lay low for today. Meanwhile, she'd keep her ears open. If there was going to be a council, she'd hear of it.

Then there was Nodd. Why did he have to come up the mountain after all this time? If he was discovered it could ruin everything. She regretted that she wouldn't be able to show him just how skillful she'd become; he would be so proud! But she couldn't take the chance, and would have to keep him away from the games at all cost. Once she won the tournament, Borrac would announce her as his intended, the marriage to take place immediately after his sickening blood sport. Nodd would never let that happen. She must think of some way to get him to go back down the mountain.

****

"Eleanor wants you to take the luminaries back to the lower village. She says it's not safe here for any of you." Nashor stood in the doorway having returned only minutes after going on duty again that evening. He glanced anxiously between Nodd and the luminaries, who were with Lavina by the fire in the boarding house's main sitting room waiting for Eleanor's return. She had sent him instead. "She said you should leave tonight - now."

"We cannot leave yet!" exclaimed Aryelle. "We came for the council. Eleanor was supposed to see Borrac and-"

"Maybe that's why she wants you to go."

"You've seen Eleanor then?" Nodd asked.

"Didn't you hear what I said?" Nashor huffed indignantly. Glad as he was to be free of Borrac's bloodline, knowing he shared this deformed old goat's was no comfort. With effort, he tore his eyes away from Nodd's exposed forehead.

"I heard you son, but you can't get rid of me that easily. I knew it would be dangerous before I ever hiked up this mountain, and so did these youngsters. We can't deny them their chance for this council they're looking for. It's hard to believe Borrac could be involved, but we'll just have to see for ourselves now, won't we?"

"Eleanor won't like it if you don't follow her orders."

As if marveling at a newborn, Nodd gazed at his son. "As dark as Jode is fair," he said, nudging Lavina, "and just as wet behind the ears!" He grinned up at Nashor. "So... Eleanor sent you as her errand boy?"

"I'm not! I mean, she's my commanding officer!" A flush crept up his face as he floundered under Nodd's scrutiny.

"Be a ram, lad! You already have her trust; now earn her respect. So she's got an advantage on you by a few years, and rank too. You've got to make up for it if you want to win her heart."

"Her heart?" Nashor's flush deepened.

"You're green yet, but you'll learn. A ewe only fancies someone she can respect... that or someone she can twist around her finger. Be the first kind - it's what you were meant to be," Nodd advised. Leaning toward Lavina he whispered, "Confidentially, the first time I laid eyes on him I knew he was the one for Eleanor. Her and Jode, they were raised too much like siblings. This is better."

For once Lavina was too overcome with emotion to speak.

Aryelle was growing impatient. Waiting the entire day for Eleanor's return had been torture. The longer they waited, the more uneasy she had become. She couldn't let it end here. "I have to find that council! If we leave without doing that, our journey will have been a waste. Is Eleanor coming back here tonight or not?"

"She has other business to attend to, but said she'll stop in before the games tomorrow to make sure you're gone," answered Nashor.

"Then she'd better not find us here" said Nodd with a wink.

"Don't worry- she won't!" confirmed a gruff voice behind Nashor's back. Nashor turned. A beefy fist crashed into his jaw and sent him sprawling across the floor. Nodd leaped to his feet, shielding Lavina and the luminaries.

Torc swaggered into the room followed by a handful of armed patrol, burly and battle scarred rams obviously still loyal to their former commander. They stepped over Nashor's prone body.

"Well, if it isn't Ragor of lower! Thought 'cha had me fooled with that backward business and turban an' all. Didn't know as ya snuck back inside the wall though. Should' a stayed below where ya belong, freak!" His lips curled into a satisfied smirk. "The Chief's gonna be mighty pleased, yep, mighty pleased when I haul yer carcass in to him. Or better yet, maybe we'll surprise him tomorrow with an early weddin' present, aye boys? Might even reward me by givin' me my old rank back. After all, there's soon to be an openin'."

"What do you mean 'an opening'? Where's Eleanor?" Nodd demanded, ignoring the comments about himself. "Have you hurt her?"

"Not hair or fleece of the iron maiden have I touched," said Torc with a mock bow. "I came fer the fairies. Taking 'em to the council hall, I am."

"Taking them by force? Doesn't sound like a very friendly council to me."

"Jest escorting em. Figured they wouldn't know their way around yet."

"Then why hit Nashor?"

"Had it comin' fer not being on his guard. Somebody's gotta teach that boy somethin' or else he won't be no use to anybody. Besides, he mighta tried to be a hero and keep me from takin' *you*!"

"What about Eleanor?" Nodd repeated.

"You'll find out fer yerself at the games tomorrow, now won't 'cha? She puts on a pretty good show, but it's what comes after you'll be interested in. Take him!" Torc barked to his men.

It took four rams to hold and subdue Nodd who, even weaponless, put up a good fight. Not one of them escaped injury; the only patrol without a show of blood limped noticeably as they bound Nodd and dragged him away. Nashor stirred starting to come around, and Torc gave him a kick to the head, knocking him senseless again.

"Leave him alone!" cried Aryelle. She and Karril watched helplessly, their arms pinned to their sides by the two remaining guards.

"Ain't none of your concern, little lady. Don't worry; we'll treat you dignitaries right nice."

"I am the ambassador! Leave my cousin here with Lavina."

"Got my orders, miss," he said ignoring her protests. He turned to Lavina, her quivering mass glued to her chair. "Sorry 'bout yer boy ma'am, but don't you fret none. We'll fix him up. Now he's learned his lesson, I'm sure he'll be right co-operative, jest like you need to be. Otherwise, this poor lad might meet with a few more.....difficulties." He lowered his voice menacingly. "You tell Eleanor when she comes by that these folks got off jest fine. You understand what I'm sayin'?"

Lavina cringed peeking under her horns, and nodded. Torc jerked his head toward the doorway and the luminaries were ushered none too gently in its direction. Aryelle sought Lavina's fear-filled eyes, sending thoughts of encouragement as she was forcefully escorted into the night.

Torc performed another mocking bow. "Pleasure doin' business with ya ma'am. An' if you ever get tired of runnin' this here boardin' house, ya jest come on down to the Shattered Horn and I'll set ya up right nice." He hefted Nashor's unconscious body easily over his shoulder leaving Lavina to weep after them.

Outside, the night was crisp and cool. The moon tossed distorted shadows across their path as the guards led them through a maze of alleyways. Aryelle attempted to reassure Karril though her senses screamed they should flee. Gently, to avoid detection, she probed her guard's mind, but his thoughts had already drifted to the mugs of ale waiting at the end of his shift. The other guard was the same. Torc must have fallen behind or taken another route; she could not sense him at all. When she tried to communicate with Nodd and Nashor, there was only void.

Eventually they approached a sprawling inn in a section of the city grown derelict. The Shattered Horn was once a grand estate, the Chieftains' residence before Borrac built his mountaintop complex. Neglect had taken its toll. Now the dilapidated building served as a den of vice. Raucous voices fouled the air, a belligerent outburst rising above the rest. Garish light spilled from its open doorway, and clouds of foul, dense smoke wafted out into the night. Torc waited just outside the door, Nashor slumped at his feet.

"Take him round back and keep him quiet," he ordered. "I'll show our guests to the council chamber." Their guards left, dragging Nashor between them. Nodd and the other guards were nowhere to be seen. Torc wrapped a fist around an arm of each luminarie. "It's right through here, but you best stay real tight." The stench of his unwashed body was nauseatingly close. "The crowd sounds a little rough - probably excited 'bout the games tomorrow."

The unholy clamor inside the crowded barroom was deafening, the odors even more rank. Sweat, ale, and greasy food aroma mingled with acrid smoke that hung in a heavy blue cloud. Revelers greeted one another over the din. Writhing lewdly on a stage in the center of the room were heavily decorated, bare-chested fauen, male and female. Games of chance and challenge involving dice, knives and many horns of ale took place all around them.

They might have gone unnoticed in the crowd, which was scattered with races other than Aurrac. But as Torc escorted them across the room, a body sailed through the air and landed with a sickening thud at their feet. The crumpled carcass was covered with coarse, thick fur, its lanky limbs ending in sharp, curving claws. A wolf man! Aryelle gasped. Torc released his hold on her and grabbed a fistful of the creature's mane. He jerked its head back. Blood seeped from its muzzle. A heavy stone blade stuck tellingly in its throat. The room fell silent.

"Who did this!" he growled, scanning the room. A sea of empty excuses stared back. But against the near wall, one burly fauen was bent over a patch of earth. When he raised his head, a dirty wooden peg protruded between his clenched teeth. He spat it out, soil and saliva dripping in his unkempt beard.

"We both lost," he grunted.

A burst of bawdy laughter careened around the hall. Though still reeling, Aryelle noticed only the Aurrac joined in, foreigners in the crowd looking decidedly uncomfortable. Her gaze returned to the body sprawled in front of them. Torc released his grip on the creature's fur… and it melted away like water down a drain, leaving behind the form of a beautiful, silver-haired woman. Karril choked and turned away. Blood glistened on her lifeless lips and slickened the black handle of the knife in her throat. Even some Aurrac blanched now.

Aryelle bent toward her; perhaps there was yet hope. But before she could even tell, Torc shoved her roughly out of the way. He drew the knife free, wiping it on the dirty fleece of his flank. With a flick of his wrist, he threw it across the room. The blade struck a wooden post, quivering inches from its owner's head.

"Save it for the games, Sorcha of Dorn" Torc warned. "The blood moon rises soon enough!"

The other ram wrenched his knife from the post. He spat a wad of phlegm on the earthen floor and contemptuously turned his back.

By now, there were murmurs running through the crowd. Aryelle heard the words Wulfen and fairies repeated over and over. Karril huddled closer. Torc heard the murmurs as well, and was reminded of his young charges. He grabbed them firmly by the arms again, and dragged them further into the teeming mass. Aryelle peered over her shoulder, but the woman's lifeless body was already blocked from view.

"Whot'cha got there?"

"Ain't they pretty, now?"

"Dem's fairies, ain't they?"

"Never saw the likes 'afore!"

Torc ignored the comments as he dragged the luminaries roughly through the throng. Aryelle could feel a bruise forming under his grip. Jostled by the crowd, she held her wings as close to her slender body as possible, wishing that they were bound. She cringed when a grubby hand reached out to touch one.

"Hands off, ya slug! These here are fer the council tomorrow!" said Torc.

"Is that what yer callin' it now?" asked the grizzled fauen who had touched her. "Aw, I'm too old fer the games, but this money pouch here might be worth a little time with one of 'em. I'll treat 'em real gentle-like, so's they'll still have fight enough left in 'em!"

"Quiet, fool!"

But Aryelle had heard and understood his meaning as the murderous intent of the crowd pressed in upon them. The council was a sham. They were to be part of the entertainment tomorrow, handed out like prizes at the end of competition.

They were the blood sport.

She struggled, using her free hand to claw at Torc's arms and face. Catching on quickly, Karril did the same. Torc bellowed and threw back his head. Angry red welts rose across his leathery skin, but he only tightened his hold, yanking them forward the final few steps. Fauen all around them broke into laughter and scattered applause. A door was thrown open and the luminaries were hurled through it. They fell to the hard-packed floor. The door slammed shut and a bolt slid solidly into place.

Chapter 18 – Scattered Light

Kayanna thanked Quinna and took the cone made from a wrapped valleo leaf. She drained the simple cup, then flattened and rolled it into a straw as she had seen the Naturra woman do. Ripping it carefully in two, she handed half back to her. Both women placed their half of the straw inside their lips against their lower teeth. Saliva flowed and Kayanna swallowed it, savoring the spearmint-like aftertaste and the warm rush that flooded through her body. Soon her headache would ease and they would be able to travel on again.

The boy, Jonquin, stood off at a distance, peering uneasily into the yellowing wood. Kayanna thought how like Karril he was, excited and anxious all at once about the journey he was taking. The two were close in age, though Jonquin seemed much older.

"He has never been in the New Forest before," explained Quinna following her gaze. "Jonazat and I were afraid that if he saw what life was like in Ka'Andharra he would want to stay. It is why we agreed to take him to the Summit. To give him a chance to see the world outside of Wellwood, but not where he would be tempted to never return."

"But now you are taking me back to Ka'Andharra. Are you not still concerned?"

"The *Dru'noch* has changed all that. There is no village left for him to return to. Perhaps now it is best for him to stay in the city."

"But there are other Naturra settlements. The one we just passed through…"

"I will return there after seeing you home. But we have decided now that Jonquin must make his own choice. When Jonazat returns for me after the Summit, perhaps he will wish also to remain in Ka'Andharra."

"You have sacrificed much to help me." Kayanna placed her hand across her heart, acknowledging her gratitude. "I am sorry that your husband had to go on without you."

"Had we not lingered in Wellwood, we would have missed finding you. It was for the best. And he may yet see your niece and son there."

"I know he will," answered Kayanna. "Elazaryn sent his bel to Aryelle to guide and protect them."

"You do not believe what we told you?" asked Quinna.

Kayanna frowned. When she found Aryelle in the tent unconscious yet moaning, she had immediately assumed her pain, sparing no thought for her own safety. Never had she experienced such intense suffering! There had always been others to share the task when the need was great. Reeling from the pain she had taken into her body, she stumbled from the tent into the night. The Naturra family had found her dazed and wandering, not yet quit of the pain though days had passed. Quinna, Jonazat and Jonquin had healed her, sharing the horrible effect of the assumption between them. It was only afterward that she learned the truth. Instead of peace and comfort, Elazaryn's bel must have somehow transferred to Aryelle the pain and suffering that he was undergoing back in Ka'Andharra. Kayanna took it from Aryelle and the Naturra from her, and between them, they had been able to disperse it into the ether. But like a sieve that filters out only the largest particles, a residue remained, causing an ache between her eyes and at the base of her skull. She wondered what effect if any the others still felt.

"I had forgotten. My head is still not entirely clear," said Kayanna.

"We have seen this before, though you have not. It must have been a shock. The need would have to be very great for an Elder to send his suffering to someone else." Quinna eyed her with concern. "We could rest here for today," she suggested.

"No," said Kayanna. "It will subside soon, and Elazaryn still needs me. He would not have endangered his daughter unless all of Ka'Andharra was threatened. I must return as soon as possible. I am sure Aryelle will make it to the Summit. She is very determined."

"I am sorry we could not fully ease your pain. After what you did for our village…" Quinna's voice trailed off.

"You have done more than enough, cousin. And this helps," she said taking the rolled leaf from her mouth.

"Good" said Quinna, removing her own leaf. Kayanna returned her brave smile, knowing her teeth must look the same lovely shade of blaiz.

****

Rachaan's nerves jangled. He gripped the delicate handle of his teacup so tightly Ladhonna feared it would snap. She resisted the urge to take it from him, knowing well enough not to touch him when he was in such a state. But it did not prevent her from provoking him further.

"I told you it would not work. But would you listen? Sometimes you are just as bad as he is-"

"It should have worked! There was no reason for it not to work! Unless you made a mistake with your ingredients…"

"I made no mistake!" indignation lit Ladhonna's face. "You must have administered it incorrectly."

"Or… Elazaryn is stronger than we thought" Rachaan replied, unwilling to consider his own incompetence.

"Either way, now he suspects. He has not allowed me into his chamber since."

"Nor I. Gaelen alone has been in council with him, and he says Elazaryn seems young as a fledgling again. His candle burns brighter than ever!" The muscles in Rachaan's face twitched as he clenched and unclenched his jaw.

"You have spoken with Gaelen?" Ladhonna asked, incredulous.

Rachaan glared at her with contempt. "Of course. The groveling idiot may have Elazaryn's confidence, but he fears me."

"He distrusts you."

Rachaan shrugged. "He tells me what I need to know."

"But what does he tell Elazaryn? You would do well to not underestimate Gaelen as you do." At the mention of his name, Ladhonna's blood had run cold. He had been in the gardens near her herb shed the evening she mixed her potion. She remembered how his tuneless whistling had distracted her from her task.

"Perhaps I have overestimated *you*, my dear. What are you hiding?"

"I just…if Gaelen suspects anything, your intimidation of him will not further our cause," she replied nervously.

Just then, a knock came from the outer door of Ladhonna's apartments. Her hands fluttered to her face as Rachaan dropped the delicate teacup. It shattered noisily across the floor, contents spraying the room.

"Is everything all right?" called Gaelen from the corridor.

Rachaan held a finger to his lips. Stepping gingerly so as not to slip, he disappeared from sight.

"I …um…I am all right. I will be right there" called Ladhonna. She stooped over a shard of the shattered cup. The sharp edge bit into her finger and a line of ruby beads appeared. She sucked in her breath.

The door to her apartment opened. Gaelen stepped into the room.

"I could sense your distress," he excused himself sheepishly, for it was not good form to enter the Lady Ka'Andharra's rooms uninvited. He flushed with embarrassment at finding her hunched over the floor. "My Lady, allow me to do that."

He knelt to pick up the pieces of glass and noticed her injury. He touched her hand.

Ladhonna pulled away. "It is nothing."

"Shall I call a Kandharril?" he asked with concern.

"I said it is nothing!" she snapped. "It would be a waste of flame."

"Not for the Lady Ka'Andharra! I would gladly make the sacrifice if you would allow-"

"What are you here for?" she demanded, bringing her hand to her mouth. She sucked the warm droplets from her finger, grimacing at the salty blood taste.

"Oh, yes....um....Elazaryn wishes to see you now. He would have sent a page," he explained hurriedly, "but I was coming this way anyhow. Rachaan is to be there as well."

Her frown grew more pronounced as he bent to retrieve the remainder of the broken glass. "Should you not go tell him then?" she asked, her voice becoming shrill.

He raised his head slowly and looked at her with knowing eyes. "I think I just did."

****

-*We are not alone*- thought Aryelle, wrapping her arms protectively around Karril. He edged closer. Their eyes quickly adjusted to the gloom. Other captives huddled nearby. Aryelle and Karril shrank back against the wall as a figure rose and approached them through the darkness.

"*Beni*, you are here. I can use your help. There are many who are injured, but none fatally so. Several will be unable to flee unless they are assumed. Focus on those first."

"You are Empayan!"

"I am Naturra," said the voice's owner drawing closer.

Aryelle looked up into the stern face. Of course he was Naturra! His coarse clothing and glowing aura marked him as one of her wilderness cousins, but hearing the familiar dialect was like a taste of sweet nectar. She and Karril scrambled to their feet.

"Our guide was Naturra-"

"There is no time for pleasantries," he rebuked her. "A tunnel is being dug for our escape. We must be ready by the time they break through." He walked away, but turned back when they did not follow. "What is the matter? Are you *phrachaan*?"

"No, we are not frightened."

"Then move! You are able to heal, are you not?"

"I do not think-"

"Obviously not, if you think I am going to stand here while these people need our help. Get busy!"

Aryelle stared at him. Just who did this arrogant Naturra think he was giving orders to? "I am Aryelle, daughter of Elazaryn and heir to the Seat of Ka'Andharra," she said to enlighten him.

"I know who you are. I assume the future El'Kandharre is up to the task."

Aryelle was dumbfounded. "My... my cousin is too young-"

"I can do it!" protested Karril.

"-he has not yet been tested."

The Naturra looked them over and shrugged. "He looks strong enough. So do you. Come – we are wasting time." He faded into the shadows.

Her eyes followed his softly glowing silhouette as he squatted down next to two huddled forms. Karril moved to join him, but Aryelle laid a restraining hand on his arm. "Why should we do what you say? How do I know we can trust you?"

"What do you need to know?"

His words triggered a memory. For a moment, she was back in honeyed halls of Ka'Andharra.

-He forbids it because he fears what it will do to me.-

-Because he loves you!-

-But I am ready! I am strong enough!-

-The entire Circle has tried-

"The Circle loves too little and fears too much! Their fear weakens them, and their weakness makes them even more afraid."

"But why should we expend our light?"

"Because he has come to us!"

"But we do not know-"

"We do not need to know any more than that…."

"Why have you not done it yourself? Why do you need us?" Aryelle asked coming back to herself.

The Naturra rose, his gaze penetrating her defenses, evaluating her. She shifted uncomfortably as he spoke. "You should help because you can. Your gift is not for you. Whether you trust me or not, your light is needed. I cannot do it alone."

Aryelle swallowed the lump that rose in her throat. "I will help you, but my cousin must not risk-"

Karril shook off her hand and walked defiantly over to the Naturra. Aryelle flushed and stood wondering what to do. The Naturra spoke again, surprising her further.

"Thank you Karril, son of Kayanna."

"How did you know my name? Have you seen my mother?" asked Karril hopefully. He bent down beside him, barely glancing at the other figures.

"Yes" he answered. "She is with my wife and son. They are taking her back to Ka'Andharra."

"She is well?" blurted Aryelle, bending toward them.

"Yes, but we will speak later!" His tone brooked no argument. He turned his attention back to the figures in front of him, one cradling the other. Whispering in soothing tones he reached out slowly to touch the nearest of them. With a savage snarl, the creature whipped its lizard-like face to one side, nearly ripping off his hand. Aryelle and Karril jumped back in alarm, but the Naturra remained calm, his voice losing all edge and flowing together like the song of lapping waves. The creature eyed him warily, a low growl rumbling in its throat. It hissed with its forked tongue when he tried to move closer.

The Naturra kept up his soothing pattern of speech, switching to Empayan. "She does not trust me. Her mate is already dead, but she will not leave him. I have probed, and she has a broken foreleg and crushed tail – she will not make it out unless we heal her. I need to make her sleep. The two of you can assume her injuries while I do so."

Aryelle started to protest, but the Naturra's sharp glance and creature's hiss silenced her.

"What is she?" asked Karril.

"She is Dezrot, from the Northern Waste. Her people trade with the Aurrac and sometimes take part in their Games. Enough talk" he raised his hands peaceably as the Dezrot snarled at him again. Rows of sharp teeth lined her wide mouth. The Naturra slowly brought his fingertips to his temples and rolled his eyes back into his head. Almost immediately, the creature's head slumped forward.

Aryelle hesitated. She looked at Karril's determined face and saw compassion written there as well.

"There is not much light so I suppose it will take both of us. But leave most of it to me" she said, giving conditional permission.

Karril nodded and together they began the assumption.

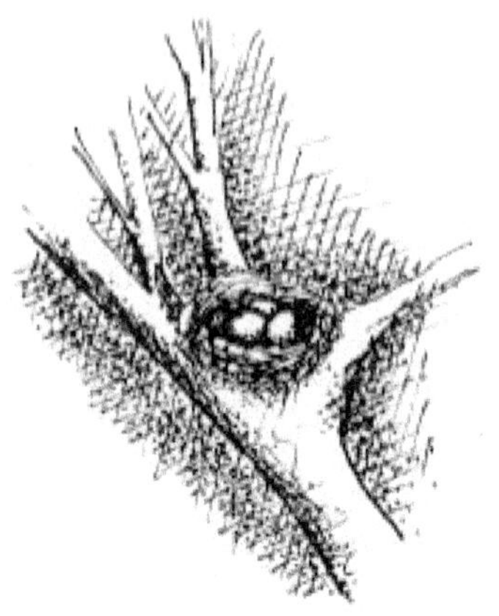

Chapter 19 –Let the Games Begin

The next morning dawned fine in the Upper Village, which lay strategically above the tree line, yet below Mt. Cor's final incline. Near its southern wall rose a coliseum large enough to accommodate nearly everyone in the city. The Aurrac, being poor record keepers, had no idea how long the coliseum had actually existed. Legend had it the gods themselves had placed it there, near enough the heavens that they could see and enjoy the sport that took place within. Long before this day's Games were scheduled to commence, the coliseum began filling with a boisterous crowd. Older rams and those too young to participate flooded in, telling tales of glory and waving colorful banners. Bets were placed, currency beads changed hands. Occasional fights broke out, forerunners to the day's entertainment. Dressed in gay costumes, beads and imported ribbons, ewes flaunted their latest finery, chatty and excited about the upcoming events. It was a time to see and be seen, by peers and potential suitors alike. Though Borrac could and often did lay claim to any ewe in his herd, even he couldn't service them all, try though he might. The climax of the festivities only began with blood sport. When it was over, dominant rams would have first choice among the bevy of beauties so blatantly on display. Many a union would be established as the Blood Moon rose, and the following spring's offspring conceived.

Eleanor scoffed as a group of giddy ewes not much younger than herself paraded by. They whispered among themselves, breaking into a fresh fit of giggles as they hurried past. She realized she was the object of their laughter, but convinced herself she didn't care. Won't they be surprised when Borrac chooses me, she thought, though her insides churned, lurching dangerously. How she loathed him, how disgusted she felt when his hands caressed her or his lips burned against hers! How she longed, especially during this season, to return the desire of some strong, handsome young ram. Instead, she denied the passions that raged within her and focused each festival on the games in which she was the lone female to compete. To the Games she poured out her energies, shunning the subsequent blood sport and mate choosing, vowing to keep her virginity and her dignity intact. Was she saving herself for that monster Borrac? No, though it certainly appealed to him that she was yet pure. His obsession with ruining her self-imposed innocence had helped further her plans, while her status at the games kept unwanted suitors at bay. A vision of Nashor popped into her head. She shook the image aside and set her jaw determinedly. First, she would carry out her plan to bring Borrac to his knees. Then, one day perhaps she would see. It would take more than just good looks and an incredible physique for her to give her love away.

Turning the corner toward Lavina's she stopped short. There stood her favorite aunt framed in the doorway, blubbering hysterically and waving away a persistent old peddler who was trying to jam his hoof inside. With her full weight, Lavina stomped on the intruder's hoof, causing him to howl in pain and draw back as she slammed the door in his face. Eleanor hurried over as the peddler ranted, hurling insults at the closed door.

"What's going on here? What's wrong with my aunt?"

"How about what's wrong wit' poor me?" cried the peddler. "That mountain just came down on me hoof wit' no reason! Cor, that hurts!"

"What do you want here?" demanded Eleanor without sympathy.

"I was just deliverin' a package from the peak, that's all, and a message-"

"What's your message?"

The peddler decided her fierce stare was reason enough to share the information. "There's a weddin' dress in this here wrapper, an' I was told by Borrac's steward hisself that the lady who's stayin' here's to be the Chieftain's new bride! Confidentially, I can't see as *she'll* fit into it though!"

"I'll take it," said Eleanor, ripping the package from his hands. He started to protest, but she reached for her blade.

"Yer that fierce one, ain'tcha? Might fit you," he said backing away as she glared at him, "but I don't s'pose you'd be the one wearin' it. Could ya see it gets delivered inside? Yer auntie said she's the only one there- that everyone else has left. Off to the games like me, right?" He continued backing down the alleyway. "But prob'ly someone will be back and lookin' for this package afterward. I'll just leave it in yer care then." With those words, he reached the end of the alley and dodged out of sight.

Eleanor sheathed her blade and turned the package over in her hands. She tugged at the hide string holding it closed and peeked under its wrapper of coarse paper. Inside was a soft chamois gown, beaded and beribboned, dyed a brilliant shade of her favorite blue. Eleanor traced a finger across a velvety sleeve, and just for a moment, indulged a desire to envelop herself in its luxurious folds. Chastising herself for such foolishness, she thrust the package under her arm and continued down the alley in the direction the peddler had taken. He had said Lavina was alone. The others must've gone as she had instructed. To avoid a lengthy explanation, she would take the dress to the barracks and hide it there. Besides, she hated a teary scene. She'd send someone later to make sure Lavina was all right.

Nashor awoke with a splitting headache. He squinted against the sun's glare and rubbed his aching jaw, then slid a hand to his throbbing temple, where blood had dried and crusted. He groaned and slumped back against the wall of the barracks. The last thing he remembered was taking a message from Eleanor to the deformed stranger, his sire. He'd been insulted and embarrassed by the ugly lowlander in front of the fairies, guests in his mother's house. But then a fist had come at him out of thin air. How he had gotten here he no clue. He was finding it hard to think clearly. His eyes blurred as he knuckled them with both fists and stretched the cramped muscles in his legs.

"Hey, wotchit!" exclaimed a voice. "You nearly tripped me up, there!" The old peddler limped back a step, and then bent over the young guard. "Cor, what 'appened to you?"

Nashor staggered to his feet, accepting the peddler's hand. He steadied himself against the side of the barracks and took a wobbly step. His knees buckled.

"You're a mess, chap! Here, lean against me." Even stooped over, Nashor towered above him. "Guess you're in no shape fer the games then, are ya? Too bad! I'd have wagered a fair spit on a strapper like you."

"I'm all right," Nashor mumbled. His jaw hurt even more when he talked.

"Well, come on to the Games wit' me then. Ya might be sittin this one out, but no sense in missin' the show altogether now, is there?" He wrapped an arm around Nashor's back and the two slowly hobbled off.

Eleanor would be at the games. Nashor had a sick feeling there was something he should tell her, but his head just wasn't clear.

"Name's Dornub" said the peddler by way of introduction. "Kinda like doorknob, which some folks has said I resemble, though I don't rightly take their meanin'. Maybe its 'cuz I'm a peddler by trade. Had more than a few doors slammed in me face, that I 'ave! It's been a few shakes since I come round these parts. Jest deliverin' a weddin' dress fer the Chieftain, I was. Well, not *fer* the Chieftain exactly, but his intended now, don'tcha know. Cor, isn't that a story! Here, lean a little that way, yer breakin' me shoulder! Now what was I sayin'? Oh, yeah! A mountain came down on me while I was deliverin' it! You should'a seen her..."

As Nashor and the peddler turned down another side alley, Eleanor turned onto the barracks road and hurried toward the guardhouse. Once inside, she shoved the package into a wooden chest that held her few belongings. She headed for the door. Suddenly she paused. There was still plenty of time till she had to be at the arena. Before she could change her mind, she retrieved the bundle and went into a smaller room to change.

When she arrived up at the arena a short time later still wearing her plain doeskin halter, a secret smile played around the corner of her lips. A strip of brilliant blue chamois had replaced her simple leather armband.

****

"Let the Games begin!" Borrac's voice trumpeted from the ceremonial horn. A roar of approval thundered through the coliseum as the High Chieftain returned to his seat. His steward Gorron and Accora the High Priest flanked him on either side. Behind them sat the eleven lesser chieftains. As ranking lord, Borrac would not participate in the games, though if challenged by the day's victor, he would don his battle gear to defend his position. And he would crush the contender, who would already be battle-weary. Rarely did a challenger vanquish a reigning lord and a new chieftain come into power, though one of his offspring was expected to eventually. Borrac had himself defeated his sire in a similar contest. Perhaps some young ram from his bloodline was already dreaming of such a victory. He smiled to himself. Or perhaps not. Four times now, Eleanor had proven her dominance in the Games. Clearly, she was expected to remain undefeated, though she would never be allowed to rule the patriarchal Aurrac. Borrac's lordship had gone unchallenged, and he alone enjoyed the spoils of blood sport, his right if the victor of the games declined it. But other chieftains had come this time, not only to witness their head chieftain's marriage, but because they had been promised a share in the fun. The Aurrac means of appeasing the gods and punishing lawbreakers rolled into one gory, entertaining event.

Clouds were gathering to the southwest beyond the enormous raised water tank abutting the wall of the enclosed coliseum. Stocked with fish for use in the games, later on its contents would be used in the ritual of sacrifice. Once the bloodlust of the clan-herd was sated, blood of the dead and dying would be mingled with the water and sluiced out over the southern face of the mountain where a stream bubbled to the surface. The river would run red. Cor would be appeased.

The first games of the day were simple contests between the most inexperienced rams. These included rock climbing, leaping, hoof races, obstacle courses, and stone throwing. Knife and spear throwing, archery, sling, and falconry made up the category of fishing and hunting skills. These were fielded by the next level of competitors. Weaponry and combat were left to seasoned members of the patrol and those foolhardy enough to risk sparring with them. It was not uncommon for the hard packed arena to be slippery with the blood of many rams before blood sport even began.

After the initial parade of contestants, Eleanor and the other return athletes left the field to the newcomers. She feigned interest as young rams dodged and darted around obstacles designed to highlight their agility. Last time Nashor had done poorly in this event, having interrupted a major growth spurt. But his new size had been an advantage in both rock climbing and stone throwing, causing Borrac to notice and select him for the patrol. Now, twelve moons later he was to compete with the rest of them in the hunting skills category. She looked down the line of seated competitors. She hadn't seen Nashor since she'd sent him home last night, nor was he there now. Where could he have gone?

"If you're looking for Nashor, he's not here," said the ram to her left. "Last I saw him, he was bleeding against the barracks wall, courtesy of ol' One Horn, I hear."

"And you did nothing?" asked Eleanor.

"You might not be afraid of Torc, ma'am, but I am. He's not one to mess with."

Eleanor snorted with disgust.

"Besides, I heard he just wanted to teach him a lesson, not hurt him bad."

"You hear too much and do too little, Narwag! Live through these games and I'll see to it you get the demotion you deserve!" Eleanor strode purposefully down the row of contenders. As she reached the end, a hand shot out, grasping her firmly around the wrist. It was Torc.

"Where ya going, Ellie?"

In a move that surprised the older ram, Eleanor twisted her wrist, bearing down with the side of her hand like a knife. His grip was immediately broken.

"None of your business, Torc" she retorted. "Touch me again and you won't live to regret it."

"Maybe not be my business Ellie, but it sure is the Chieftain's, and he's a watchin' ya right now."

Eleanor looked into the stands where Borrac sat in his private box. His eyes were fixed not on her face, but on her colorful new armband.

"If'n yer worried about that pretty boy Nashor, you can stop. I didn't hurt him....much. I s'pect he'll have a bit of a headache is all." Torc was still rubbing his wrist when she turned back toward him.

"He wasn't at the barracks. I was there right before I came here." She glared at him angrily.

"Then he's prolly still at the Shattered Horn sleeping it off. Sit down; he ain't goin' nowheres and neither is you. Borrac said keep him comfortable till after the games, then send him home to his mama." Torc congratulated himself on this fabrication, having actually forgotten all about him. He'd had more important matters to attend to.

"Why should Borrac care about Nashor?"

"Because *you* do, Lambkins."

She shot him a murderous glance. "And why should I believe you?" she asked.

Just then, a cheer went up from the crowd. The first event of the day had a declared champion.

"Cuz I've got everything to gain and nothin' to lose if I let'cha go. Maybe this time I'd even give Borrac a run fer his beads."

"And maybe this time I'll finish what I started" said Eleanor, fingering her knife sheath and returning to her seat.

****

"Get up, ya lazy old goat! You got a party to attend."

Nodd ignored the gruff voice of his jailor, squeezing his eyes shut attempting to recapture his dream. Lavina and Althea had been taking turns braiding his beard and feeding him oatcakes with honey and warm, sweet milk.

A bucket of icy water splashed Nodd's face. He bolted awake, coughing and choking on the dirty, wet gag stuffed in his mouth. His hands and hooves were bound as well. Memory of the previous evening flooded over him, and stiffness crept into his joints from the cold, stone floor. Groaning, he rolled over and curled back against the wall.

"Oh, no ya don't!" barked the jailor, swinging his scruffy leg toward Nodd's midsection.

Faster than a flash flood Nodd grabbed the jailor's hoof with his bound hands and twisted. The jailor's body slammed against the hard granite a fraction of a second before his skull bounced off it. It was the last sensation he ever felt. Nodd pawed over his matted wool in search of a weapon, anything to cut his bonds. He found nothing. Struggling to his feet, he hopped awkwardly through the open cell door.

"Wake up. They will be coming soon. We must be ready."

Aryelle and Karril were immediately alert. It seemed only moments ago Jonazat bid them rest. They had spent nearly the entire night healing, pausing only to allow their sufferings to leave them. He must be near exhaustion himself though he did not show it.

Aryelle opened her eyes even wider, but she could barely make out even the faintest outline. *That is strange*, she thought peering through the gloom. She could feel it teeming with life, and heard several languages whispered in the dark, though the ambassadors spoke Common while addressing one another. In hushed tones, they had plotted their escape, judging time by the level of the din in the barroom outside.

The door had opened just once since Aryelle and Karril were shoved through it to admit a silver-haired man in a midnight blue robe that sparkled in the light of the doorway. He was Wulfen, and had volunteered to join the captives knowing his choice meant death. His mate was gone, and now he had lost his taste for living. It mattered little that the others planned to escape; he, like the Dezrot, would stay till the end. She also was unwilling to leave her fallen partner, both of them thrown in here after another barroom brawl. Aryelle had learned that the more aggressive races often came to compete with the Aurrac, others simply to watch the annual games. It was always a gamble to do so. One never knew when they might become part of the concluding sport.

Aryelle stood and brushed the dirt from her robe, her surroundings slowly coming into focus. She recognized the Naturra who had eventually introduced himself. Jonazat bent and retrieved her shoulder pouch, handing it to her. She noticed his wings were bound with webbing similar to her own, at least, to what she was accustomed to. She wished hers were still bound.

As if reading her thoughts, Jonazat pointed over his shoulder and said, “I will need your help with these. It would be better if our wings were bound while we are in the tunnel, but we may have need of flight on the other side.”

He turned so that she could reach his bindings. "Your aunt helped me into them before I left her with Quinna and our son."

"I am anxious for more news of Kayanna," said Aryelle. They had been so busy that there had been no chance yet.

"When we are clear of the city there will be time."

"Will you stay with us?" asked Karril.

Aryelle had never heard her cousin sound so tired. She wrapped an arm around his shoulder. "I am sorry for getting you into this Karril," she said remorsefully, her weariness matching his. "I never should have brought you here. Everything I have done lately has been wrong."

"You would be wise not to dwell on the darkness of mistakes already made. Look toward tomorrow's light instead." Jonazat's gentle reprimand sounded just like something Elazaryn would say. Aryelle blinked back tears. "Yes" he said answering Karril, "I will stay with you. You and I know it is better to flee from death, whether our own or our enemy's."

A brilliant light bobbed through the gloom toward them followed by the strangest creature the luminaries had ever seen, and they had seen many that night. Hopping on strong back legs, forelegs held forward so that its tiny paws hung under its nodding head, the praircat bounded over. Its face was banded with a mask of dark fur edged in white, while the rest of its body was covered with a silky, golden pelt. The ridiculous length of its torso is what caused it to look so odd. Stretched to its full height, tufted tail to pointy snout, the praircat reached almost to Aryelle's waist, yet was barely larger around than her arm. It stopped in front of them, remaining upright, waving like a reed in a breeze.

"We're through, Captain," the praircat reported. "Just need to widen it a bit, just a little bit."

Jonazat smiled indulgently. Everyone had accepted him as their unofficial leader. "Very good, Rona! Spread the word quietly, smaller Emrysians first. They will be able to pass through more quickly."

The praircat saluted him briskly and disappeared into the darkness. Bel, no longer needed to illuminate the dig, slipped into Aryelle's pouch which Torc had neglected to take. Perhaps, thought Aryelle, knowing luminaries carried no weapons.

Someone else approached out of the gloom. Aryelle thought him very handsome in his human form.

"I will stand guard," said the silver haired Wulfen.

"The Dezrot was helping the praircats dig. I will send her back here. May your sorrow make you both stronger," said Jonazat, laying a hand upon his shoulder. The aura surrounding him spread to envelop the Wulfen. Then the luminaries went to join the others.

Aryelle looked back and heard a low growl. Though she could no longer see him, she knew the Wulfen had resumed his animal shape. With fangs bared, he guarded the door.

Chapter 20 - Humiliation

Eleanor was glad for the chance to catch her breath. With the first and second rounds of competition completed, an intermission allowed the competitors to prepare for their final events. Acrobats and buffoons entertained the crowd while they checked their weapons and secured their battle gear. Eleanor did neither. She preferred not to wear the heavy, protective garments most used to shield their vital organs, and her weapons were in perfect condition. She should know; she'd just used them to win every competition she entered. In archery, she embarrassed her only opponent by shooting his arrow out of the sky and still managing to strike the target's bull's-eye. Similarly, she humiliated the other contestants in knife throwing; the handles of her blades, thrown with either hand, quivered in their targets before the rest were unsheathed. She had elected not to compete in sling this season, though she was certain to have won. It was Nashor's best category, and with her out of the running, he might have easily taken it had he shown up.

Instead, another ram took the top award. Torc bested the field in spear throwing, though his accuracy was better than his distance. It was the one event Eleanor never entered knowing her smaller size left her at a disadvantage. But falconry had fallen to her as well, her whistled commands to Hornet obeyed almost before they sounded.

Borrac was smug, boasting to the other chieftains, some of whom had chided him for allowing a ewe to enter the games. Laughing boisterously at the lewd suggestion offered by one of them, he glanced Eleanor's way, eyes smoldering hungrily. She pretended not to notice, looking elsewhere.

Torc had his back to her and he was shaking his head. An older ram, not in the games but clearly still loyal to his former commander, whispered something into Torc's ear. The effect was immediate. Torc lunged at the ram, grabbing his jerkin and lifting him nearly off his hooves. With an angry roar, he hurled him against the wall of the competitors' box. Before Torc could reach him again, the shaken ram scrambled to his hooves and fled.

Eleanor grinned. Whatever the message had been, Torc wasn't pleased, and that pleased her.

Nashor came to for the second time that day leaning against a wall in a dead-end alley near the arena. His head still felt as though it would split in two, but his inquiring hands soon discovered that it had been expertly bandaged. The peddler was nowhere to be found. Nashor remembered hobbling this far with him before the need to stop and rest became overwhelming. Dornub's rambling commentary had done nothing to help matters, but the bottle of spirits he produced seemed to dull the ache a bit. What happened next was no mystery. Unaccustomed to such strong drink, Nashor had simply passed out dead drunk.

He squinted through the slits between his fingers. Morning's crisp autumn air had given way, and a spattering of low clouds drifted across the azure sky. The breeze was a warm breath.

Nashor braced his hooves against the paving stones and inched his way upward against the wall. He turned toward the arena's entrance. Just then, a roar went up from the crowd.

He had better hurry.

The first captives poured from the tunnel's exit and darted into the deserted streets. Nearly everyone in the Upper Village was attending the Games. Karril, Aryelle and Jonazat were the last in line, being among the largest of the Emrysians due to their wingspan. To their good fortune, the room that housed them had been built on hard packed earth rather than solid rock, allowing the burrowing praircats to dig with little difficulty. To their dismay, it had also been constructed over a former latrine.

-Suffocation is still possible- thought Aryelle, holding her breath. She crawled forward through the foul air of the tunnel. Ahead of her, Karril squirmed back and forth using elbows and toes to inch his way along. An occasional clod of dirt fell as his wings brushed the low ceiling. Aryelle was able to keep her wings folded more closely along her back and sides, as was Jonazat. Such control came with age.

Finally, they made it to the tunnel's further end, coming up against a wall of solid rock. The space here was wider and angled steeply upward. Using the rough stone for hand and footholds, first Karril, then Aryelle crawled out of the hole. A furry face greeted them.

"Rona! What are you still doing here?" asked Jonazat, the last to poke his head above ground.

"Just making sure you make it, Captain, just making sure," the buoyant creature answered.

Aryelle and Karril brushed the dirt from their clothing.

"No time for that- Go!" Jonazat hauled himself out of the tunnel and sprinted down the narrow alley. Rona followed on all fours. Aryelle and Karril held back. As the praircat reached the corner, he turned and stood upright beckoning to them.

"Come on! What'cha waiting for? What'cha waiting for?"

"Our companions…we have to find them," said Karril.

Jonazat looked back over the praircat's head. His eyes were set in a strong, tanned face. How good it felt to see the familiar features of her kind, thought Aryelle. Surely, given the chance their people could make peace. But others needed her now. Jonazat's face swam before her and then came sharply back into focus.

"We must go!" he called.

Aryelle shook her head. "Thank you for all you have done."

"I will not leave you behind" Jonazat said, coming back for them. Rona was at his heels.

Jonazat had almost reached them when a shrill whistle and the drumbeat of many hooves ricocheted off the alley walls. He was in the air in a heartbeat, but Aryelle and Karril were too startled to move. Rona darted back into the open tunnel.

"Take wing! Take wing!"

The words were like nonsense to their ears.

"Erilith! Erilith!"

In their native tongue, it finally registered, but too late. As their wings snapped open, a weighted rope net sailed over them, knocking Aryelle and Karril to the ground.

A cry echoed inside the tunnel. Rona shot out of the hole, only to become entangled in the net. Several aged but still menacing patrol rams circled as the luminaries and praircat struggled to free themselves.

"Glad I brought my butterfly net now, ain't I," laughed their grizzled leader. "An' we even caught us a caterpillar too!" He bunched the net so the praircat couldn't escape and reached out to stroke its silky fur.

"Ow! The little bugger bit me!" he cried putting a bloody finger to his mouth.

"Bit me too" said another guard climbing out of the hole, "right on the end of me nose!"

The rest sniggered.

"Always stuck out too far anyway."

"Should 'a bit it clean off!"

"Too bad the brownie got away." That made the others look to the sky, but the 'brownie' was nowhere in sight.

"Captain?" Rona whined.

"It's alright; we nabbed a few, didn't we? We'll round up some more. And don't forget that pretty little fishy they caught trying to swim upstream the other day! Should still be plenty a sport fer the chief."

They jerked their prisoners roughly to their feet, untangling the net and binding their hands behind them. It was as effective as clipping their wings. Rona they dumped into a large sack.

"Take 'em to the holding cells, 'cept that one in the bag. I'll make a hat outta him, I will!" said their leader, still sucking his wound.

"Borrac won't like it. We already lost too many."

"What Borrac don't know won't hurt him, now will it? Or you," he growled threateningly. The other ram backed down.

-He is gone- thought Karril. *- He said he would not leave us.-*

- What does it matter? - Aryelle returned. – *He was a traitor, just like our guide.-*

Her emerald eyes glazed over as she and her cousin tripped forlornly toward their doom.

Eleanor's first opponent in hand-to-hoof combat was from another herd, perhaps a little older than she was, and with impressive horns and clumsy hooves. Twice already, he'd stumbled almost disqualifying himself. The object was to be the first to upend your opponent by yanking a leg out from under them without catching a kick to the head. It was in this game that Torc had lost a horn to her, lucky then that her aim had not been as accurate as it now was. He no longer competed in this event, though she would be facing him later in Poles and possibly Blades. The second was far more dangerous. The final event of the competition, it also served to increase the bloodlust of the crowd. In it, the four highest-ranking contenders would vie for the honor of being declared Champion, battling hand to hand with progressively shorter blades. Points were doled out for each draw of an opponent's blood.

Eleanor dodged out of the way as the big horned ram lunged for her ankle. She leaped agilely over his back and gave him a quick kick in the hindquarters. He struggled to regain his balance, heavy horns pulling him forward. Taking advantage of his awkward position, Eleanor turned and reached for his ankle. Confident of a win, she was caught totally off guard when he somersaulted, a hoof grazing her cheek as it left the ground. In a surprise move, he twisted sideways, grabbing both her ankles and pulling them out from under her. She fell on her back with a thud.

A hush fell over the crowd. Eleanor had been bested! As the contestants got to their hooves, half of the crowd cheered. The other half jeered.

"Cheat!"

"He was down!"

"Shine his hooves while yer down there, girlie!"

"Stick 'im one, Eleanor!"

The big horned ram strutted around her, hands clasped high in victory. Eleanor brushed the dust from her fleece. Without a backward glance, she stalked from the field. The crowds' remarks followed her.

"Should'na never been allowed to compete…."

"Don't know her place…."

"Borrac's whore, I heard….."

As she entered the competitors' box, her eyes challenged the other contenders to comment. No one did. But an echo of Torc's satisfied smirk danced at the corners of several mouths.

The next contestants took their places and the games continued, but the atmosphere in the arena had changed, intensified. Would this be the year? Would a new champion arise, a challenge be made for chieftain? Those who dwelt near the summit of Mount Cor had prospered under Borrac's leadership; that was undeniable. But they had suffered as well.

One witness in the stands looked at neither contestant. His head was wrapped in white cloth, and his eyes were fixed on the glowering Aurrac chieftain. Why, he wondered, would Borrac be anything but delighted to see the ewe put firmly in her place?

The crowd cheered as a final winner was declared. A lone contestant returned to the box. The other was dragged unceremoniously from the field, a crimson trail staining the earth as his head bumped along the ground.

"Get in there!" The guard jostled the luminaries toward a narrow doorway. "And don't try no tricks neither, or ya won't even make it till the blood sport! When they open that other door, there'll be weapons waitin' fer ya inside the arena. Course, you won't be able to use 'em with yer hands tied now, will ya?" He made to untie them, and then changed his mind. Why bother? There were never enough weapons for the prisoners to defend themselves with anyway. He laughed. "Fight fer yer lives or run like rabbits; it won't make no never-mind!"

The guard thrust them roughly inside and bolted the door behind them. The only difference from their former prison to this was that here it was not only cramped, but floored with stone. The crowd outside was still drunk, but with a different kind of draught.

Aryelle's wings brushed the roof of the cave-like room. Stooping, she moved cautiously forward, nearly tripping over a shaggy body that lay on the cold, stone floor. A low growl rose from it. She gasped and backed away, bumping into Karril. They flattened themselves against the wall.

"Is that you fairies?" croaked a voice in the darkness.

"Nashor?"

"Ow….yeh, it's me. Over here."

"There he is!" said Karril. Aryelle could still not see him. She edged sideways, avoiding the body on the floor, and found Nashor leaning further along the wall.

"How did you get here?" she asked.

"I walked..… stumbled mostly," he stammered. "My head hurts. The light…." He seemed to fall asleep.

"That was a Wulfen back there," said Karril sliding down the wall beside him.

"A Wulfen?" Aryelle peered back through the gloom.

"Careful" cautioned Nashor, rousing. "…vicious when they're injured."

"I think we may know this one" she replied. She took a step toward it. An angry rumble issued from its throat.

"Don't touch me! Your healing powers… aren't welcome here." He labored to inhale. His growl came out quite different from Common, yet she understood.

"But you are hurt-"

"And dying too, I hope. I sent… a good number of them… ahead of me. I'll chase them… all the way… to the Hills of Yonder."

"But if only my hands- Nashor, can you untie me?"

"I said I don't want your help!" the Wulfen snarled. Then more gently he added, "Unless… you can make the end to come sooner…."

"I am sorry" Aryelle answered. "It is not for me to end your life. There may be yet for you to do with whatever time you have left." She hung her head knowing time was running out.

There was silence for a moment outside in the arena. The Wulfen whispered painfully, "Then if you would, stroke my fur… give me the comfort… of a friendly touch… as I die."

"Don't trust him" grunted Nashor.

"I am not afraid," said Aryelle. She motioned toward her hands, still bound behind her. The action caused him additional pain, but regardless Nashor drew a blade from the sheath at his side, and sliced cleanly through the rope. Aryelle flexed her fingers and rubbed her wrists where the rope had bitten into her skin.

"I will be back to help you, Nashor. Wait for me, Karril." She knelt beside the injured Wulfen and began to stroke his thick gray fur. A lost and lonely whine escaped him as he laid his head in her lap and closed his eyes.

Eleanor waited impatiently on her end of the suspended plank bridge. Her opponent was less nimble now that he spent the most of his time at The Shattered Horn. Torc finished the climb and stopped to catch his breath. Finally, he moved onto the staging at his end, signaling he was ready. Eleanor squared off opposite him, eying the intentional gaps in the span of swaying wood and rope, some large enough for either or both of them to fall through to the jagged rock-studded platform below. The bridge had no sides. She stepped onto it, hooves testing each slat as she advanced. Though falls were seldom fatal, injuries were common, often eliminating rams from further competition. Eleanor refused to let carelessness add to her earlier humiliation. Halfway across, she retrieved the combat stick she would use. The smooth pole was a standard length and fit comfortably in the palm of her hand. Boned to a rocklike finish, it was nearly unbreakable.

Torc reached his weapon and bent over, taking time to minutely inspect it. Eleanor advanced, taking advantage of his slothfulness. Every nerve in her body tingled. She was determined to make up for her earlier lapse, but she would do it with skill, not trickery. She had never faced Torc in poles before, but she had watched him fight, studying his moves against the day when she would eventually draw lots to spar with him. He preferred to allow his opponent to tire himself while presenting a solid defense of blocked attacks. Then with unexpected swiftness, he would twirl the sturdy rod in one hand high in the air, catching his unsuspecting foe with a forceful blow to the head. An additional prod to the belly with the end of his weapon would throw them further off balance. But she would not to fall victim to such tactics. Stopping just shy of a gaping hole, Eleanor waited for him to rise. She wanted him to come to her.

"What'sa matter, girlie? Afraid to come an' get it?" Torc taunted, above the noise of the crowd.

"I've never been afraid of you, Torc!"

"Aw, that's right. But yer slippin' Ellie. Gord got the better of ya, and so will I. Time fer ya to hang up yer horns, girlie, and let the rams be rams!"

She would not be goaded. Torc pointed the end of his weapon at her.

"'Or maybe ya figure on takin' a *real* ewe of yer own, someone fine and fancy…..The chieftain might wanna rethink makin' you his bride if'n you got other preferences."

Eleanor glared at him with loathing. "What do you know about anything?" she demanded, leaping across the gap before her. She reached out with her pole and knocked Torc's to the side, making first contact.

"Yer not the only one Borrac favors. He done right by me, settin' me up with the Shattered Horn, ya know. And could be there's plans afoot you don't know nothin' about." He took a step closer.

"I know you *had* hostages, presumably for blood sport. But they got away, didn't they?" She ducked as he swung wildly over her head. Her guess was right on target. "Borrac won't be pleased."

"What makes ya so sure?" He parried her blow and returned one, which she met.

"You're the one who's slipping, Torc. I saw it in your face when you got the message. I can smell your fear!"

Torc backed over another gap in the bridge as Eleanor pressed forward. The clash of their poles rang out. Jarring vibrations coursed down her arms. Holding firm, hands a body-width apart, she used the rod like an extension of her arms to slap and block, forward and up, down and back.

"There'll be blood sport a 'plenty, enough for Borrac and a dozen chieftains," said Torc. He stopped, panting slightly, holding the pole level in front of him. "Those pretty fairies of yourn might go down easy, but the Dezrot and Wulfen ought' a put on a good show." A sneer curled his lips. "Them… an' Nodd."

Surprise registered on her face sparking a satisfied gleam in Torc's eye. Suddenly, he jerked his weapon up and over hers, a circling paddle. It broke the grip of her nearest hand, flinging her pole in a downward arc. Torc bore down with a blow intended to shatter her raised forearm, but her reaction was swift. She sliced her arm through the air, and the end of her pole deflected his blow. Spinning her weapon over her head, she swung it toward the side of his, using his own strategy against him. He avoided it easily and stepped back another pace. The gap was directly in front of her. His eyes challenged her to cross it, his rotted teeth bared in a nasty grin.

"So what's he to ya? He's a freak – a monster! You been goin' down the mountain to him when you's s'posed ta be on patrol, ain'tcha?"

"The only monster I know is Borrac!"

"Aw, now girlie, yer a fool to go talkin' 'bout yer intended like that. He might not take kindly to it."

"I'm not afraid of either of you!"

"Then yer a bigger fool than I thought!"

He thrust again engaging her in battle. Poles clashed, the crowd cheered, the rope bridge jerking like a storm-tossed wave. Eleanor countered Torc's strength with speed and skill. The match appeared stalemated. Finally, Torc showed signs he was beginning to tire. One of Eleanor's strikes landed squarely on his shoulder, the dull thwap of wood against his padded leather jerkin breaking the rhythm of wood on wood. Torc bellowed and feigned an attack. Eleanor leaned back to escape the expected blow. It never came. Instead, Torc retreated. She followed, determined to press her advantage, first one step, then another. Torc backed away. Eleanor took another step and the slat gave way, clattering to the rock-studded stage below. Her leg slipped painfully between the remaining slats and she fell forward, forearms slamming onto the planks. Her weapon flew from her hands and slid along the bridge toward Torc. He stopped it with his hoof, and then kicked it nonchalantly aside. It spun through the air, landing off to the side in a cloud of dust. Eleanor raised her head. Torc charged, his pole aimed at her chest like a vaulter's pivot. Instinctively, she grabbed the edge of the bridge, swinging her hanging leg and rolling her entire weight sideways. The bridge heaved, knocking Torc off balance. He teetered for an instant trying to regain control, arms flailing wildly. It was no use. He fell, using his pole to vault clear of the rock-studded platform. The match was over.

Aryelle's hand stopped its slow stroking buried in the coarse fur of the Wulfen's neck. His pulse was weak, but steady. Would he die here in the cell? What about them? Would she and Karril meet their end in the arena? *What more is left for me to do*, she asked herself.

Knowing he slept, Aryelle carefully shifted the Wulfen's head from her lap. She felt her way along the wall to Nashor. Karril sat snoring softly beside him. Aryelle laid her hands gently over Nashor's bandaged head. A soft glow radiated from her tear-streaked face. She raised it toward the faint light that snuck in around the cell door, and felt the familiar energy flow through her body into the young Aurrac. She smiled wearily. Taking the blade from Nashor's wondering hands, she moved to Karril and cut his bonds.

Eleanor was certain Torc had cheated. Somehow, while pretending to examine his weapon, he had tampered with the slat and then memorized its position. His plan to lure her forward had worked, but his sluggishness cost him. The judges declared it a no-win. Eleanor hadn't used her weapon to best her opponent, nor had Torc though he had disarmed her. Both grumbling, Eleanor and Torc returned to opposite ends of the competitor's box to the rumblings of the crowd.

There was a break in the action as the points were tallied to determine which contestants would face one another in the final round of Blades. Eleanor knew she was lower in the standings than she had ever been before, her poor showing in combat lowering her overall score. She avoided looking in Borrac's direction, calculating who her opponents would be provided she made it to the final round. Only the four highest-ranking contenders would move on.

Borrac was seething. This was not the demonstration of total domination he envisioned! Eleanor must leave no questions in the minds of the other chieftains. A goddess should have no weaknesses. Then, as her master, *he* would shine omnipotent. It was as a god that he would populate the Aurracs with a divine race! But first, *she* must prove herself worthy. Eleanor was letting him down.

He brushed off a comment from a lesser chieftain and pulled Gorron toward him by his frilly collar. The steward listened carefully, and then slipped away to carry out his mission.

****

The judges announced their final scores. Ranked first was big-horned Gord, who had cleanly beaten Eleanor in hand-to-hoof combat. Second was a senior member of the patrol, the commander under whom she served. She hadn't competed directly against him, but both rams had won all of their previous rounds of competition. Third and forth on the list were Torc and Eleanor. Obliged to stand and acknowledge the judges decision, they returned to their seats as the other competitors filed out. As the last of them left for the stands or the barracks, depending on how spent they were, Gord and the commander headed onto the field. As Torc moved to follow them, a lace-cuffed hand thrust a note through the doorway. He took and unfolded it, staring at the paper as if it were gold. Slowly, he turned and gazed down the length of the bench, locking eyes with Eleanor. His look was pure evil. He crumpled the note in his fist, popping it into his mouth like a savory morsel, and his eyes never left her face. With a lecherous grin, he saluted and then paraded onto the field.

Eleanor followed at a distance.

The note contained two words sweeter than honey to Torc's mouth. Words that made him eager to face her again in competition despite the way she had humiliated him. He swallowed the last of the pulpy wad, his chieftain's message fueling him.

Kill her.

Chapter 21 – The Prophesy

A crew trotted onto the field to make ready for the final round of competition. Once they had wheeled away the framework and rigging of the rope bridge, they roped off a square in the center of the arena, placing tables at each corner, one for each of the competitors. The tables held blades of varying lengths; a heavy broad sword, a slightly shorter, curved scimitar, a short sword and a hammered stone knife. Like surgical instruments, they gleamed in the sunlight awaiting the moment they would be called upon to perform.

This portion of the games was unique. Contenders took to the field all four at once, paired for broad swords as they were seeded. They would change weapons and opponents with each sounding of a ram's horn trumpet. At the final horn, they could choose whatever blade they preferred in a wild free-for-all. Judges circled the roped off area which the combatants were not allowed to leave. The leader in strikes, or the only one left standing, would be declared Champion.

Eleanor took her place in front of her weapons table, dwarfed by comparison with the three brawny rams. Their padded leather tunics added to their bulk, offering some protection from the sharp blades soon to be thrust at them. But while sleeves shielded, they also bound. Eleanor preferred the free range of motion her simple chamois halter afforded her as she picked up her broad sword with both hands and swung it experimentally above her head. She turned to face the center of the ring.

"Shhh- let her sleep." Karril was careful not to shift and wake Aryelle. She had earned her rest.

"How did she do that?" asked Nashor.

"We are empaths. She took your pain into her own body."

"But why? She barely knows me."

"You needed healing," answered Karril as if it needed no further explanation.

It was not so clear to Nashor. "Will she die? I was pretty beat up."

"She has endured much worse. It will leave her soon." He endured Aryelle's weight against his shoulder knowing that whatever happened now, they would face it together.

Nashor looked at both with amazement. The fairies had seemed like frightened children in his mother's home. Now they possessed a calm that was unmistakable. He'd seen it before in captives being led to execution. But surely, they had no idea what awaited them in the arena.

A clarion sounded its two-note call, bellowing low and then raising an octave. Aryelle startled.

"The final game" said Nashor. "It'll be over soon, and then they'll open that door. Pray to whatever gods you recognize that Eleanor stands victorious beyond it. That's your - *our* - only hope."

Aryelle felt for Nashor's hand. "Light often shines in unexpected places," she quoted wearily, then leaned back against Karril and closed her eyes.

Torc was ruthless in his frenzied opening attack. Eleanor fended him off, shielding herself from blow after blow with the flat of her broad sword. Neither scored a hit.

The ram's horn blew a second time and they changed weapons. The curved blade of the scimitar called for an entirely different stroke. Gord bore down upon her. Gone was the feigned bumble-ness of her opponent. He fought with skill, their blades dancing a dangerous tango. Admiration gleamed in Eleanor's eyes. The signal horn sounded and their combat ended in a draw as well. She whirled toward her weapon's table to exchange blades, suddenly aware of the other dueling pair. Despite the signal, they were still engaged. The commander's left arm hung limply by his side. Torc, consumed by bloodlust, moved in for the kill. The audience roared when, scimitar still in hand, Gord thrust himself between Torc and the commander, taking over the battle. Eleanor waited while the commander exchanged his weapon. Haltingly he approached. Blood poured from his shoulder.

"You can't fight," she said, keeping her weapon lowered.

"Draw" he whispered hoarsely. His face had drained of color and his eyes grew vacant.

"No, sir."

"Fight me!" he ordered. With the tip of his short sword, he sliced at her face drawing a beaded trail of blood along her cheek. Through clenched teeth he hissed, "Don't let Torc be my victor!"

Now Eleanor understood. She struck her breast in salute. "No, sir!"

The commander gave a throaty yell. With the last of his strength, he threw himself forward. Eleanor planted her hooves and leaned her blade outward. It buried itself in his belly. A startled gasp bubbled from his lips, and a roar of approval flew up from the crowd.

"Well met…patrol ram," the old soldier grunted. His eyes rolled back into his head.

Eleanor pulled her blade free as his body slumped to the ground. The bloodthirsty lot in the stands went wild. Banners waved, stomping hooves and clapping hands coalescing into a rhythm that called for more.

Eleanor's head swam. The arena spun around her. The fleeting image of Torc and Gord locked in battle flirted at the corner of her vision. Finally, the signal horn sounded again, pulling Eleanor from her trance. Torc had exchanged his weapon for a treacherous stone blade. He moved in her direction. The front of his jerkin and sleeve were torn and stained with blood, but his wounds were not serious. Gord faded into the background.

Eleanor dropped her bloodied short sword on the ground and instinctively reached for the shortest blade on her weapons table. As Torc stepped over the dead commander's body, she whirled around to face him. Sweat dripped from his brow, his hair plastered to his head. He leered mockingly, tossing his blade from hand to hand. Knives were his weapon of choice, Eleanor knew. But they were also hers. She circled, keeping beyond arm's length. His longer reach might be an advantage, but again, she was quicker and not winded.

"Yer mine, girlie!"

"In your dreams, Torc!"

"Time to wake up, princess. Yer dead! Borrac's orders." He lunged, but she sidestepped easily.

"So that's what's making you so sure of yourself. You think Borrac sent that message for you? Think again," she said, taunting him. "Borrac wants to make sure *I* kill *you*! He wants me to make a good show of it." She could see the wheels turning inside Torc's twisted mind. They passed each other, dangerously close. "But I'm not going to kill you, Torc. I'd much rather you live to suffer the humiliation of having to worship me."

"Either kill me or be killed, girlie," he said menacingly, "'cuz I'll never bow to you!"

It was Eleanor's turn to smile, but it never reached her eyes. With a movement so quick that Torc never saw it coming, she spun toward him, ducking under his unarmed side while switching her blade to her empty hand. With a backward stroke, she sliced cleanly through the tendons in the back of his ankle. He fell to his knees screaming in rage and pain.

"Oh yes, Torc…you will!" Eleanor spat on the ground beside him, then turned and looked straight at Borrac. Electricity crackled in the air. A storm was fast approaching.

The audience went wild with calls for her to finish him. Eleanor ignored them. She strode toward the ropes as the last trumpet sounded.

"Nooooo!"

Torc's knife spun through the air, finding its mark between Eleanor's shoulders. The blow knocked her forward as the razor sharp blade imbedded itself in her back.

There was stunned silence. Eleanor's body lay twitching on the ground.

A lone ram leapt from the stands, his head covered in a makeshift turban, gray beard braided into two long strands. He ran to the center of the arena, leaping the rope barrier and bending briefly over the dead commander's body. When he straightened, he held the commander's short sword. He charged straight at Torc, who gaped, unarmed and helpless. Propelled by fury, Nodd buried the sword in Torc's chest. Blood gushed over his hand. Grasping its handle, he gave the sword a final twist. Torc's eyes and tongue bulged out of his head and blood bubbled from his lips… lips that would sneer no more.

Nodd pushed him aside and hurried over to Eleanor. She lay there arms flung wide, her belly in the dirt. He rolled her carefully onto her side leaving Torc's blade where it stuck between her shoulderblades. Tenderly he stroked her cheek, wincing at the pallor beneath her tanned skin as he streaked it with Torc's blood. Her eyelids fluttered open.

"Nodd?"

"Shhh…..I'm here, little flower."

Her eyes drifted closed and she smiled weakly, replaying a fragrant memory. "You haven't called me that in years," she whispered. "I used to ride on your shoulders…and you would pick them… little, white flowers. You'd stick them in my hair… and say you stole their name for me… because I was so pretty….."

"You still are, little flower. You still are."

"I can't feel anything, Nodd," she exhaled. "Tell Althea…. I love her. She… might not know." Her words were tinged with sorrow.

"She knows, child. She knows."

Suddenly, there was a commotion on the field. Gord upended his weapon's table and crashed through the rope that marked off the combat area. He ran along the inner wall, pushing aside a sentry and unbarring one of the cell doors that lined the arena to release the waiting prisoners. Nashor stumbled blindly onto the field. His arm shielded his eyes as they adjusted to the light. Behind him still in the shadows stood the luminaries, poised for flight.

Gord looked past them into the dark cell. "Are you fairies the ones who heal?" he asked seeing no others.

Aryelle and Karril exchanged anxious glances. Why question rather than kill them? Finding no answer in the luminaries' eyes, he turned to Nashor, who nodded reluctantly.

"Eleanor is dying," said Gord.

Nashor dropped his arm and scanned the arena. There was the old goat - his father - cradling Eleanor in his arms. Two bodies lay nearby. He looked at Gord for confirmation, and then ran on fleet hooves to where Eleanor lay. Falling to his knees, he called out to Aryelle. "Hurry! There is still time!"

Aryelle grasped Karril's hand and stepped hesitantly from the cell. A thousand pair of eyes rooted them to the spot. Then, to the hushed amazement of the crowd, Jonazat flew over the stands and landed a pace in front of Gord. Now three, not two luminaries stood before the spellbound crowd, most of whom had never seen the likes before.

"Fly, cousins! Fly! Now is your chance!" Jonazat's eyes challenged Gord to try and stop them, but the big-horned ram made no move.

"You came back!" cried Karril.

"I said I would not leave you. Now hurry! Take wing!"

"Aryelle!" Nodd called from across the field.

Aryelle and Karril looked at each other and then Jonazat. He shook his head as she spoke. "Our friends need help."

Then take wing they did, but not out of the coliseum. With hands still clasped, they flew side by side to Nodd. Nashor made room for them. Now Gord's stare challenged Jonazat as he strode past him to join the others. For a moment, Jonazat hovered before the crowd. Then a sigh escaped his lips, and he flew over to assist.

Nodd looked up with hope-filled eyes. Aryelle placed her hand reassuringly over his.

"Remove the knife," said Jonazat.

Nodd searched Aryelle's face, and then rolled Eleanor's limp body forward and pulled the blade from her back. Blood poured freely from the wound. Aryelle placed her hand over it and instructed Nodd to step back. The luminaries formed a tight circle around Eleanor, open wings shielding their movements from view. Brilliant light radiated from within them. The crowd watched in awe.

Borrac paraded onto the field flanked by two high-ranking chieftains and two of his personal guard. Nashor and Gord turned to meet them, going down on one knee before their High Chieftain. Nodd did not. Nashor watched him from the corner of his eye. Then Borrac spoke, demanding their attention.

"You dare to disrupt my games?" He addressed Gord though his eyes never strayed from the turbaned ram who remained standing.

"I would face a worthy opponent," Gord answered lifting his chin.

"Even me?" asked Borrac.

"I would challenge you, yes," he said rising, "but I would win my championship first, not be handed it by default. If the fairies can heal the female warrior-"

"You could have finished Torc. Instead you left it to this old goat."

"He wasn't worth soiling my blade."

"You're here to fight who *I* chose!" Borrac raised his eyebrows. "And you?" he asked Nodd abruptly. "Speak up! Who are you?"

Nodd glared at him with undisguised loathing. "Don't you recognize me Borrac? Perhaps if I were asleep in bed; isn't that when you prefer to attack?"

Recognition dawned on Borrac's face. He reached out and yanked the turban from Nodd's head, exposing the purple stain that had marked him since birth.

"Nodd-" he snorted derisively, "- the outcast. What are you doing here?"

"I came for Eleanor."

Borrac glanced in her direction. "What's Eleanor to you? She can't be your lover," he chided "but maybe offspring from when you still had the equipment?"

"She's not mine, though rightly she should be. She's yours Borrac, the child you tried to murder. You may have stolen my manhood from me, but your daughter lived. And I stole her heart, just like I stole her mother's!"

A new fury filled the High Chieftain. Murmurs rumbled through the crowd as they strained to hear what was taking place on the field. Then suddenly the audience gasped. Borrac's eyes grew wide. Rising into the air beyond Nodd's misshapen head, in an aura of pure radiance, was Eleanor. She stretched languidly, as if waking from a restful sleep. The luminaries hovered just below, rotating slowly, colorful rays escaping their inner circle. Gradually they descended. The light faded and the luminaries collapsed to the ground. Eleanor stood in their midst, looking around in confusion.

Borrac stepped past a spellbound Nodd, slapping him on the shoulder. "Too bad you won't be staying for our wedding," he gloated. Snapping his fingers above his head, he commanded his guards "Kill them all!"

Borrac reached for Eleanor then stopped, his hand poised midair. His daughter…how had she lived? He remembered that night, her sleeping innocence curled as she had been just a few seasons previous within Althea's womb. He had felt a twinge of regret… then raised his blade and struck again and again, just as he had with the others. She hadn't even cried out.

Surely, the gods had protected her as one of their own! Flesh of his flesh, *blood of his blood.* They had saved her, not once but now twice! And they had given her back to him as their gift … *to create a pure race with him*! This was their sign! He took Eleanor's hand. Still dazed, she allowed him to lead her away, stepping around the spent empaths as if in a trance.

The two chieftains and Borrac's guard hesitated. It was just enough time for Nodd and the others to react. Gord swung his scimitar at the belly of the nearest guard while Nodd lowered his horns and rammed the other, knocking him off his feet. Before he could rise, Nodd finished him off.

One of the chieftains charged at Nashor. He rolled backward with the movement, using his own momentum to send the ram sailing over his head. Quickly Nashor dashed to the nearest weapons table and grabbed a broadsword. He returned, swinging wildly, but by then both guards and lesser chieftains lay dead. The judges had wisely fled the field at the first sign of trouble.

Finding himself unchallenged, Gord looked around for an adversary. There was no one left to defeat. Nodd and Nashor had hurried to the luminaries to find Eleanor already gone. They helped the empaths struggle to their feet.

"Why is it so dark?" asked Aryelle, her voice shaky.

Nodd scanned the darkening skies. "Storm's moving in-" he began, spotting the remaining chieftains leaping into the arena. They had been promised a share in the blood sport, and would not be denied.

"Get them out of here!" Nodd instructed Jonazat. He and Nashor hurried back to Gord's side. Without a word, they had become comrades in arms. Together they stood their ground as luminaries staggered away behind them. Nine bloodthirsty rams approached.

"Behold!" Borrac cried in a thunderous voice. The chieftains halted and every eye turned toward the High Chieftain's box. Borrac drew Eleanor to his side. "Behold," he repeated. "The gods have spoken today in our midst! Eleanor, stolen from me in her youth, and returned under the protection of Sheala, Goddess of the Hunt, has been granted immortality in our very presence! The gods have deigned that a pure race of Aurrac should come into being; a race of gods fit to rule, or to destroy all others. Today I claim Eleanor, divine vessel of my own divinity, as my bride!"

An agitated murmur swelled through the crowd. What was he saying? Hadn't the fairies healed her, not the gods? Borrac heard their rumblings and scowled. The other chieftains muttered angrily.

"Divine?"

"She's a foundling!"

"You're mad, Borrac."

"Silence!" he roared. "You dare question me?" His crazed eyes fixed on the final speaker. "You saw her dead before you, just as I saw her dead by my own hand long ago! But still she lives! The gods have saved her again, using the fairies, as a wedding gift to me! She is fruit of my loins - the gods recognize their own! Borrac and Eleanor – WE ARE YOUR NEWEST GODS!" He motioned to his high priest. "Accora! Read the prophesy!"

The crowd grew restless as Accora stepped forward. Snowy hair and beard, lavishly curled, hung in ringlets around his face framing it like a lion's mane. A two-pointed miter sat upon his head like an extra set of horns. The wind picked up, the heavens rumbling ominously as his purple robes billowed behind him. With an extravagant gesture, Accora drew forth a yellowed scroll. His words echoed around the arena as he solemnly addressed the assembly.

"*As prophesied by Accora, Aurracan High Priest, representative of Cor and his heavenly legion: When the blood of all Emrysia cries out to the gods, then shall the portal to the otherworld open at last and a new order be established. Darkness shall vanish and death be no more when the worthy ones pass through the threshold. They shall be of shared blood and like mind, perfect though different as night to day-*"

"Shared blood and like mind!" cried Borrac, interrupting. "Do you hear? Now let prophesy be fulfilled! Let the blood of all Emrysia flow upon this sacred ground!"

Hearing his prearranged cue, a sentry on the far side of the arena hurried to unlatch a second cell door, loosing a crew of unfortunate Aurrac prisoners. They bolted from confinement, some scurrying into the stands toward freedom while others dashed toward the weapons tables to arm themselves. Around the arena, other sentries unbarred more holding cells. Foreign captives, those not fortunate enough to escape and some who had come to view the games and instead been taken prisoner, fled onto the field preferring to take their chance fighting rather than be trapped like rats in a hole. A beautiful flame-haired woman bolted from one cell followed closely by a snarling Dezrot. Above them, a self-conscious looking patrol ram upended a leather bag, dumping a disheveled praircat into the arena. Stunned, Rona swayed on hind legs, ears pricked forward, then darted toward the wall and began digging furiously.

Dismissing the High Chieftain's madness, the other chieftains attacked with undisguised glee. A free-for-all battle ensued, and pandemonium reigned in the coliseum. The excited crowd was whipped into frenzy. Prisoners attempting to escape were mobbed and forced back into the arena. A slobear grabbed the praircat by its silky scruff and tossed it further onto the pitch, hoping to distract the approaching Dezrot, who was making no distinction between friend and foe. Rona rolled across the dirt and then dashed between Nashor's legs. He raced toward the luminaries.

Suddenly the heavens opened. A blinding deluge burst from the sky, but the crowd in the stands ignored the torrential downpour. Huddling beneath makeshift umbrellas, they peered eagerly through the rain toward the massacre below.

"ENOUGH!"

Borrac's amplified bellow carried over the din of the storm and the battle. And as suddenly as it began, the rain ceased. Thunder rumbled across the mountaintop. Tension filled ozone permeated the air.

The ropes had fallen around the center of the arena where three battling pairs still engaged in deadly combat. Slipping and tripping over the muddy ground littered with bodies, Borrac crossed the field again. The remainder of his personal guard had disappeared fearing the same fate as the others. A new entourage followed less eagerly in his wake. Gorron and Accora stepped primly around the dead and dying. Between them, Eleanor gradually woke to the surrounding carnage.

A scimitar, its handle encrusted with precious stones, gleamed in Borrac's hand. Coming up behind the nearest dueling pair, Borrac drew back the blade and swung it in a deadly arc. The head of the chieftain who'd called him mad tumbled to the ground. His combatant, Nodd leaped back in surprise. Gord, Nashor, and the two remaining chieftains lowered their weapons.

"I said enough! And see," said Borrac lifting his arms, "even the heavens obey! Too bad *he* couldn't hear me." His eyes glittered with a wildly exultant gleam, twisting his swarthy features into a mask of insanity. "Ah, my warrior bride" he said, drawing Eleanor near. "I suppose now Nodd's earned the right to witness our nuptials, what do you think?"

Eleanor's eyes sought Nodd's, pleading with him to understand. He looked away, letting the blade slip from his hand. It stuck in the mud at his feet. The remaining chieftains joined Borrac, eyes searching for their comrades among the scattered dead.

Borrac surveyed the scene with a satisfied grin. "I trust you enjoyed your blood sport? Now, since you are all that's left, would either of you care to challenge me?" His gloating stare shifted from face to face, mocking them. "No? You then, Big Horn! Gord is it? How about you? You've earned the right. Or are you too spent now to risk it? Or scared perhaps? After all, the blood of all Emrysia has flowed freely here today - wait! What's this?"

A tiny movement caught his attention. His eyes fell upon the luminaries; huddled near the raised tank on the southern end of the pitch they had somehow gone unnoticed. Half drowned between Jonazat's sodden, translucent wings was the shivering praircat.

"Well, look at the pretty butterflies, too wet to fly! And even a golden, baby caterpillar safe in its cocoon! Isn't that a sight?" More cocksure than ever, Borrac winked at Nodd. "Unfinished business - I'll be right back!"

As he neared, a sleek, silver shape streaked across the muddy field. A snarling Wulfen leapt between Borrac the empaths. Borrac froze. Without turning, he called to the other chieftains.

"It seems there's plenty of blood yet to be spilled, my friends. Come! Share my sport with me."

Neither one moved. An angry Wulfen was a fauen's worst nightmare. Borrac glared at them from the corner of his eye and they edged cautiously to his side. They had seen what he was capable of too. The Wulfen paced, keeping himself between the Aurrac and the luminaries.

Jonazat shepherded Aryelle and Karril toward the rickety steps to the water tank, thankful for whatever miracle brought the Wulfen. Weaponless and in his weakened state, he had no hope of defending himself, let alone protecting the youngsters. They scrambled up the steps to the decking above while he waited anxiously below.

Aryelle looked back over her shoulder. She swayed, eyes blurring. Jonazat appeared at the end of a long, dark tunnel. Shaking her head, she stumbled forward pushing Karril onto the platform ahead of her. A pair of hands shot out of the water and pulled Karril into the tank with a splash.

Surprise lit the chieftains' faces. From their vantage point, it looked as though Aryelle had shoved Karril in. She leaned over the side reaching into the water.

"Look, she's trying to drown the other one!" complained one of the chieftains as if cheated. He brandished his sword. The Wulfen growled menacingly.

While Borrac was distracted, Eleanor turned toward Nodd, ignoring the looks from Gorron and Accora. Though both held weapons, they knew better than to try and stop her.

"It's not what it seems," she said.

"You knew! You knew all along what he did and still…" Nodd shook his head in disgust. "And how long have you known Borrac is your father?"

"Lavina slipped and told me right after the first Games when he put me on the patrol. She didn't realize Althea never had. I never meant you to know until after-"

"After what? After you *gave* yourself to your own sire? To the monster who tried to kill you?"

"After extracting my revenge!"

Nodd looked at her uncomprehending.

"I was never going to - it's not - I wouldn't have let anything happen!" she managed at last.

"Not let anything happen? Eleanor, he's a madman, a demon!"

"I can take care of myself!"

Nodd just stared at her. Then, bending down he drew his knife from the mud and wiped it on the wool of his thigh. "I would kill him if he touched you…but I would kill you before I let you wed him."

They locked eyes as though they were horns, an impasse of wills. Together they'd survived that horrible night when Borrac raided the lower village and offered unholy sacrifice to the god of his own making. So much blood! Of innocent children and children yet to be. Her blood, and Nodd's future. Eleanor would never forgive Borrac for what he had done. She could still see it in her dreams. But here in this blood-drenched arena, looking into her stepfather's eyes, Eleanor's thirst for vengeance began to fade away.

"There's been enough blood spilled here today, enough throughout my lifetime." She lowered her gaze and bent to pick up Nodd's muddied turban, handing it to him.

"Let's go home," Nodd said. He reached for Eleanor's hand. With the blade in his other, he sliced through the brilliant blue chamois covering her tattoo. The armband slipped to the mud.

Gorron and Accora had watched their exchange with interest. When the high priest saw the markings on Eleanor's arm, he gasped. His eyes sought Borrac.

Borrac and the Wulfen drifted to one side, circling each other. The lesser chieftains closed in on Jonazat.

Why had he not followed, thought Aryelle? She sat at the top of the stairs clutching the pouch at her side. Without even realizing it, she reached inside. The bel! Her fingers closed around it. The noise and stench of the arena receded. Her thoughts came clear and strong.

Give the Gift away!

"Jonazat!" she cried, and tossed the bel down the stairway toward him. He caught it in his outstretched hand. Instantly it threw a shield of unparalleled brilliance around him, blinding his attackers.

At the same instant, the Wulfen sprang.

Borrac was ready. He swung his scimitar with an underhand arc and twirled out of the beast's path. The curved blade ripped open the Wulfen's belly, spilling his entrails mid-leap. The Wulfen twisted his snarling muzzle and crunched down on Borrac's leg, snapping the bone. Borrac howled in pain, and beat the shaggy silver head with the hilt of his jewel-encrusted sword.

"Oh, my lord!" cried Gorron, swooning.

Accora steadied Gorron and the pair rushed to Borrac's aid. Passing the lesser chieftains Accora cried, "Borrac is down! Bring that empath!"

Borrac was down? The two rams looked at each other. Forget the luminaries. Here was a chance for one of them to claim the title of Aurrac Head Chieftain. They turned on one another, bloody weapons at the ready.

"But healers could ruin everything," rationed one.

"First things first," agreed the other.

They headed back toward the stairway.

Jonazat looked up at Aryelle, resignation written across his face. "No!" she mouthed as he tossed the bel back to her. The shield of light shifted.

Unprotected, Jonazat darted away from the steps, drawing the rams after him. He didn't get far. The mud was slick and he was still weak. They caught him easily. He struggled, expecting them to force him toward their fallen leader. Instead, as one, they plunged their swords into his unprotected mid-section. Pulling their blades free, they looked up at Aryelle. Blinding light surrounded her. Perhaps it would be simpler to just to finish off Borrac.

Watching them go, Aryelle let the bel slip from her fingers. It tumbled down the wooden steps, its light growing weaker as it rolled through the mud and came to a stop beside Jonazat. Aryelle stumbled down the stairway and fell to her knees at his side. Cradling his head in her lap, she lifted her face skyward.

"No child, you are too spent. Do not attempt it."

"But-" she began to argue. Jonazat's face swam out of focus.

The disemboweled Wulfen lay dead, his jaws still clamped around Borrac's leg. Borrac was out cold. Gorron fretted over him while Accora attempted to pry open the Wulfen's mouth.

"Fools!" cried Accora, as the lesser chieftains approached. "What have you done? Do you want to call down the wrath of the gods on our heads? Get the female one, and bring her to me! Quickly!"

They hesitated. Borrac was an unlikely god, but here was the gods' true representative threatening to call down their power.

Gorron couldn't wait for them to decide. He grabbed Borrac's scimitar and pushed past them, running over to Aryelle. "Come with me! You've got more important work to do!" He grabbed her by the wrist, and she was too weak to resist. Jonazat protested feebly. Gorron ignored him, dragging Aryelle back to where his Chieftain lay.

Spurred into action, Eleanor and Nodd sprinted across the field. Nashor and Gord joined them, meeting the chieftains in battle while Eleanor and Nodd hurried to help.

"Stay back Ragor of Lower!" shouted Accora. He brandished a knife over Borrac's unconscious body. "Yes, I recognize you. I recognized your mark of the accursed!"

"The gods only marked me to make me stronger, Accora! Now, let the fairy come with me and I'll spare your worthless life!"

Gorron, looking terrified, held the jeweled scimitar to Aryelle's throat.

"No! She must heal him!" shouted Accora. "The prophesy must be fulfilled!"

"Do as he says!" ordered Eleanor.

"But you - *you* are the Chosen!" Accora whispered. A look of wonder dawned in his eyes. "You bear the sign! Let me see it again!" Accora reached for her arm, cringing as she jerked it away.

"That's my mark, made when she was a child, such as all in the lower village must bear," said Nodd.

"But she's perfect, an unblemished lamb. She bears no the stain of the accursed! No--- this is a sign from the gods."

"You're wrong."

"Then they have only used your hand!"

"What are you raving about?" asked Eleanor. Pretending to be a goddess was one thing. Having the high priest believe she was 'chosen' was a different story.

Accora glanced down at his wounded chieftain, his countenance clearing as his gaze returned to Eleanor. "…and they shall be of shared blood and like mind, perfect though different as night to day, *one bearing the mark of the gods, which shall call them together*! You never knew the rest! I thought the mark was Borrac's claim of god-hood. He called the false council, gathered the ambassadors, the blood of all Emrysia…but, it's not Borrac--- it's you. You bear the true mark!"

"No wonder Borrac is mad, listening to a crazy, old rotter like you!" She pointed her knife at the steward. "Release her!"

Gorron let Aryelle go at once. Accora lowered his blade as well. Borrac moaned. He was coming to.

"He is badly hurt," said Aryelle.

Nodd drew her clear. "Don't spend yourself on Borrac; he'll live," he said, and spying Jonazat lying in the mud, "but some may not."

Leaving Eleanor to deal with Accora and Gorron, he escorted Aryelle back to the Naturra, but it was already too late. Aryelle gathered Jonazat's mud-streaked body gently into her arms and wept. Nodd guarded her back and allowed her a moment to grieve.

"Erilith zu riss, dher aya dhe," Aryelle whispered softly. Fly swiftly, my brother.

Presently Eleanor joined them, and spying it lying beside them, she plucked the barely glowing bel from the mud and wiped it clean. She handed it back to Aryelle in whose hand it grew bright again. Nodd helped her to her feet and she slipped Bel into her pouch.

As Jonazat's body slumped back into the mud, his wings shuddered. There, still encased between them was the praircat struggling to get free. Nodd pried apart the leathery-strong wings. Rona's head popped out in surprise.

"Captain?"

"Come, my furry friend. Your captain is no more."

Rona emerged and sniffed the dead Naturra's body. When Aryelle reached down, he permitted her to take him into her arms.

Suddenly, the main gate of the coliseum crashed open revealing a triangular litter borne on the shoulders of three brawny men. An ample-bodied ewe sat upon it, waving a white hanky and pointing out directions. A fourth man brought up the rear. They stopped just inside the gate, surveying the carnage.

"There they are boys!" Lavina shouted. "There's Eleanor and Nodd! Oh, and Aryelle, you're safe dear! But where's the younger one? And where's Nashor? Where's my baby?" She tried to stand, rocking the litter like a boat while the men tried to steady it. "Oh, there he is! There, by that ram with the overgrown horns! Go!" she ordered. She waved her hanky at them and pointed, falling heavily into her seat as they moved further into the arena.

"Lavina? What the-?" Nodd felt Aryelle brush past him. Rona leapt from her arms as she dashed up the stairs and leaned precariously over the edge of the water tank.

"Aryelle, no!"

But Aryelle had no intention of joining Karril. Instead, she was pulling him onto the deck, drenched but otherwise unharmed. Lureli followed, her clinging gown looking for all Emrysia like a giant fish's tail. Then suddenly, it no longer did. She swung shapely legs over the edge of the deck. The Mer saw and changed course.

"Wait, no, go back!" cried Lavina. "My baby needs me!"

Gord helped Nashor to his hooves. After quickly deposing his own foe, he had stepped between them when Nashor fell before his. The young ram, though injured would survive, but Borrac was the only chieftain left alive.

And Borrac was conscious once more. Gorron tried to keep him still. The shattered bone of his shin protruded awkwardly through his flesh. He gritted his teeth and brushed the steward's fluttering hands aside.

"Accora!" he bawled, half crazed. "Bring me Eleanor!"

The priest stared blankly, unmoving.

"I said bring her to me!"

Accora looked from Borrac to Eleanor. Then dropping to his knees at Eleanor's feet, he bowed and worshipped her.

"Get up!" she said tugging his sleeve.

He raised his eyes, not daring to touch her. "Take me with you," he begged.

"Go where you like!" she answered, releasing the purple garment as though it burned. She stalked away. Accora scrambled to his feet after her.

"Accora!" Borrac screamed in fury. But the high priest never looked back.

Chapter 22 – Aryelle's Gift

In the confused aftermath of the games, they made good their escape. Despite Aryelle's protest, Jonazat's body was left behind. Nashor and Lureli were loaded onto the litter with Lavina, and the Mer hurried from the arena as best they could. The rest kept pace, Accora trailing behind them. Borrac screamed epitaphs at Gorron when the steward tried to move him. He shouted for his patrol, but most of the spent competitors had long since left the arena. Those left in the stands had seen the unlikely crew get the better of a dozen Aurrac chieftains, and had no desire to be next. They slunk away guiltily. The coliseum emptied as the nervous crowd fled to their homes, avoiding as much as possible the route along the lower gate.

The fugitives spoke little until they were safely outside the wall. They found the gate curiously unguarded. Aryelle noticed the Mer grinning with satisfaction at one another. A few paces beyond the gate, Gord spoke up.

"I'll stay here and slow any who might pursue you. Be surefooted; the path is likely to be slippery."

"Will you join us at the lower village?" asked Eleanor.

Gord shook his head. "Your village won't be safe. Go there if you must to warn them of their danger, but I wouldn't winter anywhere in these mountains if I were you. Borrac's reputation is well known, his influence great. You should have finished him off while you had the chance."

"I may live to regret it, but at least I've got that chance, thanks to you."

Eleanor wished he were coming with them. Almost shyly she bade him well, and continued down the slope. Nodd clasped the younger ram's forearm and the two lightly knocked horns. Then Nodd also began the descent. Accora hurried past the big horned ram without a glance.

Gord turned to watch the Gate.

The descent was treacherous. They moved as quickly as they could, but the rain had made the rocks slick and patches of gravel loose and unstable. The bearers struggled under their burden. Since neither Nashor nor Lavina would make it down under their own power, Nodd suggested to Lureli that she walk. Lureli just shrugged. Her weight wasn't what was causing their difficulty. Grumbling, Nodd sidled in to support one side of the litter. Jaim already had the other. Aryelle and Karril tried to shore up the rear though both were still weak from their ordeal. Eleanor elbowed roughly in between them, and together they made their way down the mountain.

Aryelle tried not to look at Nashor's skewed limb. His nose was bleeding profusely as well. Lavina fussed, dabbing at his face with some of her own soft wool when her hanky grew saturated. Aryelle wanted to stop and heal him, but Nodd insisted they make haste. There would be time for healing when they reached the lower village. Though no longer necessary, both rams still wore bloodied turbans, increasing the resemblance between father and son.

Lureli was subdued. Given the circumstances, Aryelle wasn't surprised. She would need time herself to sort out the day's events. As they trudged downhill, she relived her shock at seeing Lureli in the water tank surrounded by swimming fish, restraining Karril from returning to the surface. It had taken her a moment to remember that the draught Lureli had given them in Wellwood would prevent him from drowning. So great was her fear that, at the time, Lureli's transformed body had not even registered. *I should have guessed*, she chided herself. But Emrysia was full of surprises.

Karril was fast asleep even before a blanket was found to cover him. Aryelle smoothed the hair across his brow. He twitched and a whimper escaped his lips. Lifting her face to the soft glow of moonlight through the window, Aryelle considered. Should she spend any more of herself tonight? Already her eyes were playing tricks on her. *But he is my responsibility*, she thought. Slowly, the aura surrounding her increased and peace flooded her soul, flowing through her into her younger cousin.

When she looked up, Nodd stood in the doorway. Aryelle rose and followed him across the hall to where Nashor lay. His embarrassment was nearly as great as his pain. Aryelle placed her hands gently upon him and as his bones re-knit, his embarrassment faded like words to a seldom-heard song. Intent on his expression of wonder, no one noticed the grimace of pain that flashed across Aryelle's delicate features. Nashor sat up, announced that he was hungry, and thanked her gratefully. She acknowledged by falling into his arms in a coma-like stupor. With the tenderness of a father for a feverish child, Nodd lifted and carried her back to where Karril lay dreaming.

Althea's delight at their safe homecoming turned rapturous at the reunion with her twin. While the rest of the weary crew feasted on honeyed oatcakes, cheese and beer, Althea and Lavina bustled back and forth to the pantry, gabbing merrily as they refilled pitchers and piled platters high with food. A houseful to feed and care for was what both loved best.

Accora sat apart from the others, silent and watchful. The luminaries slept on.

As Mer, Aurrac, and even Rona toasted their good fortune, Jode joined the party, stunned to meet the mother and brother he'd never known. Stories were shared around the fire, and explanations given. Althea launched into a rambling tale about how she had sent the bearers hiking after Lureli came up missing. Lavina took over the narrative, adding her own colorful details. She laughed till tears poured down her round cheeks recalling their reaction when she met them just inside the Upper Village gate. Of course, they had mistaken her for her twin.

Lureli fell silent when it came her time to share, staring sullenly into her horn of beer. The room grew serious. Nodd looked around at the gathered faces.

"Gord was right; we won't be safe here. Borrac may not be able to follow us himself, but he'll send out his patrol. They might already be on the way."

"Borrac may be mad, but he's shrewd," said Eleanor, speaking up for the first time since their return. "He'll wait, wanting us to think he's not coming. Once he's recovered and gathered enough force, he'll try to take us by surprise. Hopefully, the snows will come first, and by the time the passes are clear, the other clan-herds will try to avenge the loss of their chieftains. That ought to keep him occupied for a while. Either way, I say we winter here." Secretly she hoped that Gord might still join them.

"You're both mistaken," Accora lowered the curtain of doom. "Remember the prophesy - Borrac believes himself a god! He does not fear the other clan-herds, nor will he wait until he is able to pursue you himself. He will call upon the heavens. Leave or stay, the gods will find you. And he will be waiting."

"Then what do you suggest, oh wise high priest?"

He gazed through the smoke at Eleanor's face. "You are *one* of the chosen. There will be others. You must find them and pass through the portal into the otherworld. The Reign of Shadow will come to an end, as I have foretold. "

"And Borrac?"

"Do this and his reign will end as well."

"And just where do we find this portal?" Eleanor asked.

"The Stone of Seeing in the Plains of Being
Shows all, foretelling and secrets dwelling…" he intoned.

"Not again," muttered Lureli.

"Hey, I know where that is, the Plains of Being. That's my home! That's my home!" piped Rona eagerly. His long, striped tail twitched with excitement. Eleanor snorted derisively.

Suddenly, Bel shot into the room. All eyes turned.

Aryelle shuffled forward. One of her hands brushed along the wall, the other groping in front of her. Her eyes no longer sparkled like emeralds. Instead, the dancing firelight reflected off irises of milky blue. She stumbled and Nodd jumped up to steady her.

"I can do it. I am just tired," she said as he took her arm.

"Can you see at all?" Nodd whispered softly.

"N-no…but it happened earlier today too. It will pass soon."

"Is it the T'sura?"

"No!" cried Aryelle, though no one else had heard.

"What is it?" asked Althea with concern.

Nodd cleared his throat and waited for Aryelle to answer. Tears scalded her eyes. She blinked them back. Sooner or later, she would have to face the truth. "It *is* T'sura," she admitted to herself as much as the others.

"I'm sorry Aryelle. You've burned out too soon," Nodd said sadly."

"Not burned out," she explained as Bel returned to hover over her head, "just dimmed. So it often was with our Elders - as it is with my father Elazaryn - from over spending our light. My ability to heal will return when I am more rested. It may even be greater than ever, but my sight…"

"But you're still so young," Althea winced at the injustice.

Another reason why the Kandharril formed the Circle, thought Aryelle. "When I have learned how, I will be able to see in a different way, almost a better way. T'sura has many compensations." She screwed her face into a brave mask.

"But who'll teach you?" asked Lavina.

"I will return with Karril to Ka'Andharra…if someone would be willing to help us find our way." *I have so much to learn*, she told herself, *but now that I am finally ready, do I really want to?*

"I will," said Nashor. "It's because you healed me that this happened, isn't it?"

Aryelle considered - how could she explain? The T'sura was a gift, though one she was hardly eager to accept. Her pride was gone, along with the need to prove herself. She had always known that her purpose was to share her light however it was needed. But she could no longer make the mistake of thinking she needed no help. Her people still had faults, but T'sura had opened her eyes to her own. Could it be that her eyesight was a meager price to pay for that wisdom?

"It may have happened eventually anyhow," she answered, "though not for many revolutions. And I assumed others besides you."

"Like me," said Eleanor.

"But you healed me twice!" argued Nashor looking ashamed.

Aryelle tried hard to smile. "If it would lessen your burden, by all means come. But I think you would better serve your people if you stayed." She turned unseeing eyes toward Nodd and they swam again with tears. If only she had taken her own advice. "I heard your conversation from the walkway. It may not mean much, but I think everyone should leave the village. It is not safe here. Not all need journey far. Most could shelter in the caves you spoke of until word of our flight has spread. By the time snow fills the higher mountain passes, they should be able to return. Nashor, Jode and the rest could see to their well-being. If you and Eleanor leave with us, perhaps Borrac will leave the villagers in peace."

"Your vision is still clearer than most," said Nodd. "This is wise council."

"What about Accora?" scoffed Eleanor.

"He will have to come with us," Nodd answered. "We don't know where his true loyalties lie, and he's heard too much already. If he stayed it would endanger the village."

"I will come," said Accora. "Wherever the Chosen One goes, I will follow."

"Me too! Me too!" chimed Rona. "I can show you a short cut through the Plains of Being!"

"I think I have had enough of short cuts!" said Aryelle. Despite everything, a smile tugged at the corners of her mouth. "But I cannot wait to get home!"

Afterward – The Journey Homeward

Accora stalked after the others, deep in thought. He had tried to get Eleanor alone, but she didn't trust him, avoided even being near him. He had yet to get a closer look at the markings, and now she had covered them with another plain leather armband. He knew his attention made her uncomfortable, and so he held back hoping she would relax her guard. Let her think he was just a crazy, harmless old ram.

He counted the heads of his fellow travelers, not out of concern for their welfare, but willing their numbers to change. Eleanor, Nodd and himself made up the Aurrac contingent of the group. The Mermen brought their number to seven, and the luminaries made nine, the perfect number for a journey such as theirs promised to be. But then there was Lureli, sullen sea temptress, and the praircat whose annoyingly chipper prattle was the exact opposite. Accora hesitated to count Hornet, the Chosen One's peregrine falcon, and Bel, who if he understood correctly, housed a portion of Aryelle's father's soul. Thirteen in all, he mused. Far too many. He would have to rectify that, but not just yet. No, at first he would stay out of the way, maybe even be helpful and earn the Chosen One's trust. He would be there to witness the fulfillment of his prophesy, but others would not, of that he was certain.

Even if it was by his own hand.

But for now, he could wait.

Glossary – in order of appearance

**Kandharril – Circle of elite healers*

**El' Kandhar – Sovereign, the brightest candle*

**Ka'Andharra – treeborn capitol city of the luminaries*

**Empa'aya - (*Empire*): the luminaries name for themselves.*

**Kandharra – city dwelling luminaries*

**Domina – from domino. "And so shall each of the house Ka'Andharra fall in their turn, but not before they have fulfilled their purpose…."* –The Book of Illumination

**chanzu – literally "beautiful body feast". Fertility*

**Zu qualith kra'dempa. Dhe zu n'et dhruy nochta….. You are too proud cousin! I just hope it leads not to your destruction.*

**Naturra – wilderness luminaries*

**andhruypa – alien, other worlder*

**m'yana – beautiful child*

**mi'qua – my pride (*affectionate*)*

** Dadher – affectionate for father, daddy*

**candle – (kandhar) unit of time equaling a month; quarter-candle (dhe'phat kandhar)=week*

**Kra'nochta Empaana – Reign of Shadow, translated "partial night of the collective soul"*

**lororil – menstrual cycle, literally "flowing blood". The Lororil River flows from Lake Ril, birthplace of Emrysia*

**T'sura – inner sight, knowing*

**questanna – journey of the soul*

**Ra dhin n'et dher zu – "The sun circles not only you."* The third principle of truth from The Book of Illumination

**Dhe din'zu – literally "I am encircled by you."*

**Di suip – take a chance (*roll the dice*)*

**Ho'kay dhe bo'and – Okay, I agree.*

**flytes – unit of measure equal to approximately 20 feet*
**Empa dhel an'che – All will be made well (*beautiful & sweet*)*
**Zu t'sur, m'yana – You'll see, my beautiful child.*
**cha'kra –life force*
**dru'noch - plague*
**phrachaan – frightened, afraid*
**Eril'lith zu riss, dher'aya dhe – Fly swiftly, my brother.*

Empa'ayan Vocabulary (breakdown of syllables**)**
El- Servant
Ra- Sun (informal), yellow,
Aza – Father leader, authority
Da – Father (affectionate), first
Dhar or Dharre (inclusive Dharra, feminine Dhra) – Many, Five or a handful
Dhe – Me, self, one
Dher – Mine, belonging to
Ka, Kan – Light
Lumina – Vision, guide, teacher, Proper name of the Sun
Er (feminine Ar) – Air or sky
Le – Music
La – Song
Ja – Yes
My, Mi – Child, three
An (feminine Ana, inclusive Anna) – Beautiful
Dha – Mother (affectionate) teacher
Cha, Chan, Chaan – Eater, feast
Che – Sweet
Cho, Chon – Sustenance, food, to feed
Ne, Na – Soul, nine
Noch (feminine Nochta) – Night, nighttime, black

Dhil (feminine Dhel) – Maker
Dhin – Around, encircle
Empa- family
Aya – People
Kra – Part, portion
Lo – Water
Nor – Earth
Zu – Body, you, two
Turra – Wilderness
Verd – Green
Ari – Blue (from the sky)
Blaiz- Orange
Mont – Purple
T'sura – Inner sight, sounding, knowing
Ro' – Red
Loro – Blood
Ka'dhar – White (combining "many – dhar & lights – Ka)
Ril – Flowing, laughter
N'et – No, negative
Ri – Calm, peaceful
Dhon (feminine Dhonna) Sorrow
Do – to follow
Dhruy – Unknown
Pa – Here
Lith – To carry
Qua – Pride
Sur – Hope
Dhe'zu – Marriage
Kandhar – Candle
Eril - Flowing Air (Wind)

Phra – Fear

Tri – Tree (pronounced the same)

Counting – Numerical System

Dhe – One

Zu – Two

Mi – Three

Pha –Four

Dhar - Five

Jo – Six

Hai – Seven

Te – Eight

Na – Nine

Quo – Ten

Zunen – Twenty

Minen – Thirty

Phanen – Fourty

Dhra'den – Fifty

Jonen – Sixty

Hai'den – Seventy

Te'den – Eighty

Na'den – Ninety

Quo'de quo – 100

Empa'de quo -1000

Da – First

Zun – Second

Min – Third

Phan – Fourth

Dhra'de – Fifth

Jon –Sixth

Hai'de – Seventh

Teen – Eighth

Naan – Ninth

Quo'de - Tenth

Numerical Examples

12 = zu quo

57 = hai dhra'den

148 = te phanen quo'de quo

931 = dhe minen naan quo'de quo

1584 = dhar'ten pha te'den

Acknowledgements

In the years it took to bring this book to press, so many wonderful people supported and sustained me that I'm sure to miss someone, nevertheless, I must mention a few. To my husband first and foremost, I owe a debt of gratitude for his love & patience, and for filling in the gaps. Likewise my children, who put up with sharing their "Momster" with an often frustrating, literary child, and showered me with praise when I least deserved, but needed it most. Thank you to my parents, who gave me room to discover my own voice in our crowded first family, and to the siblings who helped shape that experience. Many thanks to my advance readers Roger DeKett, John Morgan, Terri DeKett, Mary O'Reilly, Linda Hartwell, Ann Lovett, Deb Keys, Jane Cameron, Margaret Penhorwood, Jenelle Barrett, and John & Cathy Walker, also Ron DeKett, Ed Rosick, Sylvia Cannizaro and David Stahler Jr. who lent their professional comments as well. Your feedback was priceless. Recognition also to those who wanted, but weren't able or allowed to read it prior to publishing – thanks for pushing me to "*just get it done already!*" Reeve Lindberg was most generous with her time and encouragement, sharing contacts and expertise, as was Sally Ryder Brady during a period that challenged both of us. Emma Dryden's experience and editing tips added polish, and her positive review bolstered my confidence. Scott Beck at *Railroad Street Press* did a great job handling the publishing. Credit goes to Cindy Lamontagne who occasionally cared for my little ones– now mostly teens! – so that I was able to actually concentrate, and to many other friends who bore patiently with my distraction. To the folks at my local grocery store: In a time when I had withdrawn from social contact so that I could focus, you were my connection to the world. Also Lu at the gas station – thanks for the trivia, free cappuccino and ever-present smile. To everyone at The Athenaeum and Cobliegh Libraries, thank you for making books and love of reading a community priority. Lastly, thanks to Sheala Jacklin, my "biggest fan", who blessed me with my first ever fan letter after seeing prints of *The Three Sisters,* and anxiously awaited the books. Here's the first – may you lose *and* find yourself in these pages.

C. A. Morgan is a wife and mother of five, artist, writer, singer/performer, former music & art teacher, blogger (http://imustbeoffmyrocker.blogspot.com/) and is currently working to put kids thru college --- in other words, a very busy woman! She earned her degree in Commercial Art from Michigan's Ferris State University eons ago, but for years has called Vermont's Northeast Kingdom home. This is her first published novel.

www.ingramcontent.com/pod-product-compliance
Lightning Source LLC
LaVergne TN
LVHW020041110826
845155LV00029B/584

* 9 7 8 1 9 3 6 7 1 1 3 1 4 *